Trail of Light

Guardians of War

Ellis Worth

ISBN: 979-8-8800692-0

Independently Published

Cover design by: Nisha at Passion Author Services

Edits by: Nisha at Passion Author Services and Jess Houseman

Formatting by: Heather at CreedReads

Library of Congress Control Number: 2018675309

Printed in the United States of America

To Jake Jewell, Operator 905, one of my oldest best good friends. The last text I received from you, voiced how proud you were of me for following my dreams, and that you loved me. Those words meant a lot then, but now that you're gone, they are everything.

When the night is long and my faith is shattered, I'll remember those words you typed. I won't ever stop trying to make you proud.

I'm so thankful that the last words I typed to you were, I love you. Because it's true, I'll love you forever and a day.

"We cannot direct the wind, but we can adjust the sails."
-Dolly Parton

Let love be your guiding light, and may it shine all your days.

Dear Readers,
   I love you, never stop following your dreams.

Love, Ellis

The Fall

With the fall of the Knights of Templar, the suppression of the evil Umbra came to an end. They could once again roam free seeking vengeance wherever they landed—the bringers of chaos into the world of men and of the Others.

The Knights, denied their right of power and need to protect, turned Guardians. They slink in and out of the shadows, defending this world against the malicious Umbra and their Queen.

Prologue

This Way, Nightmares Come

Arabella Grace St. James

WE ARRIVE at Forsyth Park only five minutes past schedule, I come here most nights to clear my head. Being late doesn't bother me but my family is a stickler for shit like that. My family undoubtedly wants to kill me, so tonight's form of torture is brought to me by jogging, which is stupid. I have trust issues against people who run for fun. In specific, I'm talking about my Uncle Josiah, who I lovingly call Uncle Jo.

At least after the cardio, I can people-watch sitting underneath my favorite tree. Uncle Jo is tagging along tonight, apparently. He missed his workout and needed to let off some nervous energy. Trouble is brewing within the factions, but they don't discuss that stuff with me.

Merrie-Beth, my best friend who is also my Healer, heard a rumor that there was a prison escape. The criminals are searching for the Chosen, which is insane because she hasn't even been born yet. Dumbasses.

News travels fast amongst our societies. We are the Lux, Pyralis, and the Kori. The Lux faction has two jobs within the three societies. The first is that we supply both the Pyralis and the Kori with special herbs, and medicines so their Healers can keep them healthy. You can't find the medications we make anywhere else. Our faction is more advanced in every capacity than the modern world where we hide in plain sight. Our second job is that during wartime, we come up with the battle plans because we are known as the "thinkers" amongst the groups.

The Pyralis are the most fearless, passionate faction. They make the swords along with most of the other weapons that we use. Their fighters start training as soon as they take their first steps, which is why they are the first to be called into battle. They simply take the risks that we're not willing to and surrendering is not an option for them, they will fight to the bitter death.

The Kori faction is a secretive bunch. They keep to themselves but share the new inventions they make with us so that we can stay more advanced. They work on everything from making the Pyralis's weapons better to making our household items more convenient.

Finally, after almost dying from exercise, I'm able to sit with my back against my favorite tree. Uncle Jo is still running, which makes me question his sanity. Even at this late hour, people are out in droves tonight. Much to my carnal delight, I've spotted two hot guys already. One is jogging, so he's suspicious. Probably a serial unaliver or something. The other one just bought fully loaded nachos from one of the food trucks. He's less suspicious because food is life.

We're on the brink of summer. Excitement sizzles through the air. The wind is even heaving out cool air. It feels good against my sweaty skin. To my left is a blonde woman in hot pink leopard yoga pants, walking her French poodle. She's talking loudly on her phone and has a thick Long Island accent. It seems her boyfriend, Kyle, has been messaging someone named Camilla. Poodle lady should have known not to mess with someone with that name because all Kyles are fuck boys. Her poodle, on the other hand, has no worries. She is holding her head high, her posture perfect. She looks every bit as regal as a queen.

To my right is the macho jogger from before, and he must be hella hot for me to find him attractive because he seems to like running. Even the woman who is yelling at her boyfriend abruptly stops walking. Her mouth is open in awe of the perfection coming our way. Kyle who? The poodle, however, does not want any part of this. She starts barking at her owner, not at all impressed by the well-muscled jogger.

The man is close enough now for me to get a better look at his face, we don't have to guess if he knows what kind of ruckus his presence is causing. That smirk on his beautiful face says it all. He's surprisingly graceful for a man so tall and built. His shoulder-length blonde hair is tied back in a ponytail, and I'd say he's in his late twenties—with brown eyes and a very shapely ass. Hello sir, can I call you Daddy? Daddy Thor is one hundred percent all male, with bad-boy appeal and a five o'clock shadowed jaw.

When the hot jogger is out of my eyesight, my head turns, and a set of beautiful emerald green eyes greet my bright blue ones. "Hello." The stranger says.

Startled, my back once again lands against the tree. My cheeks turn red because for me to have been so far from my post, I must have been seriously gawking at the hot jogger man. Did this guy witness that? Kill me NOW! Embarrassment sets in, but I push that shit down like a champ. My family taught me to never lose focus on what's going on in my surroundings. My back should have never left the comfort of the tree. The green-eyed guy should have never been allowed to sneak up on me.

Giving him a half smile, I reach into my back pocket. A sigh of relief escapes me as my hand wraps around my mini keychain of mace. If he tries anything, I could kick his ass. However, we, Lux, don't like doing that in public. We try to stay out of the limelight, and in today's world, that's hard because of all the cell phones.

3

Depending on what day you ask, technology can be a blessing yet a curse.

"Hey." I eventually respond. Realization dawns on me that this is the other hot dude from before. The one that was buying the fully loaded nachos. Coincidence? I don't believe in those.

The way "nacho guy" said hello sounded different. Did he have an English accent? Maybe. He's beautiful—possibly my age but not much older, over six glorious feet tall, with short, spiky brown hair, a slight scar is trekking down the right side of his cheek. The imperfection takes nothing away from his appearance. It actually enhances his handsome features. Not to mention, the scales tip over on the hotness meter when the boys have an accent.

I can tell he is uncertain of what to say next. For whatever reason, he seems as nervous as I feel. So, of course, the conversation drifts towards the weather. "It's a beautiful night. Not a cloud in sight." He mumbles.

Definitely an English accent. "Yeah, it's stunning." I chuckle. "What's your name?"

He bows politely. "Ethan Randall."

I've known this guy for two minutes, and I am already smitten. Ethan is cute with a side of clever, which is a nonexistent combination these days. Keep your cool, Arabella. My family keeps me under tight ropes. The only guy I've ever been with is our delivery guy at the cafe. He's a good friend at this point, there's nothing serious there. My uncle would probably murder him if he knew. "Well, my name is...Ms. None of your business, but most people just call me Nunya." I wink, but it comes out more like an eyelash is stuck in my eye.

He gives me a smirk that sends shivers down my spine. Looking down at my wrists, he takes a particular interest in my left one. "That's a beautiful bracelet you're wearing. My mum's birthday is the day after tomorrow. I think she would love one. May I get a better look at it?" He asks.

I'm only apprehensive for a second, he appears to be a nice

enough guy, my black belt proves I can kick his ass. The advisory warning for him today is to not make any sudden moves, because cans of whoop ass will be opened. I slide the silver bracelet all the way down my hand. This particular one is my favorite. It's a liquid metal bracelet, which is made out of silver nickel. It is about three inches in width with little silver crosses going all the way around the middle. When I wear it, it never fails to make me feel safe. It's a reminder that we're never truly alone, and that my parents aren't truly gone forever.

As I hand Ethan the bracelet, he only hesitates for a moment. His eyes glance down at mine as if apologizing for something that's yet to come. When he finally makes his move to grab it, his fingers bypass the bracelet altogether, grabbing my wrist instead. Quickly flipping it over to examine it, he looks perplexed. Well, this just took a weird turn. Is he a Vampiro? Because I'll stake the shit out of him, tonight is not the night, and I am not the one, sir.

At his simple touch, a wave of electricity courses through my body. The foreign surge of energy doesn't hurt as it flows through the length of my body. If anything, a small part of my mind has been awakened. A piece that has laid dormant for as long as I have been alive. Gazing up at his face, I gasp as a look of awe hovers over his handsome features. Ethan's eyes never move from my wrist. It's only after I flinch my hand that his eyes meet my what the hell stare but only for a second, he quickly turns back to my wrist. Yeah, this just got weirder.

I try to make small talk because I don't like awkwardness. "My uncle got the bracelet for me as a present for my twelfth birthday. I'm not sure where he got it from or if it would even still be available at that shop. I'm sorry."

"It's quite alright," he says in return.

I don't understand the feeling, but I suddenly want to know everything about this mysterious stranger. Who is he? And why is he staring at my wrist in reverence? "Tell me about yourself?"

Ethan bends his head down for a second, and when he looks back down at me, he gives me a heart-stopping smile. "Well, if you must know, I only talk to the pretty girls."

I give him back a stupid grin. I can see that the spikes of his hair are a darker brown than the rest of the strands. Near his roots, it's almost a sandy blonde. "How's that going for you?"

He scratches his forehead. "It's complicated."

I nod my head. "Ah. So, you're a man of great mystery?"

Ethan smiles and places his hands on his chest. "So, you think I'm a great man? I'm truly flattered."

I laugh, rolling my eyes toward the big bright blue sky. "Don't hold your breath. Great was used in front of the word mystery, not man."

He makes a face at me. "Hater. I am wounded."

That makes me laugh even harder at the way he says, hater. His English accent is to die for. "Would you like some cheese with that wine?"

We talk for several minutes until he has to go. Watching him as he walked away, may be my new favorite thing.

Chapter 1

Sweet Dreams are Made of These
Arabella

My story is not at all simple, and it begins as most of the great ones do, with a dream...
-Arabella

Present Day May 2023
Savannah, Georgia

A DREAM

 Opening a familiar set of double doors, I walk into a room that is pitch black dark. Putting my hand directly in front of my face and I still can't see it. Blood-curdling shrieks sound in my ear, and every few seconds a flash of light resonates throughout the large room. There is utter chaos. People are terrified, as they run in no certain direction. The wind catches my face as they hurriedly rush past me. A shiver works its way up my spine. I'm scared, because evil is coming.

 Panic rises, and my feet feel heavy as I attempt to put one foot in front of the other to run. It's no use, I can barely move. Surprisingly, no one bumps into me as they rush by.

 Finally, my eyes adjust to the darkness. A full-length mirror falls at my feet, blocking my path, startling me. Shards of glass tumble from the ceiling, cutting my face which begins bleeding profusely. Frozen with fear, the reflection looking back is not my own.

Slowly, taking a step back, I study the images staring back at me. There are two men that appear to be twins. They look angelic but my mind senses the sinister nature they're trying to hide. They're identical in every way except the style of their hair. Both are blonde, but one has shoulder-length locks, while the other has a short spiky cut. My temper flares, because they are both smirking, and I can't understand why. Finding my nerve, I yell at them to get out of my way. Frustration takes over because they know something that I don't. Their hazel eyes are mocking me, causing an uneasy feeling to creep into my gut. If this were a movie, they would be the bad guys, the villains.

I know this is a dream, but it's all too real. Wake up!! You can't stay here! They'll kill you! Wake up now! But slumber won't release its icy grip.

I try to get away, but heavy chains lock down my ankles and wrists rendering me unable to move. I let out an anguished cry, making the brothers cover their ears. The angry squeal breaks the chains holding me captive.

Quickly turning around, another full-length mirror hinders my getaway. I'm getting sick and tired of not seeing my own damn reflection. A different set of men stare at me now, visibly upset that my chains are gone. I give the assholes a smirk. The first man is wearing a kilt, he is ruggedly handsome with a scar that runs diagonally from one side of his forehead down to his ear. To the right of him is a giant—a bald, toothless giant who is grinning at me. Okay, dude, that's creepy.

A light flashes wildly in the mirror. I can see a woman is hiding in the shadows behind tweedle dee and tweedle dumb. She is wearing a wide-brimmed hat. She's shielding her face away from me for some reason, so I can only make out her profile. Terrible thoughts keep popping up in my mind. Vivid scenes play throughout my head of people being tortured to death, and my uncle laying in a puddle of *blood crying out in despair. The woman says I owe her. The hate she has towards me is palpable and all consuming.*

The villains are coming for me. When hope is almost lost, out of nowhere, another mirror opens up beside me. Hesitating only for a second, I put my arm over my eyes, and jump.

No glass shatters as it transports me to the far side of the room. Evil is still lurking in the shadows. I hear my best friend Merrie-Beth calling my name, it starts as just a whisper, then crescendos until she is shouting. "Arabella. Arabella. Arabella! ARABELLA!" She sounds almost frantic. Terrified even.

I have to find her, but I don't know where she is. "Merrie-Beth! Where are you? I can't find you. Merrie-Beth?"

Without warning, she comes to stand beside me. She's frightened and starts shaking her head from side to side. "Arabella, you have to listen to me. Don't be stubborn. Don't run! Stay and fight! Don't run, Arabella. If you do, we'll die!! Please, listen to me!!! Stay and fight! Stay and fight!" She shouts over and over again.

"Stay and fight!" I scream like a weirdo, sitting up in my bed. Rubbing my eyes, I give my alarm clock the side eye, because there was thirty more minutes worth of glorious sleep to be had. It's 5 flippin' thirty! Remembering my dream, I shiver with a groan, that was one of the creepiest dreams I've ever had. Not to mention, the most realistic.

My people, the Lux, believe that dreams are often predictions of the future. Hopefully the hell not, or it's going to be a bad day... for them. I've been working on becoming more confident, and less socially awkward, but at least I can fight with the best of them.

Heading for the shower I stop long enough to do my happy dance It's the last day of senior year and nothing can ruin this day. Not even psychos trapped in a mirror.

Graduation is tomorrow night and in less than fourteen hours, summer vacation will begin. In late August I'll head to college in my hometown of Luxington Valley for the remainder of my fight training for one year. Then just like my parents before me my three-year stint in the Lux Guardianship program will begin. My future has been planned out for years. Thankfully, it's what I've always wanted.

Today though, is a good day for a good day, that's my motto and I'm sticking to it. Putting on my favorite pair of ripped jeans. I give myself a once over in the mirror and not to toot my own horn, but they look good. My t-shirt choice of the day is my Aunt Georgia's vintage Backstreet Boys one. She gets a little testy when I call it vintage, but that's what it is. They were her favorite group growing up. Well, still are actually. They can carry a tune, so I'm not mad at it.

My curves are more toned than last summer, but my belly still has some flab. And my thighs have dimples, because I don't have any issues with chocolate, but I do have one to healthy things like turkey bacon and tofu. My arms are starting to get more defined though, and if they ever get any real muscle then you won't be able to tell me nothing.

Attempting to brush my unruly red hair is a challenge. I give up because my curls are beyond frizzy this morning. The humidity in Georgia is the absolute worst, so a messy bun will have to do. Rain is definitely in the forecast.

Checking my reflection for the thousandth time, I decide a little more makeup is needed on my light skin, but I refrain from looking back at my reflection. My dream is all but forgotten. Here's to pretending that the beginning of summer looks good on me.

Making my way down the hall to our tiny kitchen I hear my aunt Georgia humming. Which is amusing, because she has a horrible singing voice. Her matching red hair is tied up in a struggling pony-tail. Where mine is all curls, hers is straight and sleek. I greet her cheerfully, "good morning, you hot young thing."

"Good morning, sweetie. Last day of school. Best! Day! Ever!" She gives me a high-five. I love my little family. My Aunt and Uncle didn't think twice when they were asked to be my guardians after my parents were killed in a car crash. I was only four years old when they died. My mother was Aunt Georgia's sister, and my uncle was my father's brother. It's interesting, but it's not like they are blood related or anything.

My mind shifts to my parents, and I can't help but place my hand over my heart when thinking about them. My fingers gently apply pressure there, but my physical touch doesn't dull the ache of their absence. Though the pain has lessened over the years, it will never be forgotten.

Desperately needing a subject change, I tell my aunt Georgia about what Merrie-Beth and I have planned for our summer activities. We plan on conquering every escape room across the city and trying every pizza restaurant within a twenty-mile radius. We'll have pizza for breakfast, lunch, and dinner.

Aunt Georgia smiles in response, "You're in a super good mood this morning. I like it. However, pizza gluttony will have to wait for a day or two. You need to come home straight after school. You have a training session with your uncle at four. A recruiter from the Lux Training Center will be here to observe the session today." She hugs me and hands me my breakfast in a to go bag.

"Alright, Georgia from Georgia. I'll see you guys at four." I give her a quick kiss on the cheek and take the breakfast she hands me. Totally forgot about that training session, and why is someone wanting to observe me again? I've already received my acceptance letter.

My fight training or as we call it, fight club, started as soon as I took my first steps. That may seem extreme to most, but we are members of the world's best kept secret. It is a privilege to hide in plain sight and to fight for our freedoms. I come from a long line of warriors, and my lineage can be traced back to the first horseman of The Knights of Templar. Since we fell out of grace, the history books will never know our names, but we don't do it for fame, or for glory. We do it for justice and freedom.

Three secret Societies protect the world from the evils that lurk. Domestic and foreign. We are The Lux, The Pyralis, and The Kori. Light. Fire. Ice. The powers that be can never know about us, the treachery of those that lead is appalling. The Guardians rose with the dissolution of The Knights of Templar. We are every race, every color, and we stand united.

Our enemies are called The Umbra. They are a soulless rotten bunch that can be traced back to the fallen angels of old. Desecrations, who want nothing more than to see the world shrouded in darkness. We were formed to stop them. The Chosen is coming and with her rule they will be diminished.

Looking at my Apple Watch I pick up the pace. "Shit!" It'll be a miracle if I'm not late to school.

Chapter 2

An Ominous Dreaded Feeling

Arabella

*Stand up for your friends, and never let your
enemies see you squirm. Oh, and Sara can
kiss my dimpled ass.*
-Arabella

I QUICKLY RUN into the school but stop dead in my tracks as I notice
the two guys that were lurking in the background while we were on
our run last night. They are staring back at me from the lockers near
the bathroom. The one with a farmer's tan, is lean but not without
muscles, and wears a cowboy hat that has flames embroidered on the
sides. Okay, Cowboy, that hat is beautiful. The other guy has smooth
ebony skin, and the physique of a bodybuilder. He's got muscles for
days! Besides the cowboy hat, they are dressed the same. Black shirts,
pants, and boots. Though they give the appearance of being older
they are young like me. The cowboy gives me a huge grin while Hulk
gives me a friendly nod. They seem familiar somehow. Déjà vu,
maybe? They are dressed in the Watches uniform of all black, but
maybe it's just a coincidence and black is their thing. Within our

three societies, The Watch, is an elite task force that's good at taking names and kicking ass.

I slowly walk past them until the warning bell sounds, then my feet run like a bat out of hell to get to Mrs. Lopez's room. I slide into my seat with a gracefulness that's unusual for me, just as the final bell rings, which equals perfection. Glancing over at my best friend, Merrie-Beth, I smile. She sticks her tongue out at me, which makes me throw up my middle finger in retaliation.

At birth every warrior in our society is partnered with a Healer. Merrie-Beth is mine, her parents are my aunt and uncles. They train with us although not as hard, and even go into battle with us just not on the front lines.

"How was your run at Forsyth Park last night?" She asks sarcastically, because she knows how much I hate running.

Leaning over for dramatic effect, I etch closer to her seat. "Umm... pure hell, ten out of ten do not recommend. However, honey, I've got some tea for you! I saw two hotties, one of which I think is a stalker." Her eyebrows arch in mistrust, because she knows I like to embellish. "The first guy was Thor in the flesh. His abs had abs and I'm pretty sure he's in love with me. Oh, and this lady was cussing out her boyfriend because he had DMs on his phone from someone named Camilla. Maybe we can ask TikTok to find out who she is. They can find anyone!"

I sigh heavily for that over-the-top effect, making Merrie-Beth roll her eyes heavenward. "Interesting. But girl, inquiring minds, meaning mine, wanna know. What about that stalker?"

I laugh heartily, and glance over at Mrs. Lopez to see how much time we may have left. She is engaged in a heated conversation with another student. Poor Jeremy, she most certainly does not play.

We've probably got a couple of minutes while she's ripping that kid a new one! "Mer, he had an English accent." Pausing to gauge her reaction. She seems enthralled, so I continue. "We talked about the weather, Ethan even asked about my bracelet, because his 'mum' has a birthday coming up. Now for the first red flag. You ready?"

"Bring on the red flags, baby! Because that's what we like." She moves her hands in a come-hither motion.

We both laugh, because, yeah, she's not wrong. "Ethan Randall, if that is even his real name, asked to see my bracelet, and when I made a move to give it to him, he turned my wrist over instead and just stared at it for a whole minute. Stunned is not a strong enough word for what my reaction to that was, and that's why he almost got punched in the face."

Her expression is priceless. She is shook. "Is he Vampiro?"

I shrug it off, because I honestly don't know. Most Vampiro are docile creatures who still have a firm attachment to their human sides. The personality they had in their human life is who they are as the undead. The Watch doesn't worry about them much, the only ones on their radar are called the Forsaken. The Forsaken have renounced their humanity, and enjoy killing for sport, and blood.

Since the Sanguis Accords of 1612 Vampiro's are forbidden to drink the blood of an unwilling. It's also prohibited for humans not within our world to know about any Supernaturals. There are exceptions to the rule, when necessary, of course. Most Vampiro use blood banks for sustenance now. The males are often referred to as Vampiros while the females are Vampiras. Those who don't identify as either are simply known as Vamps. You can also say vampire, although you might get a side eye if you do.

"Ethan's eyes weren't dark gray, but he could have been wearing contacts." Vampire's eyes always shift to a variation of that color after being turned.

"True." She agrees. "Hit me with the second red flag, please."

I smile wickedly. "He knew my name without me telling him."

"He what?" She crinkles her nose in that cute Merrie-Beth way.

"Yes. As I go to leave, he says, and I quote: I will see you later, Arabella." The last part said in my very terrible impersonation of a British accent.

Mer almost squeals. "That's so creepy."

"I know!" I reply with a shrug.

"What if he's Umbra?" Her eyes are wide as saucers.

"Then I'll kick his ass." It really is just that simple. The Umbra are the anti-us.

She laughs. "Definitely. And don't worry, if he kills you, I will avenge your death."

Yeah, she will. Our wild laughter earns us a dirty look from Mrs. Lopez. "Thanks, Merrie-Beth. I can always count on you."

Merri Beth gives me a grin. "Did he really say 'mum'?"

Smiling broadly, I waggle my eyebrows. "Yesss."

"That's so hot! That shouldn't be hot, but it is!" When she's right, she's right.

Pondering what's wrong with us, I nod in wholehearted agreement. Then Mrs. Lopez decides to start class before I can say anything filthy about him. Ethan was absolutely scrumptious.

"Class, can I have your attention, please? CLASS!" Mrs. Lopez shouts.

Wow, she is not playing around today. Good thing my butt was in the seat before the final bell. I curl my lip up at Merri Beth, which causes her to stifle a laugh behind her perfectly manicured hand. Hot pink as per usual.

"Thanks and believe me I know you are all excited about graduation. But let's keep the outburst to a minimum. Jeremy, that goes double for you. What are your plans for this summer? I'll go first. In June, I will be taking an art class at SCAD. The month of July will be my ten-year wedding anniversary, and in celebration, we have decided to take a trip to Italy." Her smile is big, and she appears to be glowing.

Ten years and still in love, no small feat these days. Way to go, Mrs. Lopez! I wonder what Mr. Lopez looks like. I'd say he is tallish, with a pop belly and minimal facial hair.

As the kids go up one by one, I realize that everyone has a much better social life than we do. When Sara Whitmore, our arch nemesis walks up to the front of the room, my face cannot be held responsible for the stank expression that automatically appears. Unfortunately, she is a member of the Lux and will be attending the same college as us in the fall. Much like in the world around us, our high school is a mixed assortment of the societies and regular civilians.

Merrie-Beth shakes her head in agreed disapproval. From the outside looking in most people would think we're just jealous of the "perfection" that is Sara Whitmore. However, she's a thot and that's why we dislike her. I can't help that my eyes always seem to roll to the very back of my head when she opens her deceptive, pouty pink mouth. It's an involuntary reaction to her bullying, mean girl self. She is cruel and vile, and I don't like her. It's as if Regina George had a baby with the devil, and the creation was Sara.

I lightly tap my fingers on my desk, so my fist doesn't itch to punch her face. Sara makes nausea form in my belly as she tells the class about her forthcoming skydiving adventure and how she's going to visit Paris for the tenth time Let's not miss that she is finally going to get to meet the President, which is not surprising since her Daddy owns half of Fifth Avenue. Not only is she the wealthiest kid here at Eleanor Roosevelt High School, but she's also the cruelest. Sara loves to tell people how her father makes her go to public school, so she won't take her privileged life for granted. Well, Daddy needs a refund, because it didn't work.

Sara, who we have so graciously nicknamed **"the Bitch,"** has tortured us our whole academic career. With her little snide comments and impeccably good hair. Why couldn't she have at least one bad hair day like the rest of us do on the daily?

Standing up in front of the class is not my favorite. So, when it's my turn, I freeze. They stare at me, and I stare blankly back at them. It's a stare-off. Sweat beads form at my temples, and in my mind, I got nothing. Zilch. Nada.

"Twenty bucks says she barfs, just like when she played Little Red Riding Hood in the third grade. Come to think of it, that was on the last day of school, too." The Bitch throws her head back and laughs.

My fear intensifies, and bile begins to rise in my throat. I've worked hard to get that one incident out of my mind forever. Throwing up in front of everyone is horrible enough but add in the fact that I threw up on my crushes foot and the whole thing became catastrophic. Justin Chang had played the coveted role of the wolf. Years later, and the cutest boy in our class still looks at me like I am a leper. I should have never eaten those cinnamon rolls. To this day, I avoid the things.

Merrie-Beth's eyes shoot daggers into Sara's back. "I'm surprised you can remember that far back, Sara, considering your head is so full of air."

Sara turns, her eyes glazed over with embers of fire. "Listen, Fattie-Beth, the only thing full of air, is you."

Oh no, she didn't! Merrie-Beth starts to stand up, but I stop her. "Sara, why are you so mean? Have you not seen any of those anti-bullying campaigns? Daddy didn't love you enough as a child? I'm done with your bitchy hoe nastiness. It's sad really, no one even likes you. The only reason your little entourage hangs out with you is because they are scared of what you'll say about them. DO better! Be a better person, and you might actually make a real friend or two."

Still full of anger, I point my finger in Sara's face. "Oh, and if you ever call my best friend by that name again, you'll be leaving in an ambulance, and Daddy's sweet money will be paying for a long hospital visit. Is that clear?" The classroom is eerily quiet. Mrs. Lopez's mouth is agape in shock.

Looking at Sara, I stifle a laugh. If looks could kill, I'd be done, dead, deceased. She is quiet, though.

"Well, I think that is enough sharing for today kids. Sara, Arabella, I need both of you to stay after class." Considering the glare, she just sent me Mrs. Lopez is not happy.

The bell rings, and Merrie-Beth whispers that she will wait outside for me. I nod but don't say anything. I've never really been in trouble before. I put on a brave face and walk up to her desk; Sara is already standing there.

Mrs. Lopez glares at both of us for a couple of minutes and

doesn't say a word. She could be an interrogator for the FBI. Finally, she speaks. "I'm very disappointed in both of you. Sara, how dare you call Merrie-Beth that, and Arabella, I'm going to have to write you up. You threatened a student with bodily harm right in front of me. This is probably going to go on your permanent record, and you may not get to walk at graduation tomorrow."

Sara turns to me with a smirk firmly in place. If I wasn't so shocked, I'd have body slammed her onto the desk. How could this have happened on the last day? My aunt and uncle are going to be pissed at me if I don't get to attend graduation.

Mrs. Lopez turns her attention to The Bitch. "Don't look so smug, Sara. I'm writing you up, too. You'll probably face the same consequences."

Sara looks petrified. "Why? I didn't do anything wrong, Mrs. Lopez. That's not fair. Daddy will hear about this, and it won't be so good for your job."

Mrs. Lopez stands up and gets eye level with her, because she's a fucking boss. "Sara, you threaten me all you want, and I don't care if you tell your Daddy or my supervisor. I have nothing to hide. You were being a bully, which is a serious offense, and no one at this school takes matters like this lightly. Why don't I call your Daddy myself? He's sure to love the very detailed account of what happened here today. Especially the part about my job."

Sara is positively livid. Her nostrils flare, and she looks at me in disbelief. Then, she focuses back on Mrs. Lopez. Sara takes a deep breath and mumbles something unintelligible.

"What was that?" Mrs. Lopez asks. I can tell she is slightly amused.

Sara reins in her temper. "Mrs. Lopez, there is no reason to tell my father. Please, forgive me for speaking out of turn. I was angry and said something stupid. I'll apologize to Merrie-Beth, and I won't hold a grudge against Arabella. She was just standing up for her friend."

Mrs. Lopez clears her throat, "Sara, I accept your apology, and proposal. You may leave now. Don't forget your apology to Merrie-Beth."

Sara smiles. "Of course, thanks so much."

"Oh, and Sara, if you mention any of this to anyone, especially Arabella's involvement, I will have to tell the whole story. And nobody wants that." Mrs. Lopez adds with a cheeky grin.

Sara looks at me and rolls her eyes. "Oh, alright. I won't." She storms out of the room and yells a halfhearted SORRY to Merri-Beth, almost knocking her over in the process as she runs out.

"Thanks." I say with a sheepish smile.

"You're welcome, and Arabella, I'm going to give you some sound advice. Don't let the Saras of this world make you sink down to their level. Standing up for a best friend is honorable, but never stoop so low that you can't get back up again. That thrill that hits you after besting someone like that doesn't last forever. And honey, let me tell you, they are not worth losing who you are or what you're trying to become." She smiles at me.

I nod my head and honestly contemplate what she said. "Yes, ma'am, thank you."

"What class do you have next?" She asks.

"World History." I reply.

"I'll write Merrie-Beth an excuse, also." She sits back down at her desk to write the excused absence notes.

Heading out of the classroom, I whisper to Merrie-Beth. "Hey Mer, get your money's worth?"

She scoffs, "Are you crazy? I wouldn't have missed that for the world. Mrs. Lopez got the best of Sara. Do you realize she orchestrated that whole conversation so you wouldn't get in trouble? She's pretty awesome. Maybe we have severely underestimated her and the perks that her friendship could have brought us." She laughs. "Just sayin'."

I laugh. "Dually noted. Merrie-Beth, I am so tired of Sara. Enough is enough. Every word that passed my lips during my tirade was true. I'm done. She will no longer be allowed to make our lives a living hell."

Merrie-Beth looks like she is about to cry. She acts so strong and self-confident, but behind closed doors, I know her weight bothers her. It shouldn't. She has so much to offer this world. She is a healthy, vibrant, and beautiful girl.

"Mer, I'm sorry for what she said. She's an idiot." I say softly.

She looks up at the ceiling, and I know she is trying to get rid of the tears accumulating under her eyes. She looks at me and takes a deep breath. "Ella, I know it was mean of her to say, and I shouldn't let it bother me, but the truth is, it does. I am fat."

I hold up my hand to stop her, "You're a size eighteen, Mer, you're not fat. You have curves, big freaking deal. Every single one of us wishes we could look like someone else or that we could be someone else, have someone else's life, but we should just be happy being ourselves. Everyone has some sort of insecurity, hell parts of me jiggle when I walk, I say we should embrace our differences and love one another despite them."

Merrie-Beth claps her hands, "Slow down, rock star, no fixing the world's problems before 10:00 a.m. it's bad for the teenage brain."

I throw my head back and laugh. No one can make me laugh like she can. "We're going to change the world one day, Mer, girls rule the world, you know."

Merrie-Beth nods her head. "Yeah, we do! Well, at least we should. Here's my class, kid, I'll catch you at lunch." I hand her the excuse Mrs. Lopez wrote for her, we fist bump, and she goes inside her room.

Mr. Woods winds up grumbling only a little bit about my being late. He is in a perfect mood for some reason. He lets us talk amongst ourselves for most of the class. Guess he is excited for the beginning of summer, too.

On my way to lunch I notice the two guys dressed in black from this morning and my run last night. The Cowboy and The Hulk. They look tense, like shit is about to hit the fan.

Faking a smile and nodding at them I walk into the lunchroom. My heart drops as I open up the familiar set of double doors, because my nightmare comes flooding back to me. I don't know what it means but here's to ending the school year with a bang.

Chapter 3

Never in my Wildest Dreams
Arabella

My family has some explaining to do, that is all.
-Arabella

MAYBE IT'S JUST a coincidence that Hulk and Cowboy are now standing behind me in the taco line. Stranger things have happened, right? I've had plenty of dreams that have never come true. Its possible last night's nightmare, nothing more.

I search for Merrie-Beth, but she is nowhere in sight. She suddenly appears out of nowhere, pinching me, making me scream. My scream made Cowboy and Hulk seem even more intense.

"Really?!" I scoff.

"Yup, it's Taco Day. Anything can happen on Taco Day." She laughs.

"Smut Slut." I reply with a middle finger salute.

"Beyotch." I laugh, because Merrie-Beth hardly ever cusses, it's cute really.

We both giggle. "Mer, I have to work after school, but do you want to come spend the night afterward?" I ask.

"Of course. I'll rent some movies. Horror or Romance?" She inquires.

"Horror, in honor of my English serial stalker." I whisper dramatically.

She puts her hand over her heart and quotes a messed-up version of Shakespeare. "Ethan. Ethan. Wherefore art thou, serial stalker, Ethan?"

Nice. I swallow my sarcastic response when my stomach gives an angry growl. Feels like the line isn't moving at all. Looking over at the full-length mirror behind where the lunchroom ladies serve our food makes me nervous. I've always thought it was unusual that a mirror was placed there, but as far as I know it's always been that way.

Out of nowhere a bright glowing light appears from within the top right-hand corner of the mirror. Closing my eyes and shaking my head does nothing to fix my vision. My eyes widen as the light takes over every inch of the glass.

I turn towards Merrie-Beth to make sure I'm not crazy, but her gaze is glued to the light show. Cowboy and Hulk can see it, too. "You can see the light, right? Please, tell me you can." Needing confirmation, I whisper to her.

"Yes, and we don't do drugs, so that's real." Merrie-Beth whispers back.

"Yeah, wish it wasn't though." I'm taking deep breaths, slowly in and out now.

"What in the world is going on?" She whispers under breath, just as astonished as I am.

Glancing around the room, I'm shocked that no one else has noticed it. My dream is now running on a constant loop inside my brain. Ugly mirrors were a part of the sequence. I've had dreams come true before, but when they turn into reality things are usually slightly different, however the people and places always remain the same. A gnawing sensation creeps down deep in my belly. This isn't good.

Merrie-Beth taps me on the arm making me look at her. Instead of meeting my gaze, her full attention is on the mirror and her pink lip-glossed lips are wide open. Now whether her reaction is because she's horrified or just plain surprised I have no idea. She points in the direction of the mirror. My panicked stare follows in the direction her finger is pointing.

A mental breakdown is slowly building up and is threatening to surface because I know my eyes won't ever unsee any of this. The bright light has vanished and has been replaced by a thick sinister fog. Can fog even be described as sinister? The only answer is yes, because only something malevolent could have created this. The men will come soon and knowing that is like a punch to my gut, because my dreams never lie.

My mind begs me to run, but my inner warrior keeps my stubborn feet planted firm on the ground. Merrie-Beth is afraid and is frozen in place. Moving in front of her, I get in a fight stance no time like the present to show the enemies that are coming what kind of damage I can cause. Both Hulk and Cowboy come to stand beside us, one on either side. They casually keep their weapons pointed at the ground so as not to cause a scene before it is time. That's my confirmation that they are members of the Watch. It's comforting, but also not, because now we are not alone.

Within the various shades of the fog, four figures emerge through the lighter parts. The mist slowly fades away, leaving only the evil, otherworldly-looking men. The whole band is there except for the woman who kept her face hidden from me. My mind is preparing for battle.

The bad guys are also dressed in all black, like the Watchman beside me. Even the Scotsman's kilt is black. His shoulder-length curly black hair is tied in a man bun, and he's carrying a two-handed claymore sword. Out of the four, he looks the fiercest.

To his far right is the giant. He is well over seven feet tall, bald, and has big gold diamond studs in both ears. Terrifying because he is as big as he is tall and the fact that his weapon of choice is a long wooden club with razor-like spikes embedded on the top does nothing to help to dispel any fear. His club is similar to my favorite weapon of choice at home, the giant's looks more badass though, and that pisses me off. Unfortunately, he's not green nor does he appear to be very jolly.

The two men in the middle are mirror images from my night-mare. Evil smiles are pasted on their clean-shaven faces. Thriving on our discomfort, their eyes shine with joyous delight. In the hand of the twin closest to the giant is an ax with a double blade. The ax has a symbol in the middle, but I can't tell from this distance what it is. The other twin is carrying a bronze-plated sword.

The Hulk at my side looks at me almost apologetically. "I'm sorry this is happening; we hadn't anticipated any of this so soon. They've come to take you to her, but we won't let that happen."

Her? The woman from my dreams? A shiver runs down my spine, and my heart drops to my knees. I have so many questions and now is not the time for any of the answers I need.

The Cowboy smiles over at me. "Damn right we won't. You'll both be fine; we'll take it from here." He looks at Merrie-Beth and gives her a wink, making her blush. I appreciate their enthusiasm, but hell will freeze over before I sit back and not help with this forth-coming fight. They extend their swords out, clanking them together.

Hulk looks at Cowboy. "You ready brother?"

Cowboy gives him a lazy grin. "I was born ready, Jeremiah."

The Scotsman's creepy smile deepens. Throwing his free hand up in the air, he drops a medium sized rock down on the ground. Lightning flashes and a loud popping noise resonates throughout the lunchroom. What the hell is happening? An eerie silence falls over the room. Jeremiah and the Cowboy don't seem surprised by any of this. Looking at each other one more time, they nod their heads, then turn their gaze to me, "For The Chosen!"

Why did they say that while looking in my direction? I've heard the saying plenty of times before. It's what we say before we go to battle, it's in all our history books. The guys move to stand front and center blocking our view and shielding us from the chaos that quickly follows only seconds later. No one around us saw the fog or the men in the mirror, but they heard the thunder and saw the lightning coming from out of the ceiling. Kids are screaming and running themselves into utter chaos. Teachers are trying to calm the frantic students while they attempt to hide their unnerved states.

A cool breeze starts blowing from somewhere, gentle at first, but quickly becomes more forceful, making it almost impossible to stand. The temperature has dropped drastically in the room. Rubbing my arms up and down with my hands to create a little friction for warmth, I exhale, seeing my breath as it exits my mouth. What the hell is going on? It's summertime in Georgia, we don't do the cold. Little shards of ice form in the midst of my breath. Dark magic can be the only explanation.

My heart pounds ferociously in my chest as I realize that the men are gone. Our reflections and the disarray around us are the only images that we are greeted with now. Still in disbelief, I grab Merrie-Beth's arm, and we start running. Whether that be from my body's fight or flight response, or just a pure adrenaline rush, it's anybody's guess. To hell with the Merrie-Beth in my dream that told me to stay and fight. Staying would be bat shit crazy. I've been trained in all the ways that count, but I don't know how to fight against someone that's practicing black magic. It's not something you should face alone. Mer's been trained but not like me, and I won't allow her to get hurt. We start running towards the south exit. I hear a muttered, "shit," behind us, and Cowboy and Jeremiah move quickly to get in front of us, their weapons fully drawn.

Our run is short-lived because ten feet from the exit the Scotsman awaits. How he has managed to get out of that mirror is beyond me, but there the asshole is. Now that he is not so close to the giant, he's more muscular and taller than I thought. "They're going to block all the exits, Arabella, we need to stay in the middle and draw them to us." I don't know which one gives their unwanted opinion, but we ignore it all the same.

The Scotsman's body tenses as he spots us. He wields his Clayborn sword from side to side, then makes a move to get closer. Everything about this man is unsettling. His entire being exudes danger, and if people came with labels, the Scots would be deadly.

The Cowboy takes a lasso out of his belt making a badass firebolt shoot out of the end as it hits the floor. Catching the Scotsman by surprise he lets out a curse, as he barely escapes the wrath of the firebolt. Cowboy smiles. "I've waited a long time to kick your ass, Ramsay."

Ramsay sneers. "Son of the King and Queen of Fire, I will take great pleasure in killing you in front of your brother."

Jeremiah laughs. "Damn. That's cold."

"Real cold brother." Deen agrees with a smirk.

Ramsay takes a second sword out of his holster. "I grow weary of this small talk. Come boy, let me show you how a man fights."

Deen runs to meet Ramsay, their swords clash making sparks fly out from the sheer force of it. The Cowboy is lean and graceful, and surprisingly holds his own against the Scotsman. Back and forth they fight. The Scotsman lets out a roar when the Cowboys sword slides across his left cheek.

To hell with this, I'm done with all the gawking. Merrie-Beth grabs my arm, and we bolt. Jeremiah runs with us, rushing to get in front of us like before. Our retreat proves a pointless venture as the Giant is blocking our exit. He gives us a sneer. I'll never be the same after witnessing it. "Fee-fi-fo-fum." He chuckles a deep humorless laugh.

"Oh great, the giants got jokes." I whisper under my breath.

Merrie-Beth rolls her eyes. "Apparently. What are we going to do, Arabella? I would say run to the last exit, but I have zero doubt that those jackass twins will be there waiting for us."

I nod in agreement. "We need to split up. For whatever reason, they are here for me. I had a dream about this last night, and I can't allow them to hurt you. Staying and fighting is the only option left."

Merrie-Beth looks at me, her eyes cold as steel. I was taught that family comes first, even before duty. Family isn't always blood, and she's more than just a best friend to me. Mer is the sister I've always wanted, but wasn't given. "All of this is crazy, Arabella, but if they mess with you, then they mess with me, I'm not leaving!"

I don't like her decision but understand it completely. If the tables were turned, there wouldn't be a different outcome. "Ok, let's run back to the middle of the room like the guys said. Hopefully, that will draw them towards us, and maybe that will open the exits. With a little luck we might be able to escape before they block them again."

Jeremiah smiles up at the giant. "So, dick face, you ever heard of dentures?"

The giant smiles again, swinging his club back and forth. "How about you come and find out."

Jeremiah shrugs. "That's an invitation I just can't refuse!"

He runs toward the giant, sliding on his knees to dodge the swing of the club that was aimed at his head. He somehow manages to knock the giant off balance, connecting his leg to his knee. Keeping his momentum going he jumps up, taking his sword and slashing a deep gash in the giant's arm. These brothers are crazy, and I love it! Dark red blood flows from his forearm and onto the floor. The Giant screams, swiping his hand out and swatting Jeremiah into the wall with a harsh thump, but it doesn't stop Jeremiah He gets up with renewed vibrance shaking his head as if to clear the concussion he's bound to have.

We bolt to the middle of the room. The brothers from the Watch are still locked in battle with the evil men. Becoming impatient, my head swivels towards the last exit expecting to find the twins. I'm surprised to find no one there. Even though we can't see the twins, they are hiding around that exit somewhere, I just need to keep my Merrie-Beth away from danger.

"It's a trap." I whisper to Merrie-Beth.

"I know, and whenever we get out of here, I'm running straight to my house. Then I'm going to throw all of the mirrors away and lock all the doors. Where are those stupid twins?" Merrie-Beth whispers back.

"I don't know, and it's starting to piss me off," I say impatiently. Taking my cell phone out of my pocket, I text my uncle since calling the police is out of the question.

We are in the lunchroom being held hostage! Some of the Watch is here! Oh, and I love you both!

If this ends with us, like, I don't know, dying, I had to let them know that I loved them. "I'm not sure if they can help us, but I just wanted them to know all the same."

Mer nods her head. "I hope your family can do something before it's too late."

I nod. "Me too, Mer, me too."

Those two twins picked the wrong girls to fuck with today. I've never been involved in a fight like this before, but I won't back down. Nervous energy circulates through my veins, setting me on edge for what is to come. Keeping Merrie-Beth safe is my top priority, my only priority actually. I'm inwardly shaking, but I let confidence seep into my inner being anyway. Aunt Georgia's words engulf me, "*you only need to visualize your victory, and you will be victorious.*" She taught me that one's mind is a necessary tool in battle. We might still get murdered, hurt, or kidnapped, but they will scream out in agonizing pain before everything is said and done. I quickly pray for protection and then center myself. It's time.

"Come out, come out, wherever you are, Assholes!" I taunt.

My favorite twin, the one with the longer hair, we'll call him Lunatic, pops out from underneath a table near the last exit. "There, there, Chosen One. Are you so ready to die?"

I laugh, a dry sound coming from my throat. "I'm not the Chosen. She's yet to be born."

He grins when he sees my expression. "Fear not, we haven't come to kill you. Not today, anyway. Our boss wants to have a conversation with you. You're going to make us a lot of money, sweetheart."

I fold my arms across my chest. Reasoning with him will come to nothing. "Hard pass, and I ain't your sweetheart."

The other twin comes out from behind a counter close to where his brother had been hiding. We'll call this one, Dumbass. "You see, Arabella, it's nothing personal. We are just here to collect a paycheck, and if you come with us peacefully, then we will not harm you... much." Their tones are so casual.

My mind can't stop reeling from him calling me the Chosen. He's ridiculous. Why would this woman pay all of them to kidnap me? My family isn't wealthy, so this can't be about a ransom. If it is, the jokes on them. I look at Merrie-Beth, and she shrugs her shoulders at me.

"We have no qualms about killing your friend. She's not needed. Would that be crazy enough for the both of you?" Lunatic says with a sneer.

After hearing Mer gasp, I take a deep breath, and enter attack mode. Some long-buried instinct takes control of me. Picking up a chair, I throw it at his face. Nobody will ever get away with threatening Merrie-Beth, she's too kind. The chair barely misses his head but does clip his shoulder. My smile grows, but my eyes burn with anger. "Next time, I won't miss. It will be over my dead body before you touch even one hair on her head!"

"As you wish." Lunatic answers. He is the hotter head of the two. He looks at his ax, then back at my bestie. Arrogance drips from his voice.

"You're going to fight a girl who doesn't have a weapon with an ax?" I taunt.

"No one's ever made the mistake of calling me a gentleman. We're not taking any chances with you, Chosen. Although, I'm a little surprised to see that you're her. You don't look like much." He taunts back.

Okay, we'll add rude to his list of admirable attributes. We begin walking around each other in a circle, both measuring the other one up—both waiting to see who will strike first. I want to study him, see how he likes to fight. Taking a few punches is worth the ass kicking he'll receive in the end.

"You know what they say about arrogance?" I ask coyly.

He raises an eyebrow. "No. What do they say?"

31

"The more arrogant they are, the harder they fall," I reply.

Putting down his ax on one of the tables, his smile is cruel. "I'm going to take great pleasure in making you bleed as you beg for mercy."

A genuine laugh escapes my chest. This altercation could go one of two ways, we either make a narrow escape, or I get kidnapped. Regardless, it won't be easy for them. If it looks like I'll lose, then bargaining my surrender may be the only way for Merrie-Beth to escape.

Lunatic lunges for me, but I quickly move out of the way. My retreat does nothing to deter him. He moves his head from side to side, trying to pop his neck. Coming towards me again, he's fast, and I purposely don't move out of the way in time. His fist connects with my mouth making me cry out in pain, and I have to wipe blood away from my lips with the back of my hand. The metallic taste on my tongue turns my stomach into knots and fuels the fire for vengeance deep in my gut.

"Is that all you got?" I mock.

Amusement lightens his features. "She said we couldn't kill you, but she said nothing about me teaching you a lesson on respect for those above your station."

Now it's my turn for amusement. "Above me? Here I am, thinking I am the Chosen and all."

He scoffs. "You are not worthy to hold such a title. You disgust me."

I shrug my shoulders, because he's clearly insane. " You come here trying to kidnap me, and I disgust you? What is wrong with you, and you're fucked up brother?"

To hell with taking another hit from him. Centering myself, I punch him so hard that he stumbles back, but he won't get any sympathy from me. I don't allow him time to catch his balance, he tries to block the next two jabs to his stomach, unsuccessfully. After a failed attempt at kicking him in the balls, he grabs ahold of my foot making me fall. Quickly jumping up, I lunge for him, but he gets to me first—his fist lands on the side of my head making me feel woozy, and my vision becomes blurry in my right eye. It's taking all the strength I have left to stay standing.

Keeping Merrie-Beth safe in my mind, I push through the pain. We fight for what seems like hours when it's only mere minutes. Despite the eviler twin being beyond tired, he is still a good fighter, but not better than me. If Lunatic wins this fight, it will be because of his speed. The amount of blood pouring down his face does give me slight satisfaction.

Startling me, he pushes me up against a wall. Lunatic turns me around, his touch is ice cold, and attempts to tie my hands together. Waiting until the time is right is key. He makes the mistake of bending his head down close to mine. Allowing me to feel his breath in my ear—error number one. I head-butt him but that only makes him tighten his grip, so I repeat the motion twice more. Only after that does he let me go. He falls to the ground and is out cold. I plunge to my knees and start crawling away from him. My head is pounding. My jaw and body are aching.

Merrie-Beth yells out my name and rushes to my side. "Why did you do that?" She whispers in my ear, but blinding pain shoots through me, and I can't form any coherent words to answer my best friend back.

Chapter 4

We are Family

Arabella

*I am her, and I have more family. One makes me happy, the other
makes me want to throw things.*
-Arabella

TIME SLIPS BY, and I don't know how much of it has passed.
Seconds, minutes, hours, who knows? My head is exploding, but the
black dots have subsided from my vision. How long will it take my
family to arrive? The nausea hits with a vengeance, doubling me over.
Stone cold terror latches in my chest. The other men might try and
hurt Merrie-Beth; I need to get up. She needs my protection. Trying
to stand, I fail miserably. What will we do?

"Don't. It's okay. We are going to be okay. You need an experienced Healer." Merrie-Beth gently whispers in my ear.

"But...the men, they will hurt you." I attempt to get up again, but
she pushes me back down.

"Don't worry. They're gone." A battered and broken Jeremiah
comes to sit beside me and tries to assess my wounds.

"How's your brother?" I croak out.

Deen the Cowboy makes his presence known. "Awe, cuz! You worried about me?"

I smile sheepishly at him as my vision clears even more. He looks worse than Jeremiah does. Both his eyes are black and blue. Scrapes and bruises line up and down the visible parts of his body. My eyes stop on his hand. He is clutching the Scots man bun. My eyes tear up from the laughter that I'm too scared to allow to escape, because it will hurt too damn much.

He laughs as he sees my amusement. "I think man buns are overrated."

Jeremiah follows my gaze. Holding his stomach as he laughs at his brother. "Deen, I bet he was pissed! Please tell me there are cameras so that we can hack into them later and watch!"

Deen smiles, pointing at the apparent cameras above us. Before I can process any of this a flash of light so bright blinds us all for a moment. This light is more radiant than before. Hearing the same popping sound from earlier makes me try and climb to my feet, but I'm still too weak.

Several loud shouts sound throughout the room, calling my name and those of the people around me, which stills my movement. Looking up, I moan from the pain, the dots are back, but relief courses through me anyway, as two of those shouts belonged to my aunt and uncle.

Straining through the pain, I attempt to look up in their direction again. Disbelief battles through me, but there they are. Joy sets in all the same, while tears for a different reason sting my eyes. Uncle Jo looks at my beaten-up face and runs toward me.

His face is dark with anger. "Who were they?" He asks quietly, trying to rein in his temper.

I point to the ground a couple of feet away, but the space is empty, remembering only after that Mer said they had left. My vision keeps going from good to bad to worse.

I fight to hold back the unshed tears, but one slips down, and Uncle Jo tenderly wipes it off of my cheek. "I'm so sorry, my dear Ella.

For as long as we could, we tried to protect you, but they found you anyway, and we weren't here to help take care of you."

My aunt cries out loud when she sees my battered face. "Oh, my sweet girl. Who did this to you?" She sobs.

Now would be a good time to give her a grin, but my face hurts too much for the action. "That bad, huh? You should see the other guy."

Aunt Georgia smiles a sad little smile. "Worse than you could imagine."

My uncle wraps Jeremiah and Deen in a tight hug. He knows them. "Thank you for being here and helping them."

I attempt to stand on my own, but Deen and Jeremiah have to help me up. "Sweetheart, you have to take it easy. I wouldn't be surprised if you have a concussion."

I grunt. "Can't go to the hospital. There is no way I'm telling them that people can jump out of mirrors. It seems like my family failed to mention that to me."

My uncle looks at my aunt and rolls his eyes. "It sure didn't do anything for her smart mouth, did it?"

She laughs lightly. "Nothing will ever help that."

I look at both of them with a bewildered expression. My family's defense mechanism is to deflect challenging situations with laughter —however, my mood shifts from being grateful to suspicious. Being fed half-truths your entire life will do that to you. They have some explaining to do.

It's clear now why we've never really left Savannah, and it's because crazy people want to kill me. "Why didn't you tell me that I was her?"

They look at each other, then back to me. Aunt Georgia speaks first. "Arabella, we need to leave right now. They'll come back and have more recruits with them. We'll tell you everything, but we must return to Luxington Valley first. This is only the beginning of your calling."

What the hell is going on? I breathe in and out to try and

compose my temper. My mind doesn't want to process what she just said. My head and body ache, and I'm on the verge of a teenage melt-down of epic proportions.

Aunt Georgia senses my tension and begins massaging my back. "Trust us, Ella. We may not have told you everything, but we have always been there for you."

I know she's telling me the truth, and being pissed at them makes me feel guilty. "Okay, but I want to know as soon as we get there. It's only fair."

Uncle Jo shakes his head. "First, we have to meet with King Aramayus. Then we'll talk."

I raise both eyebrows. "We have a King?"

They both laugh. "Yes." Answering in unison.

I don't join in on the laughter but look around the room for my best friend instead. "Where's Merrie-Beth and the guys from the Watch?"

"They have already been transported to the Palace of Light. Jere-miah and Deen are your cousins." He answers. My cousins, and now they tell me I have more family. So many questions roll through my mind, but I ultimately decide against voicing any. Tonight, I'll get answers.

Looking down at my clothes makes me wince. My shirt is dirty, and there is a tear on my left sleeve. I'm not dressed to meet a King, but this will have to do. "How will we get there?"

"The only way we can. We will travel through the mirror." My aunt answers.

"Bullshit. Oh, no, we won't. I'm not going to walk through a mirror. Have you guys lost your mother effin' minds?" I turn around and start hobbling towards the door.

"It's not just any kind of mirror, Arabella. It's an enchanted one." A melodious British accent assails me from behind. Making my heart skip a beat.

Smiling, but grimacing inside, I turn slowly around. "Oh?"

My eyes lock with my British stalker who knew my name last

night at the park. We didn't get a chance to talk much at the time. He is tall, lean, and looks to be around my age. His golden brown hair once again has my fingertips itching to touch the silken tresses. Add eyes the color of emeralds, and the pointed ears of the Fae, and my body turns into hot molten lava.

He smiles, lifting an eyebrow. "Yes, people can jump in and out of mirrors. If and only if they are enchanted."

"So, are you a Guardian, Healer, or just the casual garden-variety eavesdropper?" I walk up to him and try my best not to hobble.

He grins and to my great satisfaction, blushes a bit. "I am Ethan Randall Callahan, Head Knight of the Lux Order." He does a little bow.

I whisper. "Nice to meet you, Sir Ethan. You told me your last name was Randall?"

He smirks. "Stranger danger."

I laugh, then wince. My uncle comes over and shakes Ethan's hand. "Thank you, Ethan, for coming to warn us. Otherwise, I would have never been on high alert and had my cell phone by my side. I'm usually so busy during the day, I don't check it much."

"Sorry I didn't make it here in time." He looks at me and touches my arm. "I'm truly sorry."

"No worries, I handled the situation as best as I could. My face may look bad, but my hard head knocked the Lunatic twin out. That can't be good for his bad boy image." I reply while looking into his big, beautiful eyes and damn near swoon.

They laugh, and my uncle pats me on the back. All the while directing me toward that damn mirror. "Are we seriously doing this?" I whine.

I knew that magic was real, and that some of the Others chose to live amongst us, but knowing and being a willing participant, while jumping through an enchanted mirror, is another thing entirely.

"You'll love it, Arabella, and I can't wait for you to see Luxington Valley. Out of all the places you will ever go, you will never see a view more precious than that of our homeland." Aunt Georgia gives me a reassuring smile, then looks at Uncle Jo.

I love how much they love one another. I stand in the middle of my family, and they each grab one of my hands. They know that I'm uncertain about jumping through a mirror and that I'll need the reassurances that only they can give.

Change has never been one of my favorite things, and now my world has been turned upside down. Even if I'm upset with them, I still need the comfort they have always afforded me. My aunt squeezes my hand, and I exhale a breath. Ethan makes a fist and throws what looks like a tiny rock at the mirror. Instantly, the image turns to a pretty shade of light blue. The sound of rain echoes throughout the room, and the droplets are falling softly into what I think is Lake Luminous. Which is the primary source of water in Luxington Valley and is believed to have healing properties. The sound becomes more intense as a bright light appears, and I close my eyes for a moment to relish in the warmth radiating off the mirror.

My uncle whispers reassuringly in my ear. "On the count of three, 1...2...3," and we jump. A slight pressure builds in my ears making them pop several times without stopping. That incredible light from before surrounds us, and little diamond circles float up and down. Happiness wraps around my limbs, my mind, body and soul. All too quickly, we arrive at our destination. Letting go of my family's hand, I try to balance myself. "Can we do that again?" Making them roll their eyes at me.

My gaze filters through the medium sized room that we've arrived in. It is sparsely decorated, and the furniture and decor inside is nothing too extravagant. Not even the caramel colored grand piano in the center of the room looks expensive. A desk sits in front of the window, and on the right side of the desk is a beautiful bouquet of sunflowers encased in a milk white porcelain vase. On the opposite side of the room is a fireplace, bookcase, and a chair that sits in the middle of the two.

The only art on the walls is above that fireplace. It's a painting of a boy and a girl. The girl has platinum blonde hair, and the boy has hair as dark as a raven. Her body exudes light, while his shadow leers out from his body. Could he be Shadow Kissed? That would mean he's fought death and won. The siblings have lime green eyes, which is the color of Fae Royalty. Turns out my knowledge on the world of the Lux amounts to diddly squat. I didn't know we had royalty or Knights. And my understanding of the supernatural beings that we call the Others is even more limited than I thought.

This must be the Prince and Princess of The Lux. Are they twins? If not, only a year or two separates them. They have similar features but are not mirror images of each other. The oddest sensation makes its way down to my belly. The prince is breathtakingly handsome, almost ruggedly so. He has a scar over his left eye. A blush creeps into my cheeks as I look at his hands, his big, long fingers make me shiver as I close my eyes.

Suddenly remembering Ethan, I look for him, and he's hovering in the corner by the desk. He stares at me intensely, the tick of his jaw making his expression unreadable. "Hey." I mouth. Did he witness my visual groping of the prince?

Ethan raises an eyebrow, a ghost of a smile playing on his lips. "Hey." He mouths back.

An elderly man with lime green eyes walks through the door, and I see Ethan come to attention. My aunt and uncle quickly follow suit. After a second's hesitation, I try to mimic their stances. My pain is making it difficult to stand with perfect posture.

I wish I could turn my head to the side, because I want to see what the General, or rather King looks like. Before tonight, I thought our leader was a General and not a King, but I'm assuming he's both. I'll find out more later.

"No need for all that ceremony here, not in my private study. Please, be at ease." A stern voice commands.

The King comes to stand in front of me, and I make an effort to curtsy as my aunt did before me. However, my injuries make it too difficult. He reaches for my hand and bows before me, looking stunned. "Finally, our Chosen has come home."

I say nothing as anticipation swarms through me, fizzling in and out of my bones. It would have been nice to have been able to speak with my family first, but Kings, especially immortal ones, don't wait for mere mortals. Even ones that they call The Chosen.

An older woman in black and white maids attire comes into the room and hands him a small glass of amber-looking liquid. She smiles at me then hurries from the room. The King gives me the cup. "Arabella, until Merrie-Beth can see to your injuries, this will help with some of the pain. The medicine will help only temporarily. She will need to visit you soon."

Taking the cup from him, I drink the contents without saying a word. It tastes like strawberry-flavored Coca-Cola. It sounds like a nasty combination, but it tastes like summer.

Almost instantaneously, my headache is gone, and I feel like I could probably run a marathon with how much energy the drink gave me. Ethan smirks at me over the King's shoulder, making my heart flutter. Focus, Arabella! Focus on King Aramayus.

Now that my attention is fully engaged, I can see that he is a silver-haired fox! The gray works well with the color of his eyes. King Aramayus looks like he's in his late thirties, but his eyes show too much wisdom for that to be true. With supernaturals it is hard to tell how old they truly are. His build is muscular, and he is only an inch or so shorter than Uncle Jo. When he reached for my hand, I saw a tattoo of the sun birthmark that the Chosen One is supposed to have on her wrist, but I don't have that mark. A memory of Ethan filters through my mind. One from the previous night of our run at the park when he stared down at my wrist with an expression of awe sculpted on his handsome features.

I frown as he examines the cut across my forehead, and the bruises on my face and body. "Who did this to you, Arabella?" He asks bitterly.

"I'm not sure who they were, King Aramayus. There were four

men: a giant, a Scotsman, and two brothers. The brothers were twins, and all I know is a woman wanted them to kidnap me. They explained that if I went peacefully, I wouldn't be hurt."

He laughs and has a look of admiration shining in his eyes. "I shudder to think what might have happened to you had you listened to that nonsense. You have grit, and that pleases me to see. With the journey ahead, that will only work in your favor."

I nod my head as a shiver runs down my spine. Today was a terrible day, but it could have been much worse. Merrie-Beth could be dead, and I could have been kidnapped by psychos. Ethan catches my attention once again. Leaning his back against the wall he resembles what I'd imagine pure sex looks like. His emerald eyes haven't strayed far from me. His hair is shaggy enough to cover the tops of his ears, and my fingertips itch to run my hands through the shiny locks. I wonder if he is always so bold as to stare at someone unabashedly. I quickly turn my head away, because I'm not that bold.

My aunt and uncle gaze toward the King fondly. "I'm glad you're back home. You've raised a fine girl. She's everything we had hoped for, and I understand that Arabella is not up to speed on all this. Take her to your rooms, for I've kept them open all these years. Tell her all she needs to know and start from the beginning. Our next meeting will be a briefing, where all details will be revealed. Preparations for the tournament have already begun, the new time of the Guardian has begun." The King bows before me and whispers, "For the Chosen."

"Thank you, my King. It's good to be home in the Lux Valley." My uncle bows, while we curtsy, and I follow them quietly from the room.

Chapter 5

Horrible Deaths

Arabella

What happened to my parents isn't right,
they didn't deserve to die.
-Arabella

STEPPING out of the King's study, I freeze. My eyes are glued to the extravagance, *everywhere*. I'm waiting for a TV crew to pop out and say, "Gotcha!!" This is not real life, at least not mine. My aunt has to grab my arm twice to get me to start walking. Her easy smile lights up her beautiful face. "It's breathtaking, isn't it?"

"Uh-huh," is all I can manage to say. The King's study was conservative. The palace, however, is nothing less than grandiose. Golden jeweled chandeliers line the high ceilings. Paintings line the hallways all encased in golden hand carved frames. Some of the pictures that catch my eye are of ex-Presidents. I knew from our history books who was a part of our world and who wasn't, but seeing the truth with your eyes is something else entirely. The floors are constructed of white marble with golden swirls. A golden trimmed burgundy runner lines the middle of the hallway. Everywhere, and I mean everywhere, there are carved statues and priceless antiques. My brain is too fried to comprehend or appreciate any of this right now.

Over the day's stress, I'm ready to make it to our rooms, but coming back to this part of the palace and exploring later is a top priority. It would take days, if not years, to be able to see it all. My eyes widen as we make our way to a golden staircase. Touching the banister, I look at my aunt.

She smiles, "Ever think you would walk on stairs made of pure gold?"

Shaking my head, I mentally freak out. This is the coolest thing! "No way, I have to show Merrie-Beth! Where is she?"

My uncle rolls his eyes at us and laughs. "She is with her parents, they are having "the talk" with her now. She'll be here later to doctor your wounds."

I've always known that she would be my Healer, but will it be weird for her now that I'm the Chosen? I look back at my wrist, I still see nothing. Either way Merrie-Beth is the one that holds true power, her kind have one of the most important jobs within our society. They doctor us when we are sick and stitch us up when we are at war. Their job is to make sure we are always in near perfect health. They go everywhere we go.

There is so much we will both have to learn. I'm lost in my thoughts but follow my family blindly up the stairs. When we reach the top, we turn to the right and make our way down another long hall. Decorated in the same fashion, it is just as beautiful as the last. Finally, we stop at the last door to the left. I'm ready to see what our new life looks like, as this will be our new home now.

My fidgeting gets bad when I'm nervous, so it's terrible right now. "What do these rooms consist of?" I ask.

"It is similar to the apartment we had back in the city. It has a study, kitchen, living room, dining room, and three bedrooms." My aunt explains.

Yeah, it's bigger than our old home. We never had a study or three bedrooms for that matter. I squeal as my uncle opens the door. Beautiful paintings are on the walls. Mahogany cabinets and floors, with emerald green rugs and curtains. Nothing in the room is like our tiny apartment in Savannah. They claimed the master bedroom, and didn't find it funny when I suggested that I should be the one sleeping in that big room. Hello! The Chosen is here.

Choosing my bedroom between the remaining two is easy enough, I decide on the slightly smaller one because of the view. Out of the bay window sits Lake Luminous in all its wondrous glory. Seeing this beautiful scene everyday might make up for my earlier distress of almost being kidnapped. Might! Even in the fading light of day, I can see that the water is crystal blue.

Picking up a couple of small boxes with my name scrawled on top I take them to my room and begin going through the biggest one first. My hand touches the rigid edge of my jewelry box, and tears spring instantly to my eyes. Taking it out of the cardboard I head for the red leather chair in the corner. It's been a long time since I've opened this.

I love this old thing, it's rectangular in shape and has Angel wings carved into the sides at the end. On the front and back sides is a replica of The Chosen's sun. Supposedly my birthmark, I trace the letters at the top of the box with my index finger—a sweet message in an elegant, bold script.

"Let love be your guiding light, and may it shine all your days."

A gift from my parents, the story goes that my father made it out of wood from an American Basswood tree the day after my birth. They had intended to give it to me when I was older, but they never got that chance. I wipe stray tears as they escape down my face. My father's love and dedication to me made this box possible. Were my parents really killed in a car accident, or did the woman that's trying to kidnap me have something to do with their deaths?

My aunt knocks on the door, startling me. The jewelry box and all its contents fall out of my lap and lands on the floor. "Do you need a few minutes, or are you ready for our talk?" She asks.

I take a deep breath. Am I ready? Am I prepared to hear about

47

this so-called destiny? The King called me The Chosen, and he didn't seem crazy, but what does that title really mean? I know all the stories, and about the prophecy of The Chosen. Do I even have a say in all this? So many thoughts, questions, and feelings course through me. In just a few short hours, my life has vastly changed, and I don't like it. Do Chosen Ones pitch fits, because this one is about to. Fear has a way of coming for us all, but I don't believe in running away from my problems, and I won't start now. That's how my aunt and uncle raised me, and it's the Lux way of life. Being brave is never easy. This new destiny thing could be fun. Right? Or a disaster waiting to happen, but tonight, we're being positive. "I'm ready as I'll ever be." My heart sinks down in my chest and my breathing becomes shallow. Some of this will be so hard to hear.

The closer I get to the kitchen, the more I smell the delicious aroma of my aunt's snickerdoodle cookies. This is what bribery smells like, and hell it just may work. My stomach is growling, because those assholes made me miss my tacos. Sitting down on the opposite side of where they are, I prepare myself to listen, and eat all the cookies. "Bribery will get you everything." I wink at my aunt.

She winks right back. "Some say diamonds are a girl's best friend. I say it's sugar."

My uncle's usual playful tone turns gravely serious. "Arabella, I want to start by telling you how much we love you. Everything we did, we did it for you and for the sake of our people.

I don't know what to say or think. My aunt and uncle gave up their entire identities just for me and my safety. I'm an emotional trainwreck. "I have a million different emotions running through me, but being pissed off is, at least for now, not one of them. I know you love me, and it couldn't have been easy, leaving this place or your way of life, to take care of me. Thank you."

Aunt Georgia's eyes turn misty. "You see, Arabella, the thing is, without you, nothing else matters. We were proud to do whatever we had to do."

Uncle Josiah takes both of our hands into his and squeezes before letting them go and grabbing a cookie. "What do you want to hear first, kiddo?"

What I'm about to ask will not be easy for any of us. However, I need real answers on how my parents died. "Uncle Jo, I'm sorry, but how did my parents really die?"

He closes his eyes for a second, and when he opens them, a lump starts forming in the back of my throat. The depths of his pain-filled eyes are covered in unshed tears. We've reached a moment where I know my uncle is done hiding the truth from me. "They were murdered, Arabella."

A heavy gasp escapes my lips, and my chest burns in anguish as dark fury fills my cold numb limbs. No words will form, and hearing the gory details will be the hardest thing I've ever had to sit through, but for them, I will listen. My parents' story deserves to be told. I squeeze Uncle Jo's hand, to let him know it's okay to continue.

It takes him a minute to rein in his emotions and work up the courage to explain "I'm sorry, Ella, once I tell you, your life will never be the same. We have kept you sheltered these past few years, because protecting you was our main goal. We needed you to see all the good things this world had to offer before seeing the evil that lives amongst the shadows. I don't know where your journey will take you, but now that the time has arrived, I'm not sure we made the right choices. Maybe we sheltered you too much. I fear we might have hidden you from our real world for far longer than necessary."

"Uncle Jo, isn't that the job of any good parent? I wouldn't trade my childhood for all the money in the world. I look at how you prepared me to face those evils. You taught me how to fight and how to defend myself. A grown man's ass was kicked today because of those lessons. Mer and I are here because of the both of you. Don't think of the things you didn't teach me. Think of all the things that you did." I can't stop the tears from streaming down my face.

My uncle nods. Looking at my aunt for encouragement, she smiles at him, and he begins. "Your parents received an invitation to dine with Mayra Narissa Blackwater the night before their murder.

She was a rising political star here in Luxington Valley. The re-election was days away, she was looking to gain more supporters. Mayra was well-liked and charismatic. When she began talking about starting a New World Order, one in which the Lux would rule over the world, people I had known my whole life, good and honest people, started joining her cause. The ones who disagreed, like our family, just stood back and watched while her opposing numbers grew. We did nothing, because she wasn't seen as a threat. On the night in question, I begged your father not to go. I had gotten a hold of the guest list, and every name listed on the paper were of non-supporters. That didn't sit right with me because if it were to be a regular dinner party, you would invite both. Your father decided to go anyway, he thought he could change her mind. It was no secret that Mayra thought she was above anyone who disagreed with her. However, no one knew how quickly her indifference had turned to hate and just how much that hate consumed her."

Pausing for a minute, Uncle Jo searches my face. Finally, he continues. "The part of the story about you being with us that night is true. Your mother called around 9:00 to check on you. Isabella didn't sound like herself though. She wouldn't say what was wrong, but asked if you could spend the night with us. That was no problem. We loved having you here. At around 11:30 that night I woke up from the worst dream of my life, drenched in sweat. I watched as your parents were being tortured by that evil Bitch while all her supporters were in the background cheering." My uncle gets up from the table and begins pacing back and forth beside the table.

I don't want to ask him this next question, but I have to know. "Uncle Jo, how did they die?"

He shivers but doesn't hesitate in his reply. "There's no easy to say this so I'm just going to come out with it. Mayra put a paralytic-causing herb in their food. She tortured them by waterboarding and because they still refused to join the cause, she sliced their throats."

What a horrible way to die. I cover my ears, and try to scream, but can't make a sound. My parents were drugged, tortured, then executed by a madwoman who escaped prison, and my uncle had to watch it all, I can't breathe with the thought, for our dreams are far too often true.

The next thing I know, my aunt and uncle are at my side. My aunt is holding me, and my uncle is rubbing my back. I'm sobbing so hard the collar of my shirt is already wet. "I'm so sorry you had to see that."

"It's the way of our people, and our dreams are from above. They show us many things. Had I not dreamed of her treachery we would never have been able to arrest Mayra. The herb she used is untraceable. It would have never shown up in the autopsies, but because of my vision, we found that not only was it growing on the premises, but there were also traces in her jumpsuit pocket." Uncle Jo leans down to kiss my cheek.

I wipe my eyes with a napkin. "I'm okay," I whisper, but I'm not. Their expressions are full of worry. "I'll be fine, there's more to discuss tonight." I reassure them, with more bravado than I actually feel. "Were my parents the only ones to die that night?"

"Twenty others lost their lives. Ethan's father, and the King's wife were amongst them." My aunt replies.

My sadness turns to anger. What a raving bitch. "I know Mayra got life in prison but what happened to her supporters that cheered while she was killing my parents."

Uncle Jo's face turns dark with anger. "They got what was coming to them. Arabella, the districts are more advanced in every way you can imagine. We have technology that can wipe your brain clean of everything you know, and we can give you new memories to replace the ones you had. They were cast out of our society and given new identities."

I'm somewhat comforted by this, but I still think they should have served jail time. I will never feel sorry for them. They made their choices, and with certain choices comes consequences.

Chapter 6

A History Lesson

Arabella

It's weird seeing yourself in a history book, I'm not sure I'll ever get over it.
-Arabella

"WHY DOES everyone keep calling me The Chosen?" I ask. My aunt sighs in relief, clearly happy about the change of subject. She hands me a book and tells me to turn to page 431. The thick leather-bound book is titled "Guardians: A History of the Most Famous." Intrigued, I quickly turn to page 431. Pictures of me align the top and bottom of the page. In the middle is a picture of an old scroll.

January 28, 1779

On the twenty-eighth day, in my fifty-eighth year, I, Reverend John William Lightfoot, The Great Leader of the Lux, dreamed a dream. This dream is a sign of things that will come to pass after a time. Dreams are a gift. May we always have strength to pick up our weapons and fight, "For The Chosen".

The Prophecy of The Chosen

A baby girl will be born of both fire and light. The sun will kiss her left wrist and will be with her always. Through the years, she will grow strong in both wisdom and combat. Before the Great War a tournament will be held in all three sectors. Two by two they will be chosen, and she will be their fearless leader. The Guardians of War will defeat an evil darkness, which will settle upon the world. The mighty enemy will unleash an army so lethal it will be unlike anything we have ever witnessed, but in the end, she will lead the societies to victory. They along with all nations, people, and tongues will win the Third Great War; therefore, restoring the peace and unity that once ruled this Earth."

The prophecy I had been taught as a child had been revised significantly. My mood is somber as I quickly read all five pages dedicated to me. They know everything—friends, training, favorite movies, extracurricular activities, etc. Paparazzi have been following me for years, and if they'd been snakes, they would have bitten me. My family is patiently waiting for a response. What am I supposed to say? I don't know what to think or feel. Shocked maybe, unworthy, but also, can I just tag someone and say, "not it?"

Holding up my left wrist I ask the question that's been burning a hole in the back of my mind. "I have no sun. Is magic covering the mark?" That's the only logical explanation.

"Smart girl." Aunt Georgia smiles.

Since the beginning of time elemental magic has existed. The very core of our bodies are made up of water and dirt. We are a part of nature, as it is a part of each of us. As generations passed most of mankind abandoned the old ways, and allocated all magic as evil, but that's not the case.

My family, and all the societies practice magic in some form or fashion. That is, except for me, I was born without a gift. Most of our kind has the ability to manipulate light. My uncle can form lightning bolts and shoot them from the sky, and my aunt can produce massive amounts of electricity out of her hands. They're quite deadly separate but put them together in a fight and they are damn near unstoppable.

Uncle Jo takes a drawstring pouch out of his pocket. He takes my wrist and places it palms side up. Opening the pouch, he takes out a muddy red substance and warms it up in between his hands. Then he lays it on my exposed skin. He leans down, whispering, "Revelare," three times before sitting back up. I don't know what ingredients make up the stinky red mud, and that's probably a good thing. A tingling sensation begins on the edges and slowly sweeps through the entire circle. Sparks fizzle as the substance begins to dissolve, reminding me of fireworks on the Fourth of July.

The red mud leaves behind my perfect *Sun* mark, though it appears more hand painted than a birthmark. My heart squeezes inside my chest. Meticulous detail is in every curve and every line. A secret treasure that I never knew existed, it's the only thing about me that isn't plain or ordinary. Everything about my birthmark is perfect, and for once in my life I feel beautiful.

I still can't wrap my mind around the fact that I'm the Chosen. Me! "Obviously, there is no mistaking this sun, but everything about this is insane. Have you never witnessed the awkwardness that is me? Especially when it's my turn to talk in front of a room full of people."

My aunt Georgia rolls her eyes at me. "Just because you were born The Chosen doesn't mean you're perfect. Ella, we don't choose our destiny, fate has a way of doing it for us."

My eyebrows rise to almost my hairline. Yeah, that really doesn't answer my question, but I let it go. My frazzled brain is starting to hurt again. "Is Luxington Valley really in the Alaskan wilderness like you told me? There's no snow on those mountain tops."

My aunt bites her lip and tries not to laugh. "Luxington Valley is located in the heart of the Blue Ridge Mountains, in one of the valleys between two of the tallest mountain peaks. Technically speaking, it's located in a valley of the Brasstown Bald, which is in Georgia."

My head is starting to throb. "So, that's why you told me Alaska, because I wouldn't have understood why we couldn't visit."

My uncle nods. "Bingo kiddo. Listen, you know that when the Knights fell, the Guardians arose to power. We scattered to different parts of the world, but what's not commonly known is that quickly after, a massacre against our kind occurred, during the Great Slaying thousands were slaughtered. The Umbra sought to obliterate our numbers and they almost succeeded. That's when we went into hiding and began recruiting. John William Lightfoot was found, and became the first leader of the Lux."

We hide in plain sight; we work where you work and go to school where you go to school. We're your leaders, and we're your friends. This is the cross we must bear to keep you safe. It's hard living in the shadows. "Why was I sent away? Wouldn't I have been safer here?" I finally feel like everything is beginning to click inside my mind, but I still have questions.

Aunt Georgia takes a deep breath. "The night your parents died a hit was put out on you, and the king ordered us to leave. You were always heavily guarded even though you didn't realize it."

A lump forms in my throat, because finding out psychos want to kill you is pretty intense. My mind is spinning in a million different directions, and the headache has returned in full force. I knew that we worked closely with the Others, but I'd never been told that they were a part of our societies. "When did the Supernatural's join our ranks?"

Uncle Jo shrugs. "They've always been, most of The Knights of Templar were Fae."

I have a million more questions, but I don't have it in me to ask tonight. "May I be excused? I'm exhausted."

Aunt Georgia comes to my side and gives me a hug. "Of course. I love you, sweetie, goodnight."

"Goodnight." I call out to them.

"Ella, remember, Merrie-Beth is supposed to come and doctor

you, so don't fall asleep yet. I'll tell her parents you're ready." My uncle makes his way to the front door.

"I walk into my room and decide to put on my PJs. Merrie-Beth has seen me at my worst, so it doesn't matter what I'm wearing. I pace back and forth in front of the bed. I'm so glad Merrie-Beth is here too. It's nice to still have something from my old life in this new world with me. I'm nervous about seeing her, though. With these new roles we play, I can't help but wonder if it will change us. Will it change our relationship?

Footsteps come barreling down the hall, so I sit on the side of the bed that faces the door just as Merrie-Beth runs into the room. She grabs me in a bear hug, and my earlier fears about our friendship dissipates. She will always be my best friend. "Merrie-Beth, you can let go of me now." I laugh and shake my head.

Her grip on me tightens. "No, I can't! You don't understand. When I saw you head butting that evil man over and over, I thought you would have brain damage for sure. Don't you ever scare me like that again. Just look at what you did to your pretty face." She reluctantly lets me go.

I look over at her parents. Henry and Rebecca Kincaid quickly rush over for a hug. They've always reminded me of a couple from a 1950's sitcom. They have an endless supply of cardigan sweaters, matching pairs of black-rimmed glasses, and I swear I heard her dad say, "Golly jeepers," once. The Kincaid's have been my second family since birth, and I adore them. Her father looks at my face and winces, "Arabella, you saved our little girl's life today. We will be forever grateful."

My smile broadens. "Well, it was mostly for my benefit. I'm not sure what I would do without Merrie-Beth." Every word is true. Merrie-Beth takes a black remote-looking thing out of her pink shoulder bag on the floor. Her mother gives her an encouraging smile. She walks over to where I'm now sitting. Will this hurt?

Mr. Kincaid moves his wrist from side to side to show her what to do. "Remember, sweetie. You have to move your wrist like this. That's the only way it will get an accurate reading."

He genuinely smiles as she begins to move the remote the way he told her to. "Yes, you've got it, Merrie-Beth!" He looks over at his wife, his face radiating happiness. "Look, honey, she's a natural."

Mrs. Kincaid claps her hands together and smiles lovingly at her husband. "Yes. Oh, Henry, she is amazing."

I look at Merrie Beth, and she gives me the death stare. Her eyes dare me to say something sarcastic. I giggle, which makes her raise one of her perfectly groomed eyebrows in response. "What in the world is that thing?" I ask.

Mrs. Kincaid answers. "This scientific gem is the Franklin 3000." She takes the remote from Merrie-Beth and hands it to me. "To the untrained eye, it looks just like your average TV remote, but it's so much more than that. With the mere flick of your wrist, it can detect if there is anything harmful going on inside your body. After detection, it tells us what the best course of treatment is."

A deep baritone voice sounds from the machine. "There are no broken bones, and the cuts are superficial. I suggest an ointment of three onion roots, two garlic cloves, honey, and Aloe Vera. Also, I recommend you put some plantain leaves in the mixture to reduce swelling." I can't believe what I just heard. Everything about this gets crazier and crazier.

Mr. and Mrs. Kincaid say their goodbyes, and Merrie-Beth tells them she'll be home in a minute to make the salve. I look at my aunt and uncle and silently plead with them to give us some privacy. I need to talk with my best friend. My uncle wants to say something in protest, but my aunt drags him out of the room.

Chapter 7

The Letter

Arabella

Full moons have never scared me, but what's floating below the surface of Lake Luminous might.
-Arabella

WHEN THE DOOR CLOSES, I turn to Merrie-Beth. She's admiring the picturesque view out of my new window. The waters have turned a darker shade of blue now. As bright as the moonlight is tonight, the water appears to sparkle like a thousand diamonds are on the surface. A half smile tugs at the corners of her lips, and I sit on my bed and wait for her to join me.

She finally comes to sit at the foot of my bed and sighs. "Ella, did you expect this place to be so beautiful?"

I'm surprised that's her first question, but I answer anyway. "Never in a million years, Mer. Did you see that staircase? We are living in a palace. An actual fucking palace. I bet our place is finally bigger than the Bitch's!"

She throws her hands up in the air. "Boom Beoytch!" Laughing with her this way, like we always do makes some of my anxiety melt away. I believe our relationship really will survive. The world around us may change, but our friendship never will. That's a comfort not easily afforded to anyone. Merrie-Beth starts tracing the floral design on my new comforter with her finger. "I have so much to say. I'm just not sure where to begin. This is so..."

I shrug my shoulders and give her a tired smile. "This is so weird." I finish the sentence for her. I'm not offended because it's hard to believe I am The Chosen of anything.

She smiles back at me but shakes her head in disagreement. "I'm not using weird in the same context that you are. It's not that way because you're special, Arabella. The weirdness stems from us being a part of something even more classified than we realized. We're a part of a freaking prophecy."

I rub my temples, because my head is starting to feel like a jackhammer is jabbing me in the skull. Grabbing Merrie-Beth's hand, I squeeze it. "Please, promise me that you won't ever treat me differently. I don't know what the hell is about to happen, but at least we get to take this journey together."

She pinches my arm with her other hand. Classic Merrie-Beth. "You know that I won't, oh, Chosen One. I'll do as you wish." She starts bowing her head and waving her arms up and down while she chants, "I'm not worthy."

I laugh, grabbing her arms to make her stop. "Don't make The Chosen angry."

Merrie-Beth laughs and hops off my bed. "I've got to go make the salve and bring you that strawberry concoction. Mama says that will help you to heal more quickly. See you in about ten, Slut."

I throw one of my pillows at her as she walks out of the door. Maybe the salve and the drink will help make my head *NOT* feel like death. I lay down on the one pillow still on my bed, and it's just not comfortable. Sitting back up, my gaze hits the pillow on the floor. Ten measly feet away. I'm torn between my need to be lazy and my need for comfort. Groaning loudly, I make my choice. Black dots line my vision as I bend down to pick up the pillow. With the motion, my attention lands on my jewelry box that fell to the floor earlier, making me growl, I feel like a teenage grandma.

I usually wouldn't be so careless with my most coveted possession, but my mind had been on finding out about not only my past but my future. Uncle Jo's words about me being changed forever come back to haunt me. This day has been too long, and I just want to sleep.

My pulse races as I notice the heart on the left side of my box has fallen off, I should've been more careful. "Shit!" Suddenly, my sadness turns to curiosity when I notice a small latch where the heart was. My heart rate hits a catastrophic level. As I pull open the secret compartment a piece of paper falls lazily to the floor. Quickly unfolding the paper, I watch in astonishment as magic hidden within lifts it out of my hand. A light so bright fills the room, I have to shield my eyes. After a moment, I take a peek through my eyelashes, but the brightness has only lightened a fraction. The piece of paper is lying flat in the air. Reluctantly, I wave my hand above and below the article. Nothing happens, but I can feel warmth coming from the luminescent light. Nothing about this damn day has been normal.

My next line of defense is to grab the paper to examine the contents. I tug it lightly, and nothing happens. Using a little more force, I tug it again careful not to rip it. Thankfully, it doesn't tear, but it doesn't move at all either. It's a letter that's addressed to me, and no matter what I do, it won't budge. Which is annoying.

Biting the side of my mouth, I contemplate my next move. Looking down at my birthmark, I wonder if it's literally the key to everything right now. Closing my eyes, I place my birthmarked wrist above the paper. An explosion of light permeates throughout the room with such force I am thrown back against my bed. Sitting back up, I catch the paper as it slowly glides toward the bed.

There's a blur of letters but because of unshed tears I can't read the words. I'm scared to read this letter. If I cry, my already aching head may explode right off my body, but the tears gather anyway. Swallowing the lump in my throat, I take a deep breath and steal myself for a letter that I know could possibly break me, but I hope it helps me also.

My dearest Arabella,

The happiest day of my life was the day you were born. You have given us so much joy these past four years. If you are reading this, then we are no longer with you. I asked my dear friend Eleanor to hide this letter in the secret compartment your father built if anything should happen to us. I'm so sorry, my dearest one. Each of us has a calling that is full of danger. But take heart, and never forget you are never alone. my precious Arabella. All that is to come to pass is for the greater good. We must stand for what is right, no matter the cost.

Take this note and throw it into Lake Luminous on a night when the moon is full, and the hour is midnight. It is there you will reunite with my dearest friend, Eleanor. Fear not, for she has been my most trusted friend and confidant these past ten years. In her hands will be a gift that will help you in the darkest times of your journey. Our Chosen One, what a difficult burden you will have to bear. Always remember when the shadows of darkness begin to fall; where there is shadow, there is also light. The night will never be able to defeat the day because when it's the morning the darkness must flee. We will love you, forever, our beautiful, amazing girl. Until our next meeting.

With all my love, your mother,

Isabella Grace St. James

I wipe the tears that have flown freely. "Oh, Mama." My agonizing cry bounces off the walls.

Merrie-Beth opens my door and barges in without knocking. Worriedly, she runs to my side when she sees the tears. As I show her the note, she holds me while my body shakes with grief.

It takes a while for my anguished soul to will the tears to stop. Merrie-Beth dries my eyes with a cloth and places the salve on my cuts. It burns, only intensifying my emotional state. Merrie-Beth walks to the window and looks out. She gives me a syrup that tastes a lot worse than the strawberry coke from before. "Arabella, you realize tonight is a full moon, don't you?"

Getting up, I walk to the window. "Heck no, I hadn't. What time is it?"

She looks at her watch and smiles. "Exactly 11:51, are you going?"

I nod. "I have to, Mer, and the parental units won't allow me to go on my own. I need to do this by myself."

She nods in agreement. "Okay, so how can you get there? We don't know our way around the palace yet, it's too massive."

I open the window to inspect how far down it is. We are at least four stories high, so jumping would be impossible. A smile forms on my face because on the right side of my window there's a trellis. I look at Merrie-Beth, who is staring at me wide-eyed. She pulls me back as I start to climb out of the window. "You have got to be out of your flipping mind, Arabella. Nope. There has to be another way!"

Merrie-Beth has never been a fan of heights, so I understand her reaction, but we don't have time to argue. Time is quickly ticking away. "You don't have to like it, Mer, but this is the quickest way. I'll still have a three-minute run once I reach the ground."

She sighs. "Please, be careful. If you're not back in one hour, I'm telling your aunt and uncle. You have ONE hour... so, you better leave now." She helps me out the window and accidentally looks down for a split second. Her knees buckle, and she falls with a thud. Merrie-Beth doesn't look well at all. Her skin has turned kind of green. "Don't mind me. Since I'm already down here on my knees, I'll start saying a prayer that you don't die," she whispers.

That makes me giggle. I feel kind of bad leaving her in this present state, but meeting with Eleanor, takes precedence over puking best friends. As I climb down the trellis it begins to shake, but thankfully it doesn't break. After what seems like forever, my feet finally touch solid ground. I break out into a run, as my mind races—full of a thousand thoughts. This meeting has to happen tonight, because who knows where I'll be when the next full moon comes.

Chapter 8

The Lady of the Lake
Arabella

Eleanor is beautiful as starlight,
and warm as the sun.
-Arabella

MY CHEST BURNS WITH EXERTION, but I don't stop until my feet reach the water's edge. I bend over, putting my hands on my knees, and try to catch my breath. Running sucks ass, and I loathe it with a passion. It has to be near midnight. The night is clear with not a cloud in sight. The stars shine a million times brighter in the country. Living in the city made it difficult to see the stars, but they shine in abundance here. A giant yellow ring outlines the full moon. Uncle Josiah says that's a good "omen," whatever that means.

With sadness, I look at the note. If only there was more time to memorize every line my mother poured into this letter. Once I throw the note in the water, it will be unsalvageable, but there is no time for sentimentality. With regret, I ball the note into the palm of my hand and throw it as far as I can into the water, which isn't very far.

Standing there, I look anxiously into the water. My mind pleads for something to happen, and it feels like an eternity has passed. The note didn't tell me how long to wait on Eleanor.

The only sound around me is that of the crickets. At least, I think it's crickets, I've never really been in nature at night. I jump at the screech of an owl as it flies deeper into the woods surrounding the lake. This place is beautiful, but homesickness punches me in my gut. I miss the smell of the pizza place down the street. All there is to breathe in now is the fresh scent of nature. Don't get me wrong, it's nice, but it's not home. I miss the sounds of the city, too. The car horns, the drunken people yelling, and the high-pitched sounds of sirens going off as they speed down the street. I keep looking in every direction, but still no sign of her. The letter didn't tell me how long to wait. It's been years since my mother wrote the letter. Could Eleanor have left the palace? Could she have died?

A log sits on the right side of the bank, so I decide to sit and wait a few more minutes. Merrie-Beth wasn't kidding when she said I only had an hour before she told my family about my shenanigans. That can't happen, because they will lose their shit about me coming out here alone. Especially without my phone! I forgot to grab it off my nightstand, and I also forgot to put on clothes, so yeah, I'm about to meet my Mamas best friend in Iron Man lady pajamas. Winning.

My family would have every right to yell at me though. I do have a bounty on my head, my eyes roll as the psycho twins invade my thoughts. Assholes. Especially the one I've officially named Lunatic.

The sound of rippling water draws my attention back to the lake. About twenty yards out, I see a woman with light platinum blonde hair emerging from the depths. Surprise consumes me. My mother said something about not being afraid of Eleanor, so I put on a brave face. I've opened and shut my eyes a million times today in hopes that what I'm seeing isn't real. Once again, the action proves futile. Eleanor is still walking toward me. She is very real and not a figment of my imagination.

Why isn't she soaking wet? Her hair is as dry as mine. Is she Maritime? They are basically creatures of legend. I've only read about them in books. Legend has it that we were once all Maritime, which means we could survive in both land and water. When the Ice Age came, we were forced out of the water and when the age after began and the waters thawed some decided not to return.

Biting my lip, I put my sole focus on not fidgeting. Eleanor stands a few feet before me now with a giant smile. Her wavy silver blonde hair cascades down her back, stopping shy of the end of her waist. She is lovely, and her skin has a slight glow. Her dress is baby blue and glimmers in the moonlight. It has three-quarter-length sleeves and is a close-fitting lace material that flows down to the ground. The dress looks almost magical, it sparkles brighter than any diamond shining in the midst of the sun.

Eleanor's smile is infectious, so my expression mirrors hers happily. I stand there, looking all kinds of awkward because what are words? Thankfully, she takes pity on me and speaks first. "Arabella, I can't believe this day is finally here. You look so very much like your mother. You could be Isabella's twin." Eleanor has a thick English accent. At the mention of my mother, her eyes fill with tears, but after a moment or two, she reels them back in.

My eyes shimmer with fresh tears. It's been an emotional day. "How did you meet my mother?" I ask.

Her lips pout in sadness. "I met her on the eve of her wedding. She was sitting on that same log. My mother had sent me into the woods for some berries for the pie she was making. We startled each other, and both screamed. Afterward, we had a good laugh. A wonderful friendship was born that night." She explains.

"What were my mother and father like? My aunt and uncle have shared many stories with me, but I want to know things that only a best friend would know." I'm basically pleading with her for as much information as she is willing to give me.

She gestures for me to sit back on the log. "Let's have a seat."

Sitting next to me, she takes my hand in hers. Eleanor somberly looks over the water while she gathers her thoughts. "Your mother was a spitfire. She was in every capacity what a Pyralis warrior should be, and she was the best fighter of her generation. I've watched her take out a hundred men by herself. She only thrived more after the marriage to your father and becoming a member of the Lux. Isabella loved her new life at this palace very much, she especially adored the King. He was good to her and became her mentor of sorts. He made her his personal Guard, the first Guardian to be chosen for such an elite position. You see, that was usually a Knights job. The years passed, and as happy and in love as she was with your father, she missed her home immensely. Your Aunt Georgia was here, but Radix, their brother, was not. They only saw him at joint Pyralis and Lux celebrations. Isabella talked often about the palace at Dragon Crest City. She said that the Lux, Palace of Light, paled in comparison to the Pyralis, Palace of Balefire."

Eleanor stops for a moment and wipes some tears that escape down her cheeks. She squeezes my hand, "Your father was a wonderful man. Very kind. He loved your mother with his whole heart. Victor was as easy going as he was passionate. They were opposites in many ways, but that worked well for them. He didn't mind that your mother was the better fighter. He was proud that she was the best. He once told me that if he couldn't be then he couldn't think of a greater person than his better half."

I laugh at that. "So, my dad was a bit of a smooth talker, huh?"

She smiles. "I'd say so. Isabella always blushed when talking about him, I found that rather endearing."

"What does my mother's brother do in Pyralis?" It's weird having more family.

Eleanor smiles. "Radix is married to the Queen of the Pyralis. He was once a fine Guardian, and rumor is that he is an even greater King. They have two sons who are mighty warriors. They will undoubtedly win the Fire tournament and become your companions in the Guardians of War. They'll be loyal to you, Arabella. To win this war, you'll need them by your side. The brothers are the best of the best, the most fearless of this century, even better fighters than your mother was. Some say they even have dragon's blood mixed in their veins."

She's talking about Deen and Jeremiah. My cousins that saved me during the lunchroom attack. They held their own against Ramsay and the toothless giant, and I could learn a lot from them. They are brothers in every sense of the word except in looks. "Are they adopted?"

She nods. "In a way. Their mother, Queen of the Pyralis, your aunt Adalia, was barren. She desperately wanted children, and one morning, after she returned from helping a dragon maiden escape death, the two boys were found on their palace balcony. The newborns had been carried from the depths of the Alpine Mountains on the back of the maidan dragon. The dragon was instructed to stay and watch over the city. He, along with a few others, still reside there today."

I cough because my mouth has been open in surprise so long that it feels dry. I'm amazed. "Eleanor, that's amazing. I thought dragons were extinct."

She shakes her head. "Their numbers have diminished, but thousands are very much alive."

"I have so many questions that I need to ask my family." I take a deep breath and look out over the water. I'm happy to know that I have a family. Aunt Georgia and Uncle Josiah never revealed too much about either side of our family. They said it was for their protection, but I know now that it was probably for mine.

All this new information is overwhelming. My uncle is a King. My cousins are the most fearless warriors of our time, and I'm just a simple girl from the "mean" streets of Savannah who likes eating cake and writing bad poetry. My entire family is famous for being exceptional, and my fame comes from being born with a birthmark of a sun on my wrist. That's not the same and I don't want to disappoint anyone. Pressure builds up in my chest to be perfect, but that's not me. How will I live up to the expectations of what they need me to do?

"Eleanor?" I ask.

"Yes." She replies.

Feeling the need to lighten the mood, I change the subject. "Umm...so I'm assuming you live underwater?" My question comes out a bit awkward.

Eleanor gives me a reassuring smile and pats my hand. "I know all of this is very difficult for you right now. It won't be easy becoming a leader to those who know more of this world than you do, but don't doubt yourself. You can do this, Arabella Grace St. James. You have the strength of the Pyralis and the wisdom of the Lux burning deep within you. All you have to do is believe."

My smile is genuine because not only have her words given me strength but have also calmed me. "Thank you, Eleanor," I say quietly.

She nods her head. "As for your question, we do live underwater for the most part. However, we do have the capability to live on land if we so choose. Most of us prefer the water."

I sit still for a minute, trying to let that sink in. "Of course, I've heard of Maritime before, but I know so little about your kind. How many of you are there? Why do you prefer to live mostly underwater?"

"My tribe is twenty thousand strong. As a whole, around the world, the last number I heard pushed around had us just below a million." She slightly hesitates before she answers my next question. "Most of my kin do not trust humans. I don't share in their ignorance."

"Why do they not trust us?" My curiosity not caring about the audacity of the question.

"It stems from an argument between our leaders many years ago. My father, the Governor, believes that given a chance, you Landers, that's the name they call you, will destroy us all." Eleanor rolls her eyes.

I want to ask more questions, but I sense she doesn't want to divulge specific details. I'll have to gain her complete trust first. "It was probably hard being best friends with my Mama," I gently squeeze her hand.

"My tribe has long ago learned that I will not be bullied into doing what they wish of me. So, my father made me an ambassador of sorts, and now I trade information back and forth between our palaces. I believe your King is a good man, Arabella." She says with a quirk of her eyebrow.

"I'm so glad we got to finally meet. It may be months before we get the chance to see each other again. In a few weeks, I'll be traveling to Dragoncrest City for their Trials. My new journey will soon begin." I'm not ready to say goodbye, but Merrie-Beth will alert my family any minute.

Eleanor gets up and motions for me to do the same. "The hour is late, and you must be getting back soon. Arabella, this will be a most difficult journey, but you are stronger than you think. I'll help you along the way and protect you with my life if need be. You will discover many new friends, but remember, enemies will often wear a disguise of a friendly face, those are but wolves in sheep's clothing. Keep your heart closed, and your eyes and ears must remain alert at all times. Most of Pyralis and the Lux will fight to the death for you, but the Kori's waters have grown dark as of late. We are not allowed to enter there anymore. Trouble is brewing, and they are a society divided, and a kingdom divided will not stand for long. Their true King was overthrown sixteen years ago, and another one now rules in his stead. His heart is cold and wicked. Do not trust him, Arabella. I will not be able to protect you there."

I embrace her with a long hug. "Thank you, Eleanor. Until we meet again." I don't know what else to say, and I turn to walk away before tears stain my cheeks again. She puts her hand on my shoulder to stop me. As I turn, she takes something out of one of her pockets. Eleanor lifts a heart-shaped locket over to me. Trimmed in white gold, it glows in the moonlight.

"I almost forgot. You must never take this off. It is a light that will protect you in your darkest hours."

Putting the necklace around my neck, I tuck it in my shirt. "Thank you. It's beautiful."

"See you soon, Arabella. I'll be watching over you. It's nice to have a piece of your mother and father back in this place. Now, I must get back to the Governor's ball." She starts walking toward the water. My face remains impassive as I watch her descend into the blue depths. It's nice to have another piece of my mother and father with me, also. As I turn around, my chin crashes into a hard, muscular chest.

SEBASTIAN

Chapter 9

The Shadow Kissed

Arabella

He is infuriatingly wicked.
-Arabella

A MASSIVE SET of hands gravitate to my shoulders to steady me. Lifting my head, I find the Prince of the Lux staring down with a menacing snarl that makes me shiver and back away slowly. Much like Ethan's first touch on my tawny skin, electric shockwaves spread throughout my body. The veins in my arm contract as it sizzles down, feeling like static electricity. Sparks fly from his fingers, and black fingertip marks are left on the curve of my shoulder. It feels almost violent in a way and a direct contrast to the gentle way Ethan's surged through me.

The way his jaw tightens, he clearly saw and felt the same intense shock. However, that's the only sign he gives. The prince grabs me by my arm, and with a yank, we begin our trek back toward the palace. My temper flares, because not only is he "manhandling" me, but he does this without saying a solitary word. No, hello, who are you, or kiss my ass given. Who does this jackass think he is? Being the motherfucking Chosen trumps being an asshole Prince. Pissed off me already sounding entitled, but I'll work on that later. "Excuse me, Prince Asshole, but I've got it from here."

Three times, I try to pull my arm out of his firm grasp, but that only makes him tighten his grip. My temper reaches the inferno setting. If Sebastian doesn't voluntarily let me go, then me stomping my size nines on his big ass foot should. The prince howls in pain, and I smirk, but not before making a run for the palace. I'd bet he didn't see that coming. I'm not some child who can be dragged around. Why would he care if I'm outside of my room anyway? We are nothing to each other. My feet tread faster knowing with his long muscular legs, it won't take him long to catch up to me. The sound of my heart thumping is so loud in my ears that I can't hear anything else. My mind tries to shut out the fear threatening to radiate its ugly head. I don't know what will happen if he catches up to me. Little is known about the shadow kissed, but they aren't known for having good temperaments. That's bound to happen when you've walked among the dead and lived to tell the tale.

Wariness seeps into my bones, and my body craves rest. I'm physically, emotionally, and mentally drained. Arguing with an asshat can wait for another day. Tonight, I'm still Arabella Grace St. James, an average girl from Savannah, Georgia. Tomorrow starts my new life as The Chosen, and I just don't feel like being a boss bitch right now.

The exertion of this run is kicking my ass. Glancing behind me, I check on his location. A gasp escapes me because there is no sign of him. Where the hell did he go? Before my mind can react or even scream, a movement in my peripheral momentarily catches my attention before my feet go out from under me. This fucker has tripped me! I close my eyes as the scene plays out in slow motion, bracing myself for falling to the hard ground that never comes. The prince lifts me instead into his muscle-filled tattooed arms. Shadowed wings flutter behind him, keeping us afloat.

My gaze wanders up into his beautiful lime green eyes, and I am tempted to forget his earlier asshole behavior. The prince looks back intently into the depths of mine, and it'll be mere seconds until I am lost. That can't happen. Before he can cast a spell on my senses, I break out of his warm embrace and fall onto my ass.

"Who do you think you are?" Recovering quickly, I poke him in his beautiful...solid, I mean, ugly solid chest.

He stands up to his full height, towering over me. The scowl once again spreads across his handsome, scarred face. The prince says nothing, and I have to give credit where it's due, he's intimidating.

"Cat got your tongue, jackass?" I taunt him with a roll of my eyes. It's infuriating when someone gives you the silent treatment. Why won't he talk to me? "You're not going to answer?" I ask.

"No." He shrugs. A shadowed finger brushes a stray hair off the side of my cheek.

"Where's Ethan?" My voice comes out squeaky from frustration and nervous energy. I sure as hell don't like the prince, but that doesn't make my treacherous body any less attracted to him.

"You sure do roll your eyes a lot." Sebastian licks his lips and ignores my question.

"And you obviously don't have a filter!" I challenge. His voice is smooth like velvet, making other parts of me tingle.

"Filter?" The Prince's English accent is more polished and regal sounding than Ethan's. Rich bitches.

"Yeah, over your mouth. You just say whatever you're thinking. So rude!" I accuse and poke his chest again—his nice, hard chest. A skull tattoo peeks up from underneath his black tank top.

Sebastian grits his teeth and takes a deep breath while pinching the bridge of his nose, "Listen, I don't have time for this shit. Let's go, you're coming with me."

He grabs my arm, but I move out of the way just in time. "I'm going back to the palace. ALONE! I don't need an escort. Thanks, but nah." I turn to walk away, but he stops me.

"We haven't even been properly introduced, and you're already being a nuisance. Just do whatever the hell I tell you to do, and we'll get along fine." He snaps.

Standing on my tiptoes, I grab his shoulder-length raven-black hair and yank him down until we're at eye level. "I don't answer to you, Jackass. As soon as you understand that we'll get along just fine."

I revel in the fact that he's seething. Sebastian takes his hand and grabs my hair at the nape, applying pressure to the point of pain. "I like my hair being pulled, do you, Arabella?"

Fuck. The wetness between my legs proves that I apparently have a new kink. "N-No!" I lie.

A beautiful smile spreads across his angelic face, and his other hand pulls me closer to his body. Sebastian's massive erection hits my belly. "That's a lie, Arabella. I can smell your arousal." He leans forward and places his nose into the curve of my proffered neck. "Your blood smells delicious. It calls to me like a siren from the shores of Azure."

My pulse accelerates, but not from fright, as his elongated fangs graze my neck. Do the shadow kissed drink blood like vampires? I've heard just one bite from a vampiro can give you long-lasting pleasure. Sebastian licks the spot that he's nipped, and embarrassingly, a moan passes through my lips. His seductive smile answers my question that he heard. Looking up into his lime green eyes, the desire there mirrors my own. The dark Prince lets me go, shaking his head as he does. A look of hostility replaces the lustful one from seconds before.

My lip curls in irritation, and his scornful gaze is like a splash of cold water on my want for him. "You always lick people you've just met?"

He grunts. "As I recall, that elicited a pretty moan from your lips. You're welcome."

I draw in a deep breath, but not before turning around in an attempt to hide my blush from him. With no other words, my feet carry me towards the palace. He follows me quietly, both of us lost in our thoughts. No one has ever made me feel the way Sebastian just did, and I'm not okay with that. He reeks of danger, and I have enough trouble coming my way. No extra drama is needed in my life, so it's best if we steer clear of each other. Ethan would be a more suitable choice for stress relief.

Sebastian growls behind me. Can he read my thoughts? Please. God. No. One of his shadows slinks up and down my arm in a gentle caress.

His answer not only makes me cringe, but it makes angry as well. "Yes, shadow kissed are gifted with many abilities. Mind reading and control are in the mix. Don't tell anyone, not even my father. Nobody knows."

I slap his shadow away from me. "Don't read my mind again, Sebastian."

He laughs. "You're cute when you're angry, Bells."

Putting my hand on my hip, I turn around to face him with my resentment. "Don't give me a nickname, I don't like you."

"I don't answer to you either, Bells." He taunts as his shadows turn me back around and pushes me to start walking towards the palace again.

Uncle Jo rushes toward us, giving me a death glare as he nears. Yeah, I'm not going to like this conversation. His face is dark with anger. "What the hell are you doing, Arabella Grace?"

Damn. He said my middle name, that's not good. I stand up fully, not one to walk away from pissed-off uncles. This is not my first time in the hot seat. "I found a letter in my jewelry box from my parents. It told me to meet with Eleanor, so that's what I did."

His face softens at the mention of my parents, but the intense look he gives me doesn't. "Meeting with Eleanor is fine, going by yourself is not."

My eyes roll, and Sebastian talks to me inside my mind.

Next time you roll your eyes in my presence, both of us will get a reward. Stay away from Ethan, Arabella. He's not who you think he is. Oh, and your tits are perfect in that see through top.

I cover my boobs up with my arms, and his chuckle sounds through my head, sending fire straight to the apex of my thighs. My uncle shakes Sebastian's hand, thanking him for finding me, and I'm once again lost in my thoughts. Can I trust anything the dark Prince tells me? Ethan has been friendly, but I'll be cautious. This new game I've found myself a part of seems to be more complicated than I anticipated. Uncle Jo doesn't press me for conversation as we return to the palace. Beyond grateful for that. When he's not angry, I need to ask him more questions about the court and the politics of this new place, but first comes sleep because in the morning begins my new life as the society's Chosen Poser. The last thing I want to happen is for me to disappoint anyone, and right now, I'm not ready for this new life.

Chapter 10

First Meetings

Arabella

Meeting someone who looks so much like your lost loved one is not a blessing but also a curse.
-Arabella

DESPITE MY LATE NIGHT, I wake up early. I'm nervous about today and I'm starving. After my shower, I put on my favorite pair of jeans and a dressy shirt. I'm not sure what meeting dress codes are, but this will have to do.

Heading to the kitchen and making breakfast is next on my agenda. I'm not a great cook like Merrie-Beth is, but my omelets are always on point. Beautiful mountains surround Luxington Valley, so sitting on the terrace while stuffing my face sounds like a perfect idea, and a big cheesy smile is in order because this view is flawless. Magnificent pine trees line the palace and go as far as the eye can see. I've never seen anything as beautiful as this place. My eyes look over in the direction of Lake Luminous. Has Eleanor told anyone about my arrival? Considering most of her people don't care for Landers, I'd imagine she hasn't.

My next thoughts are of both Ethan and Sebastian. They are so different in not only looks but in stature. Ethan is more strength, while Sebastian has more lean hard muscle. Both are hot as hell, and I'm attracted to both equally, well, almost equally. The tingle returns to the apex of my thighs when I think about Sebastian's assault on my neck. He's an explosion of fire, while my desire for Ethan is more of a slow-burn type of flame.

Sebastian's words about not trusting Ethan slaps me like a dick to the face. I'll keep my eyes and ears open, but is Sebastian even trustworthy? Or could he be warning me away from Ethan for some other reason? Palace and politics go hand in hand. Everyone has an agenda. What's his?

Darker thoughts send a cold shiver down my spine. Those men are going to come for me again. Am I prepared? Maybe I can ask my cousins from the Pyralis if they will help train me. Eleanor thinks they will win their tournament, and she says they are the fiercest fighters of this century. I could use a little bit of that, a whole lot of that actually.

My uncle opens the French doors behind me. "Arabella, it's almost time for us to meet with the King, but we need to have a little chat first."

I finish eating and clean up. "Is everything alright, Uncle Josiah?"

"Yes, but you need to be made aware of who will be at this meeting today." He mumbles as he helps himself to some orange juice.

"Great way to keep it vague, man." I laugh nervously.

To my surprise, he laughs. "I'm sorry, sweetie. As you know, it's just been a rough twenty-four hours. I may have aged fifty years." He motions for me to sit at the table, and I comply. My mind races. It's been less than seven hours since I last saw him. What else could have happened in such a short time? Is this about my would-be captors? I patiently wait for him to grab a breakfast pastry and more orange juice.

Finally, he comes and sits in front of me and starts babbling. "Arabella, as you've come to guess, your mother and Aunt Georgia have a brother. He's king of the Pyralis and a great man. I'm sorry we kept him from you, but none of us had a choice. We had to disappear, and while he knew about your whereabouts, you were left in the dark."

"Because I would have sought him out?" I guess aloud.

"Yes." He answers truthfully.

"Uncle Jo, Eleanor told me all about that last night. I understand because that's exactly what would have happened. You guys had to keep me safe. What we didn't talk about is you and Dad. You've always changed the subject when I brought up your family. Do you have any close living relatives?"

He sighs. "Your uncle Radix will be at the meeting today, Ella, and he is staying here until after the Trial. He wants to be the one who will personally escort you to the Pyralis capital, Dragoncrest City. He wants to ensure you are taken care of. We know you'll be safe with him."

Butterflies infiltrate my belly as nervousness moves in. He still isn't answering my question. I lift one eyebrow at Uncle Jo. "And, as always, you have evaded my question. What about your family? Or I should say OUR family."

He looks at his half-eaten pastry. "Our family is a different matter entirely, but I'm sure you'll meet them soon enough. Until then, I won't answer any questions about them."

I take deep, even breaths. He's stubborn as a damn mule. Doesn't it matter to him that I want to know about them? They are my family, too. He doesn't care. His mind is made up, and once that happens, it can't be undone. What he doesn't know is that I have other people to talk to now, and there are various ways of finding out information.

I look around the kitchen. "Where's Aunt Georgia?"

"We have been given orders to lead a search team for the monsters that tried to kidnap you. Georgia is assembling our team now. She will be leaving tonight, and I will accompany her as soon as this Trial ends. We may be unable to stop the impending war, Ella, but we can make it hard for them to assemble their armies." He shakes his head but doesn't say anything else.

This new bit of information feels like a punch to my gut. I don't want to be alone in this new, strange land. They can't leave me. I'm not ready. "Can't I go with you, Uncle Jo?"

He sighs deeply, and by the look of sadness that crosses his face, the answer is no. "My sweet Ella, I'm sorry, but no. We're on two different paths now that lead toward the same common goal. We'll fight for you, with you, and if need be, we'll die for you. This sucks, but don't be discouraged. We will never truly be separated because our love will always lead us back to one another. We are family."

I wipe the few tears that have escaped down my face. "When will I see you again?"

He shakes his head. "Only God knows, little one, but I believe it will be soon. You'll be in good hands. I've already spoken to your two cousins, and they have agreed to pick your training up where we left off."

Feeling the need to try and lighten the mood, I grin. "I thought about asking them to help me train. Eleanor said they are the fiercest fighters of this century. I can't wait to see if they really will enter the arena riding on lions during the Fire Trials."

My uncle laughs. "Rub it in, Ella. Try to video some of the tournament or something! That's hardcore! I'm brave enough to admit that I'm not man enough for that."

We both laugh and then I look at the clock. "It's almost time." I somberly say.

"We should head over there, and Arabella, don't be nervous. Just be yourself. That is more than enough. You are enough." My uncle helps me up from my chair, and we move toward the royal part of the Palace. My head feels so much better than it did yesterday, and the cuts are still on my face but are not as deep. The salve appears to be working.

The palace looks even more breathtaking in the light of day. There are rooms upon rooms full of antiquities. As we pass one of the many rooms, I see a bright light coming from one of the objects. I turn to get a better look, but the light has disappeared. When there's more time to explore the palace, I want to start with that room first. Looking up at the top of the doorway, I see a dreamcatcher in the shape of my sun hanging between the ceiling and the top of the door. No other room is marked. That must be a clue to something.

As we reach the door to the King's study, my uncle places his hand on my shoulder. "Ella, you'll hear and see things today that I wish you didn't have to, but it's necessary. You need to know how horrific each one of these individuals are." I nod up at him, and then he opens the door for us to head inside. This entire thing is going to be hard on everyone but especially hard when the conversation turns to Mayra. It won't be easy for my uncles either because Aunt Georgia warned me before bed that they would be talking about the slaughter of our family on that dreadful night. I'll be strong for our people. We'll be at war soon, and whatever that means will be more challenging than this. Taking a deep breath, I focus on not tripping, something mundane to help ease the tension radiating throughout my body.

I look around the room nervously and my heart skips a beat when my gaze locks on not only Ethan but Sebastian as well. They are leaning up against the wall. I nod my head at them, and Ethan smiles at me while Sebastian wears a smirk. Ethan looks adorable, while Sebastian looks like sex with a side of danger.

Sebastian whispers in my mind. *You look good enough to eat.*

I glare over at him. *Stop looking inside my head.*

He shrugs. *I could teach you to block me out, but what's the fun in that?*

He chuckles when I growl back at him. *Asshole.*

Forget about him, and focus, Arabella. I turn my attention back toward the middle of the room. A small circular conference table has been set up in the center, and all the chairs are full, minus two. I follow Uncle Jo to the two empty chairs, and we sit down.

As I look in front of me, my breath catches. The man who has to be my uncle is sitting directly in front of me. He has the same wavy red hair and bright blue eyes. Not to mention our same god-awful nose, which is crazy. Uncle Radix is smiling at me, then grimaces as he looks at my face. He stands and bows. "My dear Arabella, we will catch the individuals responsible for this. Death will not come swiftly enough for them."

My body shudders as I think about the men. "It's not as bad as it looks," I reply with a nervous smile.

"Arabella, as I'm sure you've guessed, I'm your Uncle Radix. You look so much like our Isabella. I didn't expect such a striking resemblance." His eyes fill with tears, but he quickly regains his composure.

I give him a sad smile. "We both do, Uncle Radix. I didn't expect that either."

Chapter 11

Villains

Arabella

*The villains in my story will pay penance for
what they've done.
-Arabella*

KING ARAMAYUS BEGINS MAKING introductions to the people
sitting at the table. "The woman to my left is the Lieutenant General
for the Lux United Armed Forces, Kamila Kelli." She has jet-black
hair and bright red lipstick. She nods at me then turns her attention
back to the King. She appears to be no fluff and all business. I can
respect that.

King Aramayus moves on to the next "The man next to Kamilia is
Greyson Kelli, her husband." He also has jet-black hair and a full
beard. He is the Armed Forces Major General. The two men sitting
to the right of my uncle Jo are both Captains in the Armed Forces
under Kamila. The blonde one is Ryder Sing, and the older man next
to him is Luke Smith.

The King pushes a small button on the side of the table, and a
plasma screen TV comes down from the ceiling. Fancy. "Arabella,

everyone is up to speed on what you told me of the vicious attack yesterday. Kamila, you may start the presentation."

Kamila walks to the front of the table with strategic precision, reminding me of a panther, beautiful yet deadly. "Thank you, my King. The message we are about to play for you is what we received from Queen Adalia after the prison escape from Inferno. It's been broadcast all over the Underground Guardian Network and viewed worldwide. The word is out, and we will find the perpetrators. The world is searching high and low." She slaps her hand on the desk as she continues. "War is imminent, but we will not make it easy for them, Arabella. We will aid you in any way you see fit. King Aramayus has so graciously agreed to give you reign over his armies once the Trials are over. Although, we'll be at your command even now."

I nod at her, hoping I look impartial, like most adults I know do. So, I'm basically in command of a whole army now? That is either the coolest thing ever or a disaster waiting to happen. A dry, humorless laugh tries to bubble up my throat. I bite my lip to keep from screaming.

The lights darken as the TV turns on. An Asian man with a bright, red-colored Mohawk appears on the television screen, dressed from head to toe in black leather. He looks fierce. "Calling all people of the three great societies. By way of Dragoncrest City, Queen of the great Pyralis, Adalia St. James, has a most urgent message."

Queen Adalia is definitely on the top ten list of the most beautiful women I've ever seen. Her gorgeous, ebony skin shines bright on the screen. She has soulful golden-brown eyes and appears in her early thirties. Something in her demeanor contradicts that assumption, the way she holds herself gives the impression she is wise beyond her years. She has long, silky black hair with red highlights, and a gold ruby-filled crown sits upon her head. Power and strength radiate from her.

She wastes no time, "King Aramayus, King Diodyous, and people of the great societies around the world, it is with much sorrow that I must inform you of a most unfortunate occurrence. At approximately 5:45 this morning, Mayra Narissa Blackwater, the "Terror Twins" Keaton and Cohen Wiley, the giant Pollux, and Blaine Ramsey escaped Prison Inferno. In the two hundred years of the prison's existence, no one has ever accomplished what these five have done today. They are ruthless terrorists who have killed men, women, and even children. Due to the items the criminals left behind, we have reason to believe they are coming after our Chosen, Arabella Grace St. James. We have since learned that Mayra has offered them a ten-million-dollar payday to capture her. We are calling on all Guardians to assist in the arrest of these dangerous individuals and for the protection of our niece. My husband and sons are in hot pursuit of the prisoners. My dear friend, Aramayus, I urge you please, allow Arabella to come back home. The trials must start earlier than any of us anticipated. This was an act of war, and they will not stop until they've taken her. We must prepare her and our people. For The Chosen."

The TV goes dark, and the letters UGN light up on the screen. This must be the Underground Guardian Network that Kamila talked about. I guess it's like their news station. It makes sense that we would have our own news channel. Having more family is weird. Uncle Radix seems pretty cool, but what kind of personality will my Aunt Adalia have? Will she be all business, like Kamila, or warm and loving like Aunt Georgia?

Looking over at my uncle Radix, I give him a shy smile because he's staring back at me. He gives me a warm grin in response, he has an easy way about him that makes me feel calm. Being away from Uncle Jo and Aunt Georgia will be torture, and I'll need that extra piece of comfort.

Kamila makes her way back up to the front of the conference table. She nods her head at someone in the back of the room. A man soon appears, carrying a bundle of manila folders and begins handing one to each person at the table. The folders are filled to the brim with papers and written in the middle of the folder in a big, bold script is the word CLASSIFIED.

When the man passes out the folders, he takes a remote out of his jacket pocket and hands it over to Kamila. "Arabella, although I gave everyone a copy, this was essentially put together for you. Within this folder, you will find every interview we did with these individuals. We've also given you a copy of the transcript for their trials, and we've included multiple pictures of them. A report also tells you about different habits we observed during the years they were at Inferno. You must study this. Even the tiniest detail could save your life."

Taking the remote, she changes the channel on the TV, and a mugshot of the Wiley twins appears on the screen, making my skin crawl. The one with the beard smirks in his picture, and I want to knock it off his face.

Kamila looks at the screen and rolls her eyes. She doesn't like these guys very much, either. "Meet Keaton and Cohen Wiley, AKA the "Terror Twins." Born in Romania during a time of famine, they, along with their parents, fled to America when they were only two years old. Their dad was a ventriloquist, and their mom worked as a waitress at a local diner. The brothers became orphans at ten when both parents died in an automobile accident. By eighteen, both brothers had transferred in and out of multiple foster homes and juvenile detention centers. There is a five-year gap in intelligence information between when the Cohens were released into the world and when they showed back up on our threat radar. The twins felt like the American Judicial System failed them during their time in foster care. They concocted a plan to bomb the United States Supreme Court building. We intercepted their plan, but their capture was unsuccessful. That arrest came one year later, when they donated several ventriloquist dummies to three separate orphanages. The dummies were stuffed with small amounts of C-4, and two hours later, 357 men, women, and children were killed. We were able to trace the delivery van they used, and that's how we caught them."

With each word Kamila speaks, the pictures change on the

screen. Seeing the aftermath of the bombings makes me nauseous. I was only seven when this happened, the brothers are absolutely diabolical. Thinking about the lives lost that day is sickening, and most of the lives lost were children. How could anyone be so heartless? We must capture them again.

Kamila clicks a button on the remote, and a picture of the giant appears on the screen. This, too, is a picture of his mugshot. However, unlike the twins, the giant has a big fat grin. Oh, good ol', toothless. "What information we have on Pollux is very limited. We do not know his age, birth date, or true nationality. We don't even know his last name. He showed up on our radar in 2005. Before that, it's as if he never existed. Pollux's fingerprints have even been altered. In February 2005, military personnel around the globe began to go missing. Twenty-five men, and fifteen women to be exact, all with different jobs and skill sets vanished without a trace. In late 2006, we found their dead bodies in an abandoned warehouse. Their bodies were so mutilated we were only able to identify them by their dental records. The giant had tortured and murdered them to get some of America's most sought-after military secrets. The Government covered this up because they didn't want mass panic among citizens. Some of our intel suggests he was able to obtain where certain missiles are located and in what direction they are pointed. Only when Pollux broke into the White House to kidnap the President were we able to catch him."

Unlike the twins, Pollux barely has pictures of himself popping up. The sight of the burned bodies is almost too much for me, and I can't stop the shudder that follows because these men are awful. So many lives have been lost, and they have no remorse for their actions. I'm happy, Merrie-Beth is safe.

Kamila clicks the remote, and a picture of the Scotsman comes on the screen. His first picture is not a mugshot, it's one of him and a beautiful woman with jet-black hair. "Meet Blaine and Geneva Ramsey. They are two of the most notorious criminals of our time. Blaine was born and raised in Scotland. He grew into a fierce warrior and, by the age of twenty, had become the head commander of the Highland Maritime Supreme Naval Army. He's highly skilled, and no fighter could stand a chance against him, in or out of the water. He came to America in 1936 at the request of President Roosevelt. The President had just signed the Treaty of Morsus Mihi, an alliance agreement between all Maritime and Humankind. Blaine joined our Navy and became a member of the First Five. He was the main contributing factor to our victory at the Battle of Midway during WWII, which was the turning point of that war. He was the Admiral of the USS Yorktown.

"After the war, he went dark and only resurfaced after he had married Geneva. Geneva Ramsey's maiden name was Cromwell—the daughter of Jedediah Cromwell, Governor to all Maritime people. Arabella, you'll be interested to know that Jedediah is also Eleanor's father. We discovered that Blaine and Geneva married three months after the suspicious death of Eleanor's mother. No one believes that her death was due to natural causes, but instead think that she was poisoned. Geneva was the only suspect, but after the ruling by the coroner, she was let go. Blaine and Geneva showed up on our radar two years later. They earned the nicknames of the modern-day Bonnie and Clyde, because they caused quite a panic up and down the Eastern seaboard. They robbed banks and convenience stores, even hit the Federal Reserves, and got away with every cent. They killed a total of 695 people, and that's just the ones we know about. I wouldn't doubt that some shallow graves are full of dead bodies. The couple has no remorse nor regard for life, and they are monsters— greedy monsters who finally got sloppy. We started a rumor that a prominent investor was delivering a payment of twenty-four million dollars in diamonds to a famous arms dealer. That information made them show up during "the deal." After a shootout that left several of our men dead, we were able to arrest Blaine, but unfortunately, Geneva got away, and for two whole years, she's been off our radar."

If he's a WWII veteran, why does he look so young? No one else thought that was weird, there's still so much that I don't know. I make a mental note to ask my family later. Blaine having the highest body count doesn't surprise me. Something about the black coldness in his stare scares me most of all.

Uncle Jo is frowning. He knows these awful people want to kidnap me and, by the sound of it, eventually kill me. The cold, dark feeling of panic settles in my body, making me numb. Kamila pauses and looks around the room. We all know that Mayra is up next, she is no stranger to anyone in this room. Uncle Radix's facial expression gives nothing away, he appears indifferent to the tension that's building in the room, but looking down at his hands, they tell me a different story. Both his fists are balled so tightly that his knuckles have turned purple.

Kamila sighs heavily as photos of the one who killed my parents come up all over the screen. She's supermodel pretty with chestnut brown hair and hazel-colored eyes. "Mayra Narissa Blackwater grew up on Long Island and was the daughter of a radical United States Senator. She went to Harvard University, and, upon graduation, she made her debut within the Lux's political system. The years flew by, and with each passing year, her popularity grew. She was charismatic, and even the politicians from across the aisle held her in high esteem. A year before she was arrested, her supporters formed a hate group called The Mortem 1. Her teachings are like that of the Umbras. Only they can rule. Mortem's creed was simple: they wanted the Lux to rule the world, where Mayra would be the Supreme Ruler of all. The night she was arrested, my father was among the dead. She will be caught, dead or alive. I do need to mention that with the reward she's offered for The Chosen, we have reason to believe that she's got a rich benefactor backing her. Nothing is set in stone, but all reports lead to Duvessa Raven."

I can feel Sebastian's eyes on me then, and when mine locks on his, he looks terrified for me. His whisper is gentle inside my mind. *I won't let her have you.* I can feel my eyes soften briefly at his words, but I quickly look away.

Who the hell is Duvessa? She has to be horrible for Sebastian to be upset about hearing her name. Kamila takes another deep breath and nods her head at me. After a minute, she finally addresses the Kings. "Thank you, both. If you need anything, please call me or any of my men. We will be happy to help."

King Aramayus nods his head and turns to me. "Arabella, this will be a trying journey. The odds are stacked against you, but good will always defeat evil. You must never lose hope, and prayers are always with you."

Even as my eyes fill with tears, I smile at him. "Thank you, my King."

He nods and looks around the room. "You are all dismissed."

Uncle Jo grabs my hand, and I'm at a loss for what I want to do. Part of me wants to return to Savannah, and the other part wants to find out if I can achieve my destiny. My face remains passive as we make our way to Uncle Radix. He shakes my Uncle Jo's hand and gives me a quick hug.

"Arabella, I understand your aunt will be leaving tonight. You will need time to say your goodbyes. Tomorrow, I would like to see you for a bit. Is that okay?" Uncle Radix asks.

I smile at him. "That would be great, actually."

He smiles. "Thank you."

"We must be going, Radix. Georgia will be leaving soon." Uncle Jo says.

He nods. "Take good care of our girl, Jo. Arabella, until tomorrow."

Chapter 12

A New Ally, Secrets, and Warnings
Arabella

I was once told to beware of the one who wears the Ice Dragon tattoo.
Yeah, that explains nothing.
-Arabella

I MINDLESSLY FOLLOW Uncle Jo as he leads me to where my aunt awaits us to say our goodbyes. My sole concentration is on not losing my shit. It will be hard not to cry, but Aunt Georgia needs me to be strong. After almost tripping over the edge of an elaborate rug, I am ripped from my pity party. For the first time since leaving the King's study, I notice we are in an entirely different part of the palace. "We're not going to say our goodbyes at the apartment?"

"No, we are meeting her at the Courtyard of the Fallen."

"You've got my attention, that sounds deliciously creepy. Are some important dead people buried there?" My interest is piqued.

He rolls his eyes. "It's a graveyard and burial place of our Founders."

"Remind me of how our Founder died?" I ask solemnly.

My uncle gives me a sad, grave look. "He, along with his beloved wife, were killed during The Great Siege of Luxington Valley. The

Umbra wore masks, attacked the city, and killed hundreds. Lightfoot managed to get all the women and children out of the city through a secret passageway, and they held the intruders off for as long as they could. Lightfoot's wife, Ruth, would not leave his side. She was a courageous woman, but they were both murdered. Their eldest son, Jethro Lightfoot, took up his position as ruler, and with him women were allowed to join the Guardians."

It starts coming back to me. "They never found out the individuals who did it, did they?"

Uncle Jo shakes his head. "No. It's still an unsolved murder. With every passing generation, new Guardians are assigned to the case. They dedicate their entire lives to that service. It's frustrating that after all these years and all the technology we've uncovered, we are still no closer to finding out. We have even offered a steep reward, and still, no witnesses have come forward. Money always makes people talk."

We make it to the front doors of the palace. The entryway is nothing less than perfect, and I gawk at the chandelier hanging high above my head. It is shaped like my sun, and on the end, it has rows upon rows of yellow diamonds draping down above our heads. It's beautiful.

My uncle rolls his eyes with a chuckle. He mumbles something that sounds a lot like, "Girls, making me smirk. After a short walk outside, we enter a building that is the same beige color as the palace, but it does not have the same extravagant presence.

"What is this place?"

"This is the old palace, and it leads to the courtyard." He answers nonchalantly.

"Oh." I'm a little creeped out, because this place looks like one of those old insane asylums that you see on tv. The palaces are zip codes apart. There are a few portraits of people hanging up in wooden frames and a table with a kerosene lamp on top of it, but no golden statues or fancy paintings. The staircase to the right is not made out of pure gold, it looks dilapidated, like it might cave in at any moment. My uncle guides me towards a narrow hallway. I shiver, because the temperature has dropped at least twenty degrees. I rub my hands up and down my arms in hopes of radiating a little bit of heat, it's pointless. The further we travel down, the colder it gets.

Candelabras strategically line the hallway, and medium-sized candles are placed inside each. It's like we've traveled back in time to the 1700s. I wonder if the palace looked exactly like this back in the day. The more we walk, the narrower the hallway becomes. Strangely, the ceiling also looks slightly lower. At the end of the hallway is a door about my height, made of dark mahogany wood, and it has a lion door knocker carved into it. A giant cobweb to the left side of my head makes me cringe. I'm not usually scared of spiders, but that cobweb is enormous.

My uncle turns to me. "Arabella, only a handful of people have ever stepped behind this door. You'll understand why in a minute. The King asked me to show you this room if you ever have to escape suddenly."

My curiosity is instantly piqued. What's behind this door? I look toward Uncle Jo and wait for him to explain. He doesn't finish, which is typical for him. Without another word, he grabs the door knocker and knocks three times. A slight wind starts to blow, and there is the faint sound of a lion's roar in my ear. The sound and wind end as abruptly as it began.

Did I imagine the whole thing? Uncle Jo wastes no time. He grabs the door knocker and knocks three more times, making it rattle and shake. After a few seconds, a glow forms around the lion's mane, and the sound of a roar starts slowly and increases in volume.

My uncle puts his arm around me and smiles. "It's just a little magic, Arabella."

I've been taught about the elements and the magic they can wield, even witnessed my family's gifts, but seeing this in person is impressive yet startling. There is still so much for me to learn about our world. My attention turns back to the door knocker, and the lion is giving me a raised eyebrow look.

"Hello, Arabella." The lion says in a peaceful yet harsh tone.

I give him a warm smile. Rude or not, my mouth can't form a sentence, not even if my life depended on it. Hopefully, a smile is good enough because that's all I got.

"Cat got your tongue?" He smirks and wastes no time laughing at his joke.

I chuckle. "Hello, umm, Mr. Lion?"

He laughs, but when he speaks, his tone is deadly serious. "Chosen One, you may call me Hadar. I am the keeper and giver of secrets. No one may enter this room unless they tell me one of their own."

It's no surprise that my mind is blank, and I don't want to tell a secret in front of my uncle. "I don't have many secrets."

Hadar looks toward my uncle, then back at me. He's pretty wise for a door knocker. "Josiah Gabor St. James, you will tell your secret first, then you may enter."

Uncle Jo hesitates for only a moment, then nods in agreement. "I have a twin brother, who I haven't talked to in seven years." He looks at me, then adds, "It's complicated."

They have another brother, and I have another uncle! How many things has my family been keeping from me? I look at Uncle Jo, and the pain of his secret is all over his face. He's never been good at opening up to people, he keeps everything bottled up. For a moment, I can pull back my anger, but this won't be our last conversation on the subject.

I keep it light, for now. "So, I have another uncle...huh?"

He sighs a deep sigh of relief. He thought I was going to have an attitude. "Yup. His name is Joseph."

I smile back, and it's not even fake. "So, I could call both of you Uncle Jo?"

His smile fades quickly. "No, I'm Uncle Jo. He is Uncle Joseph or just Joseph. You know you don't have to call him uncle if you don't want to."

I laugh. "That would be impolite of me, but you have my word. I won't call any other uncles Uncle Jo."

He seems satisfied by this. "I'm going to go ahead and enter. Hurry and don't take too much time. He'll make me tell him another secret if I come back out here to get you."

Uncle Jo makes a face at the lion, who stares back at him as if he's bored to pieces. Hadar yawns. It starts soft, then ends with a growl. "If you don't go inside so that Ms. St. James can tell me her secret, I'll make you tell me another one anyway. I'm of little patience today."

My uncle smirks. "Just today?"

The lion lifts an eyebrow but says nothing else. My uncle winks at me, then opens the door and rushes inside. I rub the palms of my hands on the side of my jeans because I'm nervous. Which secret should I tell? "Does the secret count if it is not my own but is someone else's? Or would you prefer I tell you something about me?" I ask shakily.

The lion stares at me for a long moment, Hadar seems torn between what type of secret he wants to hear. His mind finally made, "Usually, it doesn't matter. Today, however, I will only take a secret about yourself." I grow pale. Somehow, I knew that would be his answer.

"When you introduced yourself, you said you were the keeper and giver of secrets. After I tell you my secret, will you tell me one in return? Does it work like that?" I ask him curiously.

Hadar licks his lips and contemplates an answer. He is very methodical, which I like. "Arabella, after much contemplation, I have decided that if you tell me a secret worthy enough, I will tell you one in return, and it must be something that no one else knows. Not even Merrie-Beth."

That's not possible, Merrie-Beth knows everything. I rack my brain and come up with nothing. Then, out of nowhere, a thought occurs to me—a long-buried memory from my childhood. One I don't like to think about and haven't in years. A lump forms in the back of my throat. Taking a deep breath, I concentrate on keeping a steady voice. "The night after my seventh birthday, I had a dream. Now, I'm not sure it was a dream, because it felt so real. A woman with the voice of an angel called my name, waking me up. My first thought was that it was Aunt Georgia, but it wasn't. A woman who looked exactly like my mother stood by my bed and smiled at me, but even at age seven, I knew that was impossible. She smelled of jasmine and vanilla, the coziest of smells, and something about her put me at ease. She whispered my name once more and then brushed a hand against my cheek. As my eyes opened again, I caught a glimpse of her sad smile. It was then that I realized that she was my mother. I quickly sat in bed and silently prayed that I wasn't dreaming. She chuckled at my enthusiasm." I continued to tell him of the conversation with my mother.

"Mama?" I whisper.

Mama nods eagerly. "Yes, my love, you're so beautiful. I'm so very sorry, baby, but Mama doesn't have a lot of time to talk. I must tell you a secret."

I smile because I love secrets. Aunt Georgia tells me I'm the best secret keeper. "What is it? I can keep a secret, Mama."

She sits down on the bed beside me and holds my hand. "I know you can, baby girl, but you must promise not to tell anyone this secret, not even your aunt and uncle. No one must know. It's a secret just between us."

I like the sound of that. With my free hand, I take my index finger and cross my heart. "I promise, Mama."

She smiles, and then her expression changes to one of worry, I grab her other hand. I don't want her to worry, she may have to leave me again if she's upset, but she can't go. She gives me a reassuring smile. "Baby girl, when you are older, you will go on a grand adventure. You will meet many different people, but not everyone you meet will truly be your friend. Not everyone will be what they seem. Always remember it's what's inside the heart that matters. Some may appear nice when they are really mean. Some may appear to be bad, but they're really good. Ella, Mama must warn you, don't trust the one with the ice dragon tattoo."

I start to ask her a question, but I never get the chance. We both hear a noise coming down the hall. By the sound of the great big foot-steps, it has to be Uncle Josiah. Aunt Georgia barely makes a sound when she walks. She whispers for me to lie down and close my eyes, and I do so quickly. Mama moves to the side of my room and hides in the shadows, drawing her sword as she goes. I hold my breath. Surely, she won't hurt Uncle Jo. She must think it's somebody else. Who can it be?

My heart pounds in my chest. I want to cry because I don't under-stand what's going on. My uncle opens the door to my room, and I am relieved. Mama drops her sword and slides further into the shadows. He comes into my room and checks on me like he always does. I close my eyes again and try my best to look like I'm sleeping. He kisses me on the cheek and swiftly closes the door behind him. She comes back over to my bedside.

"Ella, it's almost time for Mama to leave. I can't stay, baby. Mama loves you, forever and always."

She hugs me tight, and then a smile appears on her tear-stained face. I smile back at her because I don't want her to be sad. Why does she have to leave me again? "Please, don't cry, Mama. I love you, always and forever." I whisper.

"Always remember what Mama said about the ice dragon tattoo. You must remember. Now sleep, baby girl." She whispers back. Mama puts her hand in her pocket and opens a small gray packet, pouring a golden powder into her hand. She brings her hand up to her lips and blows the powder in front of my face. Making me drift back off to sleep. That night, my dreams are filled with colliding ice and fire dragons.

Hadar wears a blank expression, while I feel the need to justify my secret, so he doesn't think I'm crazy. "It's very confusing." Hadar shakes his head. "Very much indeed, and I cannot tell you whether it was a dream or reality. However, I can tell you that I knew your mother. She was strong and very wise beyond her years. Isabella was my friend and told the best secrets. However, until today, nobody has ever told me a secret good enough to receive one, not even your mother. I assured her when we met that I would relay a message back to you only if you were worthy enough—well done, my dear. Not only will you get that message from me this day, but you will also receive a secret. I'm suddenly feeling rather generous."

My heart falls to my knees, and I'm nervous and scared as hell. After what feels like an eternity, Hadar begins. "One cold winter's night, your mother came to me all in a panic. You see, she was usually the very definition of calm, and for the first time since our meeting, Isabella was evasive about why she needed to go into this room. She usually told me everything about her adventures but told me for my protection, it was best I didn't know this time. Sadly, three short days later, I was informed of her death. It was very distressing. Mayra is the epitome of evil. Arabella, I must ask you. Can you remember what your mother wore when she came to you?"

I furrow my brows and frown. My expression quickly changes to a smile when I think of my mother. She was graceful. When she moved, it was like she was dancing. Funny, after all these years, I still remember every detail of my dream like it's embedded in me. I not only remember what Mama was wearing but can still hear the sound that her pants made as she walked. "She wore black leather pants and a gold shirt that shimmered in the moonlight."

Hadar shakes his head. "Peculiar, but all things reveal themselves in due time, and I do not speak of things that can't be fully under-stood. That is not the message nor the secret I will tell you this day." He stops my protest before it can form on my tongue. "I know this frustrates you, Arabella, but it is for the best. Secret keepers deal in facts, not myths. I have not yet all the information, but I will find those answers. I always do, my dear."

Sensing that arguing will get me nowhere, I ask him a question instead. "Can you tell me what Mama wore on the night in question?"

Hadar raises one disapproving eyebrow, I don't think he will answer, but he surprises me. "The outfit you described to me, shimmering gold and all."

Chills run up and down my body, and a million questions float to my mind. How could she have had the same outfit? I'm beginning to believe our encounter wasn't a dream. Some things aren't adding up though. Hadar said it was three days before her death, but that makes no sense. My parents died when I was four. When I saw her, I was seven. Nothing about this is adding up. What if my parents aren't dead?

As if he can read my thoughts, Hadar gives me a look of pity. "Arabella, your parents are dead. As I told you before, I deal with facts, not myths. I have no explanation as of now. All I ask is for you to give me some time, and I will find out exactly what transpired on the night in question."

Within my heart, I know that he's right. My parents are dead, but I don't want them to be. "It's weird. I barely knew them, but not a day goes by that I don't miss them."

Hadar gives me a sympathetic smile. "I understand more than you know. However, the hour is growing late, and I can feel your uncle's growing impatience. Would you like the secret or the message from your mother first?"

I shrug my shoulders. "It doesn't matter. I'm excited to hear both."

Hadar nods. "Isabella asked me to relay the following message to you upon our first meeting. Arabella, when you find out who will deceive you, do not let them know that you have figured out their betrayal. You must not tell anyone of the treachery until the time is right. Only you can bear the burden, and you must do it alone. Do not be discouraged, for it will only be for a short time."

Taking a deep breath, I let her warning soak in, not everyone can be trusted. After a moment, Hadar continues, "When thinking of what secret I should tell you, I chose one that will be most beneficial in helping you in the journey to come. I'm sure you have heard that the current King of the Kori is not the true ruler. Although accounts vary on how he stole the throne, one thing is certain: no one stopped him. He rules with an iron grip, do not trust him. You must remember, all that glitters is not gold, Diodyous has instilled a fear in the people unlike any I've ever witnessed in my thousand years. I do not know the horror that he keeps within the attic of his castle, but I have been told on more than one occasion that it keeps the people in line. It is how he can keep ruling from his icy throne and why no one has challenged him. Stay out of that attic, Arabella. No one who ascends those steps has ever come back down them alive. Stay no longer than necessary in their capital city of Barrowice Falls. No good thing has ever been able to stay there for long and leave unscathed. It can blacken even the purest of hearts."

His words place an unbearable weight on my shoulders. "How can I defeat such an evil man? I am only an ordinary girl who's never done anything extraordinary in her short life."

Hadar gives me an encouraging smile. "I don't have all the answers, but I know you have been chosen for a reason. I have seen mighty Kings and Queens enter this great hall. Out of all those extraordinary individuals, your inner light has shone the brightest. A solitary seed, when nurtured properly, can make the farmer's crops rich at harvest. You remind me of a passage I once read. Maybe you have been born for such a time as this. Through great courage, you will win, Arabella. Great leaders are not formed at birth but made by how they deal with the obstacles they face. Do not be afraid, my child, for you were destined for greatness."

Hadar transforms back into the lifeless doorknocker that he was minutes before. I jerk in surprise as the door opens, just as it did for my uncle. Whether I'm ready or not, my time is now.

Chapter 13

Goodbye, For Now

Arabella

*Sometimes seeing your loved one for the last time is a surprise;
however, sometimes it's not.*
-Arabella

I'm surprised to see the room beyond the door is full of mirrors, every shape, size, color, and type. Some reach from floor to ceiling, some are hanging on the walls, while others are on stands. "It's about time. I was going to give you one more minute, then I was coming after you." My uncle huffs.

I laugh. "Uncle Jo, I am fine. I think I've found a new friend in Hadar."

He rolls his eyes. "I knew you were physically fine. It was you dying of boredom that I was worried about."

I laugh loudly. "Hadar is far from boring. Uncle Josiah, what is this place?"

Uncle Jo grins. "Welcome to Locus Speculorum, the great room of mirrors. This room is the gateway to any destination you want to go to in the world. We can transport you there in a matter of minutes.

The Courtyard of the Fallen is hidden, and the only way to get there is from this room."

Oh. Fancy. "Why is it in another location? Wouldn't it be just as safe here at the palace?"

My uncle shrugs. "This is just how it was done."

That sounds strange to me, but I say nothing. Could there be another reason? My uncle takes two pebbles out of his pocket. One's a bright shiny blue and the other a bright lush green. My good mood quickly vanishes, because it isn't fair, and I don't want to say goodbye. For so many years I wanted to be someone special, now I'm not so sure.

The mirror in question is the plainest out of all the others. It's laying on the ground, and rectangular in shape. The wood is chipped, and the glass is fractured on one side. My uncle grabs my hand, as he throws the pebbles down causing a green mist to rise up from the mirror. "We have to jump."

I look up at him with wide eyes. "How far will we have to fall?"

He laughs. "It's not as bad as it sounds. It's just a slight drop. You scared?"

I cut my eyes at him. "Never."

He rolls his. "On the count of three then. One...two...three!" He shouts, and we jump inside. Pitch black darkness surrounds us. We're falling, but in slow motion. There is a bright light down at the bottom, and the closer we get, I can make out more of my surroundings. We're in a cave, and they are twenty or so tunnels that go off in various directions. Our hands are ripped apart by some unknown force, and a scream dies in my throat as I begin to fall at an accelerated rate. Finally, I reach the literal light at the end of the tunnel, where my back lands on something very soft. As a moan escapes my lips, I hear laughter from somewhere to the left of me. My eyes stay shut, as my heart threatens to beat out of my chest.

After a minute or two, I'm ready to get my first glimpse of the Courtyard of the Fallen. It's beautiful. Large white columns surround the yard, and wrapped around each one of them is little white lights. I bet it's breathtaking at night when the lights are shining bright. In between the columns, a clematis vine has grown, with little white flowers with yellow centers blooming throughout the vine. There are tall angel statues placed throughout and I also spot a few dark wooden benches. The square has a crisscross path from each of the four corners of lite-colored cobblestones. A weeping willow tree is in the middle of the crisscross. In between the pathways are the head-stones and four long gray slabs. Why are there four? We only have three founding members.

"Arabella." A voice that's deep and husky, with a twinge of southern twang calls out to me. It's not a voice I'm familiar with but wouldn't mind the acquaintance of because slight southern drawls are sexy as hell. I turn my head and meet the most exquisite big brown eyes of the ponytailed blonde hunk jogging in Forsyth Park the other night. He winks at me and holds out his hand for me to shake. H-e-l-l-o Daddy Thor! Today he's traded his ponytail in for a man bun. I'm not ashamed to admit that I'm a man bun fan, his ears are also pointed like the Fae. "Nice to meet you, ma'am. The name is Drake Murdock, but my friends call me Doc. Feel free to do so, I'm at your service."

I blush ever so lightly, he's charismatic, and has instantly made me feel at ease. "Nice to meet you, Doc. Feel free to call me, Ella."

He motions for me to follow him to the right side of the court-yard. When we reach our destination, Doc looks at his watch. "They should be arriving any minute now."

Before I can ask who, the column closest to him opens, revealing my aunt and uncle riding down an escalator. What the actual fuck? "Where did you go?" I half yell at Uncle Jo.

"We got separated, and the tunnel I landed in brought me to where your aunt was waiting, and you went into the one that led you straight to the courtyard." He laughs and tries to wipe something off my face.

My eyebrows raise. He looks immaculate, and I look like I've just come straight out of a war zone. Not fair. How did he get clean so fast? I slap his hand out of the way. "Why are you not dirty?" I ask with just a hint of attitude.

He gives me a huge smile and bats his eyelashes. "My tunnel had a lot less dirt." I'm done with him. Looking at my aunt for the first time since I saw her descending the escalator, makes my heart ache. Aunt Georgia is wearing a blank expression, she's trying to be strong, too. That makes me want to cry even more. "When are you leaving?" Knowing, but hoping I'm wrong, I ask anyway.

She smiles miserably. "Now, we have to move. They are liable to strike again soon. We want to stop the next attack before it even begins."

I walk towards her and wrap my arms around her in a big bear hug. There are so many things that need to be said. We are both going down dangerous paths and may never see each other again. How do you sum up the words to say to the woman who raised and loved you unconditionally but didn't have to? She didn't have to be there for me, but she chose to. This is not an easy moment for my Uncle either. We are his girls, and all he has ever wanted to do is provide for and protect us. I'm not ready to be separated from them yet. He joins us in a group hug. Time has stopped for each of us as we hold each other, but we are only postponing the inevitable.

When we finally break apart, our matching blue eyes meet. "Arabella, you have been training for this journey since birth. You're more ready than you think you are. Always remember that light will always overcome the darkness. Always, be strong and of great courage, Ella. The time has come for you to lead, it is who you were born to be. I love you, baby girl. Always, and forever."

The tears fall silently down my cheeks. "You give me courage when I have none. I love you, forever and always."

She wipes my tears and kisses my forehead. "I don't know what this journey holds for us; all I know is that we are family, which means that all roads will lead back to each other. Until we meet again."

I smile, because my aunt has never liked the word goodbye. She thinks it's too final. "Until we meet again."

For the first time, I notice Doc is not the only one with us in the courtyard now. There is a woman and a man of Asian descent. She is short and lean, while he is tall and muscled. Behind him is a man with a silver Mohawk, who looks to be in his forties. He's shorter than the other man but just as muscled. Mr. Mohawk looks at me with a curious eye. My teacher, Mrs. Lopez, comes off the escalator, her expression guarded, but mine is anything but, because how is she here? My mouth is wide open. I'm shocked. "Mrs. Lopez?" I am dumbfounded.

She has a hint of a smile. "Arabella, it appears I won't be taking those Art classes this Summer."

I smile sheepishly. "Guess not, sorry about that, and all."

She shrugs. "No need to feel sorry. The days leading up to the Great War are here."

I smile, although I'm not sure it's an appropriate action. I'm not very happy about this war that's coming. I understand it's necessary, and it's going to happen regardless, but I don't want to smile about it.

Mrs. Lopez looks toward her other companions. "Arabella, have you been introduced to everyone yet?"

I shake my head. "I know, Doc."

Pointing toward the first man and woman I saw; Mrs. Lopez begins the introductions. "Meet Mae Kim, the best archer that we have. She can make a target within a half a mile radius. Next to her, is her husband, Scott Kim. He's the second-best archer that we have."

His wife laughs, and he rolls his eyes. He looks at me and gives a wink. "She'll only have that title until the next competition."

Mae play shoves him. "Umm. I've beaten you in the past three competitions. What makes you think you will do any better the next time?"

Scott only laughs and shrugs his shoulders. Nothing wrong with a little friendly competition. Mrs. Lopez continues, "Finally, that handsome man right there with the silver mohawk is my husband, David Lopez. He's the best hand-to-hand combat fighter that we have."

David comes to stand beside Mrs. Lopez and puts his arm lovingly around her shoulder. "Basically, if you're ever in a street fight, I'm your guy." He has a thick New England accent, and is handsome, ruggedly so. There is a fresh cut underneath his left eye.

"If you're the best fighter, I'd hate to see the other guy." I tease.

My statement catches him off guard for a second, but as soon as he realizes I'm talking about his eye, he laughs. "Something like that." He winks.

"What's your specialty, Mrs. Lopez?" I inquire.

She smirks. "I do a little of it all. My main job is a weapons specialist. If I don't have it in stock, I'll get it."

"Nice." I love her confidence. I wish I had more—no time like the present to get some.

Doc clears his throat. "Don't forget about me, ma'am."

He gives me a wink, and I melt. Nobody in their right mind would forget about you, Doc. Not waiting on Mrs. Lopez, he explains. "We use guns only when necessary. When it's time, I'm the one they call. I can hit a target from a mile away. It's a gift, really."

I giggle. "It's nice that you've remained humble despite your success.

He smiles. "Yes, ma'am.

I'm beyond embarrassed because my lips won't stop smiling at him. Turning to my aunt, I grab her hand. "So, this is your team?"

She nods. "The best of the best. We have one more guy waiting on us at our next location.

"Good." I am genuinely relieved.

Mae looks at Aunt Georgia and points to her watch. "It's time."

Aunt Georgia closes her eyes, a look of agony crosses her face. After a moment, she opens them and smiles. "Time waits for no one, Arabella, and we must go. I meant what I said earlier, don't doubt yourself or your training. You're more ready for this journey than you believe you are. Our paths will lead us back to one another."

I hold back my tears. "Please, stay safe."

She lets me go and embraces Uncle Jo. "Take care of our girl, Jo. I'll see you after the tournament."

He kisses her forehead. "I promise you. She will be kept safe. Please, be careful. Until we meet again, my love."

Doc presses one of the Angel statues on the shoulder, and a mirror appears. Aunt Georgia takes some rocks out of her pouch, and throws them, one by one, the team journeys into the mirror. She takes one last look at us before jumping in, determination written all over her face.

I throw myself into my uncle's welcoming arms, and he holds me for a long time. "That was awful, but we both survived it. I'm not looking forward to seeing you go."

He shakes his head. "I'm not excited about it either, kiddo. Come on, let's get you cleaned up."

Chapter 14

A Prince and Princess Introduced

Arabella

I go from no prospects to two. Ethan is agreeable while Sebastian makes me want to gouge his eyes out. Needless to say, I'm attracted to both.

-Arabella

IT FEELS good to have all that dirt and grime off my face. With a bit of coaxing, Uncle Jo talks me into heading over to the main training facility so that we can get some practice time in. Maybe getting lost in exercise is exactly what I need. I can't believe I'm even saying this.

As we enter the room, everything grows deathly quiet. Every eye is on us, making my heart almost pound out of my chest. Maybe we should just walk away. Uncle Jo turns me around so that I'm facing him, he knows I'm about to bolt. "Ella, it's time to train. You need to block out every face and whisper that's about to start when they see what you can do." My face turns back toward the crowd, but Uncle Jo gently turns it back to him. "Block out everything except what we're doing. In time their curiosity will fade, and eventually, they will accept you as one of their own. You're no different than they are. You are their equal, not their superior."

Everyone in this room was looking at me in complete admiration. As if, I'd done something noble. I haven't earned their adoration.

"Focus, Arabella, focus. You can do this." Uncle Jo leads me to a cabinet full of equipment on the back wall. He takes out a set of boxing gloves and hands me the smaller pair. He doesn't need to give me directions, because we've begun our workouts like this for as long as I can remember. We do a warm-up before moving on to the hard stuff. This I know, this I can do. Putting on my boxing gloves, I get in my fight stance. The people's stares around me throw fiery daggers into my back, but when Uncle Jo holds his boxing gloves up, instinct takes over. I begin punching his hands one by one, back and forth, repeatedly, until I'm out of breath, and he has to shake his hand after the last punch.

A cocky grin spreads across my face. He gives me a smirk in return. The freestyle portion of our training session is coming up next. We gaze at each other without blinking, his demeanor is unsettling, and gives nothing away. I don't know when he will attack, but it's coming, and I need to be ready when he does. My family has taught me the importance of getting a good read on your opponent. All you need to do is pay close attention. No matter how good a fighter someone is, you can always tell. Most times, a person will slightly move a part of the body that they intend on using.

Uncle Jo comes at me from his left side. Crouching down, I stretch my leg as far out as it will go, and sweep his legs out from under him. There is no time to gloat, because he jumps up quickly and wastes no time retaliating. He catches me to the ribs once, but I block the next two attacks.

I go on the offensive, and we spar back and forth for what seems like forever. He only lands me on my back twice, which is a vast improvement from last summer when the ground was my best friend. I'm in my zone, this is my element. Training gives me a thrill that nothing else ever has. Thoughts of being The Chosen and what that means doesn't infiltrate my mind. My main focus is on my opponent, that's normal, and I love it.

With one last thrust, I flip him over my shoulder, and he lands with a loud thud on his back. Never once have I achieved that move. Uncle Jo has always been able to stop me right before the flip, and I'm the one that falls with a loud thud.

A whooshing sound comes from the crowd. Stunned, I look around the gym at all the bewildered faces staring back at me. They never saw that coming either. My eyes fall to Ethan first, then Sebastian second, making my heart thud more wildly inside my chest.

Sebastian can't help but give me his commentary. *If that would have been us sparring you would have been the one to land on your pretty ass.*

Rolling my eyes, I take my middle finger and rub it up and down my nose like I'm scratching it, making Sebastian chuckle. *Anytime you want to put your money where your mouth is, you know where to find me.*

He grins. *There is only one place I wish to put my mouth, Arabella. Oh, and don't think, I didn't see the eye roll.*

While that sets me ablaze with lust, I hit him back with sarcasm. *Yeah, like, up your ass.*

Laughter rings throughout my mind, and against my will, my face lights up in embarrassment. After helping Uncle Jo up, I give everyone in the room a sheepish smile. Their stunned silence turns into raucous applause. The first item off my checklist of impressing my peers is done.

"We done, old man?" I'm beyond ready to escape, and not prepared for one-on-one conversations with these people just yet.

Uncle Jo gives my shoulder a reassuring squeeze. He understands my reluctance and readiness to get the hell out of dodge. "For calling me old man, I should make you train for a little while longer. But since you flipped me on my ass, I'll be generous. Let's do something fun."

I'm tired, but not that tired. Fun may be just what the doctor ordered. "Fun would be nice. Especially if food is involved, I'm starving. FEED me."

He rolls his eyes. "Dramatic much? I think someone is hangry."

I make a face at him. "YES! Now feed me or face the consequences of starving The Chosen."

He scoffs. "I ain't scared of no Chosen."

A smirk appears on my face. "It's The Chosen, thank you very much."

I grunt, rubbing my arm after he pinches me playfully for my sassiness.

We amble toward the door and the crowd reluctantly makes a narrow path for us to get through. A beautiful girl with long blonde hair catches my attention, it's the Princess. She's standing next to her brother Sebastian, who is now sporting a devil-may-care smile.

As we move closer, the sheer beauty of Princess Amelia is alarming. The portrait in the King's office didn't do her justice. She gives me a dazzling smile that I find to be authentic. My Uncle shakes both their hands and holds his finger up in an, I'll be right back motion. Panic sets in, but I will eventually have to meet everyone anyway. No time like the present to pull the Band-Aid off my social anxiety ridden self.

Princess Amelia lends out her hand for me to shake. "Finally, you have come home. I look forward to getting to know you better." She sounds relieved, and her eyes show so much emotion.

I shake her hand gently. "Thank you, Princess. I look forward to getting to know you better, as well, and it's good to be home."

She waves away my use of formality. Her accent is a British one. "Please, call me Amelia, this is my brother Sebastian, or as I like to call him, Asshole."

Sebastian stares at me unabashedly and pays no mind to his sister. "We've already met. How's your neck, Bells?"

The dark Prince gives me a look so smug that I wish I was throwing him to the mat. My face turns even redder as he telepathically whispers, *please do, with pain comes pleasure.*

Turning to Amelia, I shrug. Sebastian wants a reaction, so I'll give him one. "He's crazy, do you know he bites strangers on the neck just for funsies."

She laughs. "You don't know the half of it, and it appears I don't either." She turns to her twin with her brow raised.

He gives me a sensual glare. "Some people are just too delicious not to take a sample from.

"Ready, Ella?" Ethan comes to stand beside me, making Sebastian literally growl.

I furrow my brow in confusion but hide it quickly behind a smile. "Yes, are you going with Uncle Jo and I?"

Ethan quirks his brow. "He had to take a meeting and said you were perishing, so I volunteered."

Sebastians expression is feral. *Be careful, Arabella. Remember what I told you. If he touches you...*

I whisper back to him in my mind, but Sebastian never finishes the sentence. *Then what?* His reminder calms down the butterflies I feel at being this close to them both again. My earlier conversation with Hadar, comes to mind. No one can be trusted.

Ethan places his hand on my lower back and guides me toward the exit. When we are out of hearing distance of the twins, he sighs with relief. "You have to promise me that you will only keep it professional with Sebastian. You know what they call him, don't you?" He gives me a coy look. "No, of course, you don't. The UGN has dubbed him the "Playboy Prince", and they aren't wrong. He doesn't respect woman and only wants to see how many of them he can fuck before his bloody dick falls off."

My answering laughter bounces off the concrete walls, earning me a stern look. While I'm not as experienced as most, I'm not dumb enough to think Ethan hasn't had sex with just as many women. You can respect females and still be a playboy, it's our choice whether we want to play with you or not. "Sorry, but that was hilarious. I may enjoy flirting but there is absolutely no time in my schedule for romance—of any kind."

Ethan nods his head, I'm not sure why he's rubbing me the wrong way, but he is, and the smile plastered on his face doesn't quite reach his eyes. "Sorry, he's my cousin, and he's not a terrible person or anything. It's just that his personal life is an absolute mess. You need to stay away from him."

I fake giggle. Is he trying to mansplain to me what I need to do? Because that's a dickhead move, and his words in fact make me want to do the opposite. A subject change is in need before I flip him over my shoulder and kick his ass. "Where are we going to eat? Also, since you volunteered your time, you owe me something fun afterward."

He gives me a boyish grin, his first genuine smile of the day. "Luxington Valley is small compared to the other societies, but we still have everything you could want or need. We must be careful though because of the prison break we shouldn't venture away from the palace. My favorite place to dine here is the *King's Kitchen*. It has all sorts of southern cuisine."

Intriguing, maybe he's winning me back over. "Shrimp and Grits?"

He winks. "Only the best or so I'm told."

Chapter 15

The First Five

Arabella

I'm a girl that knows what she wants most of the time, and a man
ordering food for me
isn't one of them.
-Arabella

THE KING'S Kitchen is a massive restaurant in the heart of the palace. The high ceilings are lined with giant crystal chandeliers. They're overly extravagant but beautiful, and with the way the adjacent light fixtures are shining on them, it looks like little diamonds are jumping up and down on the walls and ceiling. The walls are a cream color and have different murals painted throughout.

One mural catches my attention the most, and it's the only one painted from floor to ceiling. Both sides of the wall tell a story, and some of the same people are in both scenes. "Ethan, what's the story behind these murals? I can't take my eyes off the one on the back wall."

He smiles. "Your Mom painted that one. The King says, "Isabella was a very gifted artist."

I never knew she could paint at this caliber. The figures on the wall look like they could come to life at any moment. My eyes blink away the unshed tears threatening to spill over, they are not of sadness but of pride. Walking over to the mural, I touch the wall, it's a bittersweet moment when you're so close to something a loved one left behind.

The first scene is of an epic naval battle, there are three USS carriers on one side of the sea, Yorktown, Enterprise, and Hornet. They're massive yet graceful looking in a weird sort of way. Looking more closely at one of the carriers, sea foam is more prevalent at its side than anywhere else in the painting. With the way the water is rippling, there's an underwater missile that was just launched. Mama thought of everything, no detail was spared.

To the west of the horizon four Imperial Navy ships are off in the distance. The sky is bright blue mixed with thick gray smoke, and aircrafts are dropping missiles around the boats. She painted outlines of men on the carriers in their war-torn uniforms, a look of determination sketched on their faces.

Written in big, bold letters at the top of the mural:

The Battle of Midway: The turn of the tide in the Pacific WWII.

This battle is the one that Blaine Ramsey helped win for the good guys. Trying to take it all in, I walk slowly to the other side of the mural, to get a good look at the Scotsman. Standing in the middle of the group, he is wearing his kilt and has a haughty look of disdain plastered all over his smug face, what I wouldn't give for a chance to punch that expression off his face. Next to him on his left is one bombshell of a lady. She's young and beautiful. Her hair is jet black, and bright red lipstick is on her lips. Did she fight in the war? She wears a uniform, but girls weren't allowed to be in the Navy back then. Her uniform is in near tatters, and her right hand is wearing a bandage. I wonder what her story is.

The guy beside her has his arm around her neck and is smiling from ear to ear. Her arm is around him in a side hug. He has red hair in a military-style cut. His clothes are torn to bits, but he's smiling anyways, and I like them both instantly.

The guy furthest to the Scotsman's left is African American. He's tall and lean and wears a different uniform. Maybe the Air Force? His clothes are fully intact. That would make sense if he were flying a plane. I remember reading about the Battle of Midway, and planes dropped bombs during the mission. He looks serious and determined, a true military hero.

Lastly, the guy next to Blaine is short with wavy blonde hair. He looks tired and hurt. His side has a bloodstain from his underarm to his waist. Even though he's severely injured he still manages a smirk. My mother was able to capture the essence of who each person was.

The bottom is titled:
The First Five.

"Ethan, I heard General Kelli mention that Ramsey was a part of the First Five. But how? He looks so young. Is he like 295 years old or something?" I feel so inadequate in this world. I know next to nothing.

"He's Maritime, Arabella." He says with a shrug.

"Well, that explains nothing. What does Maritime have to do with him being so old?" I sigh in exasperation.

Ethan laughs and elbows me in the ribs. "Calm down, beautiful. The answer is simple. Maritime people have a longer lifespan than we do. The water preserves their cells and slows down the aging process. They can live thousands of years. Eleanor is well over a hundred."

Little butterflies swarm in my belly, because he's near, and I stare up at him in disbelief. "Stop lyin'! There is no way she's that old."

Shaking his head, he gives me a panty dropping smile. "I ain't lyin', girl. It's true! Just ask her. She'll be at the tournament as the goodwill ambassador for the Maritime."

"I believe you, I guess. What's the significance of the First Five?" I run my fingers across the mural, it makes me feel close to my mother.

Ethan's face brightens with excitement, he must love history as much as I do. Motioning for me to sit down at a table near the back, he begins the story, and gains my full attention. "They were the first five Guardians of Peace, and until that time only men were allowed to participate. The times were changing, and the world was at war for the second time. FDR assembled a special team, after the destruction at Pearl Harbor. One hundred boys and one girl enrolled in the program. It was a six-week course of strenuous exercises and tests. I saw some of the training exercises, and it was wild.

"The President's best friend was General Ascot, and he had a granddaughter. He met with the President and convinced him to let her join the program. Charlene Ascot, your great-grandmother, was the first female Guardian. You'll get to meet her soon. Those five are the reason we won WWII. They took out Hitler and Stalin, the Lux history books you were given were altered, because you didn't know about them yet. She's your family."

My mind already exploded when the bad guys jumped out of the mirror, but not only did my great-grandmother help win WWII, but she was also the first female Guardian of Peace. Everybody knows they were the most badass group of their time. It couldn't have been easy for her. She looked so happy in the mural, like she belonged. "When can I meet her?"

Ethan shrugs. "I don't know, she's a busy lady. I'll ask the King to arrange a meeting soon."

Squealing with excitement, I sail onto his lap to hug him, then immediately move back into my seat before it gets weird. The waitress comes to take our order wearing a smirk, yeah, she saw everything. Ethan orders us both a steak medium rare, and his sensual gaze never leaves mine. He assures me that the meat will be more tender if it's cooked that way. I always order mine well done. My mouth stays shut, even though shrimp and grits are my favorite and they're definitely on the menu. I don't mention that I prefer ordering for myself. That's a red flag move on his part. We eat in companionable silence, until he makes a snide comment about me finishing my entire plate. However, I let it slide, because the steak was surprisingly very good.

With our belly's full we walk toward Lake Luminous in silence. He's being super secretive about what we're going to do during our afternoon together. He grabs my hand, and grins at me from ear to ear. "Arabella, today, I want to introduce you to some freshwater Mermaids."

My heart almost beats out of my chest as Ethan entwines our fingers together, and not because he's holding my hand, I'm over that, because he said mermaids. "Mermaids? Minus Ariel, almost every story I've ever read depicts mermaids as being shady as fuck, beautiful but deadly. Not sure I want to meet that kind of person. Or are they fish? Person fish? Fish Person? What's the respectful way to say that?"

Ethan looks thoughtful. "Yeah, we wouldn't want those deadly mermaids to get ticked off." He rolls his eyes. "I'm just guessing here, but I think it's cool to call the females mermaids and the males mermen."

In my defense, I'm overly excited so thoughts are not coming together clearly. "Oh yeah, makes sense. I'm entitled to ask at least one dumb question now and then."

He laughs. "Yeah, but I think you've used your quota for about the next five years with that one."

I growl at him. "Hey now. I'm nervous. I'm about to meet a potentially dangerous adversary. I could totally die."

He snorts. "Ella, we're meeting freshwater Mermaids. Everybody knows the saltwater ones are the malicious and deadly culprits."

I give a shrug. Hello. Apparently, not everybody. "Must have just slipped my mind. Being as I grew up here and all."

He makes a face at me. "I like it when you're extra feisty. Freshwater mermaids are beautiful, thoughtful, and kind. They are joyful, but can be very opinionated, stubborn creatures. Too bad only a few people know of their existence, I can't wait for you to meet them. They won't just see anybody. You have to make a special appointment, and unless they deem it absolutely necessary, they will never agree to a meeting."

"Well, I am the Chosen One. I guess that's all it took for them to say yes." I assume.

"No, in fact, that's the reason they didn't want to meet you. The merfolk think you're not ready and that you need to prove yourself first before you can lead. They think before we can deal with Mayra and her accomplices, we should go to war with the Kori and take back the throne for the Fitzgerald's. They can be a bit superstitious and feel like every member of the new Guardians of War should be related to one of the First Five. The Kori will try and rig the tournament there, but I say that Douglas Fitzgerald, the true Kori heir, will be one of the top victors in the Ice tournament. Vengeance has consumed him, and he is fearless." Ethan rubs my back giving me time to digest this new information.

"Eleanor mentioned the King of the Kori, and she doesn't think I should trust him. She said that the Maritime people are no longer welcome in those waters. Have you ever met him?" I've only known Eleanor for a short while, but I trust her explicitly. She's telling me the truth. I'm anxious to hear his thoughts on the matter. My new family will surround me during my time in Pyralis. However, we have no idea how it will be during our visit, in Barrowice Falls, the Kori capital. Nausea gathers in the pit of my stomach. Not a lot is known about this King.

Ethan breathes a breath of frustration. "I've heard some stories about his early military days. He is a ruthless man who has lived on the edge of the law and got reprimanded often but never enough to get a dishonorable discharge. I've only met him once a few years ago. His eyes were lifeless, like he'd sold his soul to the devil. Don't trust him, Arabella. You have to be careful, and you can't let him suspect your distrust towards him."

My heartbeat quickens, and the air flees from my lungs. "That could pose a problem, as I'm not great at hiding my facial expressions. Do you know why he was allowed to take over the throne?"

"On the record, no. Off the record, yes. Devin Fitzgerald, the true King, is a good man, but also an alcoholic. His eldest daughter died in a terrorist raid, and he started drinking heavily shortly afterward. We were about to step in when Diodyous took over. Allowing that was a mistake, but the people seemed happy, and all was well for about a year. After that, the Kori slowly drifted away, and we have little contact with the new King now. He visits on special occasions or mandatory meetings, but we never get invited to go there."

We continue walking at a leisurely pace. "Do the freshwater Mermaids live amongst the Maritime?"

"They do. They formed a secret treaty years ago and are always welcome in their waters."

Chapter 16

A Choice is Made

Arabella

Sebastian is like a shadowed storm.
-Arabella

WE WALK until we see the lake in the distance, which is on the opposite side of where I met Eleanor. It's swampier in this area, and weeping willows line the muddy pathway through the wetlands. Our feet slosh in and out of the mud, and the crickets begin chirping under the late afternoon sun.

I scream as Sebastian comes from behind one of the trees, startling me. His jaw clenches when he notices our joined hands. Gone is the lime green of his irises. They are now black with unleashed cold, brutal fury. It doesn't take a rocket scientist to piece together that Ethan and the dark Prince hate each other.

Ethan smirks at him while I try to de-escalate the situation by unlacing our fingers. Guilt forms like icy shards slicing through my heart, but we've done nothing wrong, so why is my heart shattering into a million different pieces? I'm not sure I even like Ethan after today or why my emotions are so strong like this.

"You know that she's mine," Sebastian growls.

Ethan's laugh is cold and calculating. "She has already made her choice." He pulls me into his arms.

I push him away from me. Was he only acting like he was interested in me to get at Sebastian? "No, the hell I haven't!" The dark Prince gets in his face, and I quickly jump in the middle. "Stop!" A warm, shadowed arm reaches around me and gently thrusts me out of the way, but I'm not so tender when I place myself back into the center of all the chaos. "Y'all need to calm the fuck down!"

Ethan growls. "No, I won't share what's mine."

My glare turns icy. "I don't belong to anyone."

Ethan rolls his eyes at me. This condescending side to him is not my favorite. "You're what I say you are, Arabella."

Okay, we'll see about that, big boy. Backing up, I lean heavily into Sebastian's muscular arms. "Ethan, you can go back to the palace. Sebastian will take over as my escort."

He defiantly stares at me for a long moment. Just when I think Ethan won't leave, he walks away in a childish huff. "We'll talk later."

Sebastian is seething, his breathing is coming in and out in angry puffs. One of his shadows turn me around, his face is unreadable. "I told you to stay away from Ethan. I also told you not to roll your eyes at me again."

Swirls of black and gray float through the air around us. Sebastian has ten shadowed arms coming from his body and a whirlwind of dark confetti hovers above our heads. My words get stuck in the back of my throat, not from fear, but from the sheer beauty of the Shadow Kissed before me. His anger is palpable, and call it female intuition, but I know he won't hurt me. A set of arms pulls my plush body against him while one hand firmly wraps around my neck, making my pulse quicken, and my blood run through my veins like hot molten lava. Moisture pools between my thighs, causing a moan to escape my lips. Sebastian dares me to defy him while his eyes penetrate to the depths of my soul. "I'm through with being fucking nice, Arabella, but make no mistake. You. Are. Mine."

He releases his hand as his perfect lips crash down on mine. Our kiss is intensely violent, both fighting for control and dominance. Never has this savage raw need taken hold of me with anyone else. Our bodies are so molded together that I'm unsure where he ends, and I begin. One of Sebastian's hands reaches inside my panties and grips my mound. He hisses as his fingers feel the wetness gathering there, and I feel a prick of his fangs nipping at my neck. He plunges two digits inside of me, stretching me with the vast size of them. A primal growl sounds in my ear. "This is mine, and only mine. I'll kill Ethan if he ever touches you again. I'll kill anyone that touches you."

His naughty words should scare the hell out of me, but it has the opposite effect. The possessiveness almost throws me over the edge. My anger from minutes before is still simmering at the surface, and that makes me hold back because I want him to work harder to get the victory of my release. Sebastian's fangs find the crease of my neck, making me cry out, but the pain quickly turns into a form of euphoric pleasure. I come as he hooks his fingers at just the right place inside me. He continues to drink his fill, sending shivers down my body, and I come again.

He licks the blood away from his lips, then unbuttons his black leather pants. My mouth pops open in a perfectly shaped "O" as he begins to pump his thick cock with the come-soaked fingers that were just inside of me. He moves up and down with precision. My mouth waters as I get on my knees before him. The need to taste us together on my greedy tongue overwhelms me.

A shadow lifts my chin, directing me to look into his hungry gaze. There's a reverence in Sebastian's expression, and not because I'm The Chosen, but because he desires me more than anything he's ever wanted in his life. I'm a brazen sacrifice who is knelt before her dark Prince, awaiting his instruction. "Be a good girl and suck my cock."

Happily, I take him inside my mouth with a moan. He's so thick and long, it's difficult to pull him all the way in, but Sebastian rears his head back with a long hiss as I lick the precum off the tip of his shaft. His body hums as my mouth and hand moves in sync. He pulls my hair daring me to take him in further. I gag as his cock hits the back of my throat, making my eyes water, my face turns into a watery mess. As he thrust in my mouth over and over again. "Such a naughty little mouth. I'm about to come, and you better fucking swallow it all."

Sebastian screams his release, and I heed his command, swallowing down every bit of his release. He pulls out and adjusts himself and before I can think, he pulls me up and gathers me into his arms. Gone are his shadows, and a peaceful look is on his face. "Bells, do you choose me?"

My body tingles in anticipation, and I don't know how my heart knows but it does. My mind says proceed with caution, but this overwhelming need to accept him as my own has me throwing that caution into the wind because Sebastian has always been mine, even when I was annoyed with him invading my mind when we first met. I think I knew then that we would be together. My voice is a throaty whisper. "Yes."

The wind rustles my hair, and a bright light emerges from my necklace and swirls around us as they meet with the shadows floating above his head. A blue glittery light encases us, as a tattoo of a blackthorn vine with beautiful black and red roses forms around our wrists. Sebastian kisses my lips and then my wrist. "Now, we're Bound."

I furrow my brow in confusion. "Bound?"

"Yes." He slides away from me and with the wave of his finger, cleans us both up, and makes our bond marks translucent. Why wasn't I born with any magical abilities? Not fair. "Tonight, we'll talk." His whisper floats through the air between us. Placing a finger in front of his lips. "Your cousins are coming."

I give a slight nod at Sebastian, but we really need to talk now. What the hell does bound mean? Placing my now invisible tattooed hand in my pocket, I smile at Cowboy and Hulk. My cousins from the lunchroom battle, as they walk out of a dense part of the forest that surrounds the area near the lakes edge. They smile as we come into their eyesight.

At first glance, the brothers appear different as night and day. Watching them more closely, they are more alike than any two people I've ever met. They are true brothers, not by blood, but by spirit. Sebastian goes to stand by one of the weeping willow trees to give us some privacy.

If I had to guess, Deen is about 6'2, thanks to the cut-off sleeves of his shirt, I can tell he has a farmer's tan. He's lean, yet muscular. His hair is a shade of chestnut brown, and his beautiful eyes are a pale blue.

Jeremiah has smooth ebony skin, is about 5'8, and looks like he could bench press a thousand pounds. No joke, his arms are about the size of my head. He's sporting a silver-colored fauxhawk outlined in bright red. His eyes are an odd color. They are a little lighter than charcoal gray but not exactly silver, either. I've never seen eyes that color before, they are uniquely gorgeous. The brothers are staring back at me with the same blatant curiosity, I give them a mischievous grin.

Deen holds his cowboy hat in place as he bows slowly. "Well cuz, I'm assuming you've figured out who we are." His smile is as lazy as his thick southern drawl.

Deen's easy way puts me at ease. "I may not be the brightest bulb, but yeah, you're my cousins."

Jeremiah rolls his eyes at his brother. "Let me properly introduce us, Arabella. His name is Deen, but most folks call him Cowboy. My name is Jeremiah, and most folks call me Firestorm." His voice is deep. He too, has a rich southern accent, but it's not as thick as his brothers.

They reach out their arms to hug me, and I willingly accept. Group hugs are the best. "I wasn't certain the day of the lunchroom attack, but I've seen you two, quite a lot actually in the past year."

Deen pipes in, "Sorry about all that. We would appreciate it if you wouldn't tell our parents about us stalking you." He gives me a guilty look, then continues. "Our parents told us that they had it covered, and that we should let the grown-ups do their jobs, until it was our time. Everybody knows we'll win the tournament, but they felt like we needed a lesson in patience."

Jeremiah makes a face. "And patience is a virtue we don't want or need. You're ours to protect, the others can handle their own in a fight, but we are the best."

Deen nods his head in agreement. "I understand if you think that sounds conceited, but we'll call it confidence. We've been training since we were little kids. Our parents dreamed we would one day become a part of the new generation of Guardians. Now it is our dream, as well. We were born to fight for and protect you."

My sigh is long and exaggerated. "You both grew up in this world. I don't know what to think let alone do, then add finding out I am the key to saving the world, it's a little too over the top for me."

Jeremiah gives me a reassuring smile. "Arabella, you've done better than most would have. Don't panic, you're a phenomenal fighter already. The fact that you haven't had the training equipment that we do, and you're already a badass, says a lot about what kind of fighter you will become, that's less work for us."

Deen rolls his eyes. "Yes, Arabella, this is more than a battle between good and evil. If we fail, this will end modern civilization as we know it. The beginning of the end, one step closer to the Apocalypse. We can't let that happen. The stakes are too high."

I get that, because they are, but my brain is still trying to adjust to a world where teleportation and me being The Chosen is real. Not to mention an impending world war that I'm supposed to somehow stop. The burden is heavy. Now that I've found them, I won't have to go on this journey alone.

Chapter 17

Freshwater Mermaids

Arabella

*It appears the only thing freshwater mermaids
fear is dragons.*
-Arabella

DEEN ELBOWS HIS BROTHER. "When y'all are done come find us in the clearing."

Jeremiah grins over at me. "Yeah, we have a present for you."

Sebastian comes to stand by my side, while his shadows high-five the brothers. "The mermaids are getting restless. It's time."

Before the brothers leave, they can't help but give their embarrassing commentary. Deen points back and forth between Sebastian and I while yelling, "We're team Sebastian, by the way."

"Yeah, because Ethan's a little pussy." Jeremiah adds with a smirk.

I roll my eyes but give him a cheesy grin. "That's an insult to all of us who have a pussy."

They laugh. "My bad, my inner feminist apologizes. He's a whiny motherfucker then." Jeremiah rectifies. That comment even makes

Sebastian chuckle as we watch them walk away. What could they have gotten me as a present? I'm intrigued, but kind of terrified.

My dark Prince answers the question, I never voiced out loud. *You're going to love it, it's your birthright, there is a reason your magic has been contained.*

I almost stomp my foot in frustration. *Stop reading my mind, Bash, and what do you mean?*

He smirks at the nickname I've just given him then says nothing which pisses me off. I turn to him.

I'm tired of all this talking in riddles shit. You need to explain. Now.

He shrugs. *No. You'll find out soon enough.*

"No, that's not good enough." I'm done with being the last to know everything. Sebastian stares at me so long that it gets uncomfortable for him. I can't back down, or I'll always have to when it comes to whatever being bound to him means.

He reaches for me, so I lean into his palm. The chemistry between us is explosive! I'm left with confusion by the rush of emotions toward him that slam in me all at once. "They are waiting for you, but I promise from this moment forward to never hold anything back again, and tonight we'll talk."

I nod as Sebastian walks with me toward the edge of the water, my stomach turns nervously. The merfolk don't think I'm ready to lead. They're not wrong, but it hits different when somebody agrees with you.

"Don't be nervous, Bells. Prove them wrong." His tone is demanding.

My eyes meet his earnestly. "Sebastian, I know it doesn't matter what anyone else thinks about me. The problem is that we're in agreement."

He grabs my hand and places it over his heart. Our bound tattoos are back in full view on our wrists. "Arabella, if you thought you were good enough, then I'd be worried. Everything you need has already been placed inside of you."

Sebastian takes a rock out of his pocket and throws it into the water. The stone skips across three times, before it sinks below the service. Almost instantly, a whirlpool begins to form. "Will there be lots of them or just a few?"

He shrugs. "Not sure, the Beckett sisters will definitely be here. They are the noisiest of the bunch and won't be able to resist."

I back away from the edge as droplets of water from the whirlpool splashes ten feet into the air as it churns violently. Melodious laughter fizzles through the air. The sound makes me smile and reminds me of a chord of music I've heard before. The different octaves blend perfectly. Three rays of light shoot out of the water then quickly dive back into the ice blue depths, but they weren't quick enough. My eyes didn't miss the pastel-colored mermaid tails as they descended.

As the water stills, three mermaids shyly pop their heads out of the water. All have similar facial features, but that's where the resemblance ends. One mermaid has long wavy hair, auburn on the top, with golden brown on the bottom. Her sister in the middle has short pink hair cut in a stylish long bob. Lastly, the eldest sister is a tad more beautiful than her counterparts, she swims closer to where we stand. She has blue plaited hair, and her golden bronze skin glimmers in the sun. Her voice is commanding and direct. "Come here, child."

I do, without a second's hesitation. The mermaids brazenly look me over from head to toe. "Child, we have come to the conclusion that you're too inexperienced. What say you?"

These mermaids don't waste any time on subtlety, and I won't lie to them. "I'm not."

The three mermaid's gasp. I don't know what they expected my answer to be, but it wasn't that. The pink haired beauty speaks next. "Why do you go forth on your journey then?"

I shrug. "It's what's expected, and the very reason for my existence. I won't back down just because of my inexperience, nor will you ever see me dishonor my family name. My parents not only died to protect it, but they did so while believing in me. Fighting against my birthright would be selfish, when so many lives are at stake."

"We don't think it's fair that you don't have to compete in the Trials. Do you?" The eldest asks.

"That thought has crossed my mind, it doesn't sit well with me. I plan on speaking to the King about that tomorrow, so that I can." I answer honestly, and in my peripheral vision it doesn't escape my notice that Sebastian is looking at me like hell will freeze over before that happens. I ignore him, it could be the change in position of the sun or just my eyes playing tricks on me, but they have given me an unspoken truce. Respect is written all over their beautiful faces. Drawing close to each other they converse together for a minute. With how animated their facial expressions get and how wild their hand gestures are the conversation must be intense. However, I can't hear a sound, not even a hushed whisper. Damn it.

My knees buckle as we stand there awkwardly, waiting on them to finish. My bruised ego has already taken a hit, what will they say next? The sisters go back under the water and quickly rise above the surface. My mind turns to mush as my mouth drops open. Gone is the deep golden tan of their skin and in its place is an iridescent pastel pink. Becoming more comfortable in their presence, I sit on the bank of the lake. As they move closer to me, more of their top half rises above the surface. For the first time I realize they are topless. "Can I ask you what your names are?"

The sister with Auburn hair answers first. "I'm Alisa Beckett, the middle child. This is our baby sister Francesca. And our older sister, Sophie, has the blue hair. She is very bossy." Alisa ends her sentence with a wink, making me chuckle.

Sophie slings her long wet blue hair into her sister's face, causing everyone to laugh. "Why do you always have to say I'm the oldest! It's rude to call someone old!"

"See, I told you. Bossy!" Alisa whispers conspiratorially.

"You're only turning 45 next week, Sophie. No biggie. At least Dad lets you go on dates. I have to wait until I'm 25, and Josh Carlisle will have a girlfriend by then, it's rough being this young." Francesca twirls a piece of her pink hair around her finger. The way she loses her train of thought after saying his name, Josh must be hot. I bite back a laugh when Sebastian growls inside my mind. Serves him right for listening to my thoughts.

Man, I want to live underwater if it will make me look like Sophie at 45. "If it's any consolation, Sophie, you look amazing."

Her smile back at me is vibrant. "Thank you. We have waited many years for your birth, and now for your reign. I'm happy to report that you have exceeded all our expectations. If you do not forget us when war comes upon our shores, we have a small token of our gratitude to gift you. This token will grant you one wish."

Sophie reveals a small coin inside the palm of her hand, after seeing the look of panic that covers my face. Alisa replies. "You can use it anytime, doesn't have to be now. All you need to do is throw this in a body of freshwater, and one of our kind will answer your call. Arabella, we are a peaceful people, we quarrel with no one. When trouble arises, will you protect us if we give you this gift?"

"I will protect you with my life, regardless of whether you give me a free wish or not. Just being around you makes me happy. Thank you, that is enough of a gift." I mean every word of my answer. They have made me forget the battles that lie ahead.

Alisa comes even closer to where I'm sitting. "Arabella, may we hold your necklace that Eleanor, the Governor's daughter, gave you?" Surprised by their weird request, I do as they ask. Why do they need my necklace, though? Eleanor told me never to take it off, and here I am, taking it off. Sounds smart, but surely, they can be trusted. Sophie takes my necklace from Alisa, and Francesca hands something to her. After connecting the piece, she throws it into the air and lets it fall into the water. I panic, as they remain calm and watch it as it sinks deeper into the water.

Sophie yells. "Now!" All three shoot beneath the surface, I assume to grab my necklace. The sisters come up with a shout, all I see is splashes and hair. Finally, Franchesca untangles herself from the other two. She swims over to give me my necklace while the other two continue wrestling, not knowing she has escaped. "Here, Arabella, it's yours. Guard it with your life, for a wish to work, the token must touch the bottom of the body of water where the wish is made. Sorry for the dramatics. We had bets on who would bring the necklace back to you first. It's not always hard being the youngest, they are slow pokes and fight so much with each other that they forget about me and my mischievousness."

I chuckle, because these mermaids are sweet and fun. I look down at my necklace to see what has been added, and around my sun is now a circle. As they don't touch each other the sun is no longer attached to anything visible. I shake my necklace, and it still doesn't move.

The other two sisters are out of breath but join the conversation once again. "This necklace was a gift from my parents. How do you have a piece that fits it perfectly?" The younger sisters look at Sophie. That's odd. They don't know whether they can answer my question or not. She looks at me, I hope my eyes look pleading because I want to know.

"We're not supposed to tell you, but what's the fun in that? Our fathers were great friends. Sometime after your birth, your father came to tell ours the great news of your birthmark. You're a legend, in our eyes, Arabella. We've been told about the Chosen since birth. He gave my father this token and asked him to give it to you one day. This next part is what was forbidden to tell you. Your father asked us for our complete silence on the matter. There are three pieces to your necklace, they fit together like a puzzle. He voiced that one day, once pieced together it would save your life. That's all we know; I also heard him say these things myself."

"Why were you forbidden to tell me what my father said?" I am slightly offended because wouldn't he want me to know that. This journey will be hard enough.

Alisa sighs. "Your father said everything needed to fold together perfectly in order for you to win the war, he said you needed to find each item at just the right time, so that your life would be spared."

Shivers run up and down my spine, none of this makes sense. Sebastian tenses up beside me. How can a necklace save my life one day? I have so many questions that have been left unanswered, but I do have the second piece to the puzzle. That's something, at least.

Sebastian interjects with lethal calmness. *Arabella, we are having supper with my father in about an hour. It's time to leave.*

"Thank you for everything, I'll never forget your kindness, and will protect each of you. Also, I'm done with being The Chosen, because I want to be a mermaid when I grow up." The sisters laugh, but a look of horror quickly spreads across their faces. I lift my eyes to the sky, which is where they are looking, but nothing is there. Before the Bennett sisters can make their getaway, a roar sounds off behind me. Sebastian grabs his weapons; his shadows are on high alert as he stands in front of me. The broadness of his shoulders and his height, he hides the potential danger coming.

There is a whisper of movement coming from my left where the brothers ran off to minutes before. Then in seconds a wind so strong it almost rips me to shreds comes next, and my hair shoots upward toward the chaos. The pitter-patter of my heart runs wild in anticipation, but when Sebastian visually relaxes, I peek around his shoulder.

FALKON

Chapter 18

You Mean I Get a Dragon

Arabella

Falkon is ornery, just like any self-respecting dragon should be. I would be extremely disappointed
if she wasn't.
-Arabella The Chosen

THEY SAY SEEING IS BELIEVING, but I'm going to have to work really hard on the believing part. Standing before me is a massive red and gold ombré dragon. The upper half is blood red, while the bottom is gold. The creature stares at me with blatant curiosity, my face mirrors the same expression. I've been told my whole life that dragons are real, but their numbers have dwindled significantly throughout time. My cousins run back from the clearing. "Damn it, Falkon! We told you she would come to you!" Jeremiah chides.

The only answer he receives from the dragon is a series of dark grey puffs of smoke that come out of its nose. One of which is suspiciously shaped like a human hand that is shooting a bird, making Deen cackle and Jeremiah roll his eyes. Putting two and two together, I walk around Sebastian's protective shield. They have gifted me with a dragon. "May I come closer?"

The dragon turns its head to the side, sizing me up. "Yes, Arabella Chosen." The gravelly voice is feminine.

Walking to stand in front of her, I bow. "Thank you, Falkon."

She bows in turn, then looks over at the brothers with a huff. Deen laughs. "Don't start, Falkon. She's here and she's safe."

"Arabella The Chosen, why did you agree to go into the Trials? Don't you know that thousands will die that day." She admonishes.

Clearly, I didn't, but it's too late to change my mind now. The promise has been made. "What's done is done, Falkon."

She shakes her head in frustration, then narrows her eyes on Sebastian. "And YOU, tricking her into being bound to you before she knew the details of the prophecy."

Nausea rolls to the pit of my stomach. "What's she talking about, Sebastian?"

His face is an unreadable mask. "Tell her!" Falkon roars.

"Tonight." He stubbornly answers.

That's not good enough. I look toward my dragon. "Can it be undone?"

"No," Sebastian whispers through clenched teeth.

Unimpressed, Falkon answers me. "It can, but it's a difficult task."

One of Sebastian's shadows grabs my elbow, and his face is twisted in rage. I remove my elbow from his firm grasp. "Please, let me explain. When you were born, so was another prophecy."

Falkon recites the passage before he can. *Two Princes will battle for your hand; one will love you, the other will deceive you. Choose wisely which path you travel, for one leads to darkness, and one leads to victory.*

Another damn riddle. I get as close to Sebastian's face, that my height challenged self can. "I wonder which one will deceive me. Huh, asshole?"

He grabs my chin, at which Falkon huffs in warning. "I'm sorry, but I'll always do what keeps you safe first. Even if it pisses you off. Ethan would rather kill you than let you choose another path."

Black dots blur my vision, an indication that I'm about to lose my shit. "Ethan's not even a prince, Sebastian."

Sebastian looks behind me at my cousins and Falkon. "Arabella already knows, but due to my Shadowed status I can infiltrate even the complex of minds. That's how I know Ethan is not who everyone thinks he is." He turns to me next. "Please, give me a chance to explain tonight, after the dinner."

Looking down at my hand, I nod. "I may have forgiven my aunt and uncle easily, but you'll only get ten minutes to change my mind before I let Falkon explain how to undo this. Good luck."

His hand rubs my cheek in adoration. "Please, know that I'm sorry. But I had to do it again, I would."

Yeah, that won't change my mind. "Well, tell me how you really feel, Dark Prince." Placing my arms over my chest, all the pieces fall roughly into place. I've watched enough episodes of Vampire Diaries for his actions to be suspect. "Answer me this, did you use compulsion to get me to agree to being Bound to you?" He has the good sense to let his remorse show. "Oh my God, you did! Get out of my sight. NOW!"

He shakes his head. "I'm not leaving, you will never be far from my sight again."

"Too bad." Throwing my hands up in annoyance, because I don't want to be anywhere near him right now.

He puts his Bound tattoo in my face. "This says that you are mine. I might have used stronger means than necessary to get you there, but I meant everything I said before."

Falkon leans her head over my shoulder, and snarls at him. "Arabella The Chosen told you to leave. That means—leave."

Sebastian grabs his weapon, and his shadows slink to the surface. Falkon chuckles a dry humorous laugh. "Well, that's one way to become unbound." We look on in horror as she rears back her head breathing in deeply. While Falkon looks back at us her eyes are rays of fire. She means to incinerate him. Without any thought for my well-being, I jump in the middle of them, and scream for her to stop. Sebastian grabs my waist to push me out of the way, but it's too late.

Lava like fire shoots out of her mouth, instinct wills me to grab my necklace, causing me to go into a trance.

Time eases by slowly, almost freezing in place, and going on with nothing but some long buried inclination within, I hold my hand above my head, aiming it at the water. The cool liquid flows into my hand as I form it into a ball. Then disperse it into the fire, extinguishing the flames with one thrust of my arms. As time returns, my cousins rush to my side while Sebastian moves in front of me. A loud screech comes from Falkon, when the water hits her face, making us cover our ears. I can't believe it, but I've found my magic.

I'm not over what Sebastian did to me; however, he earned a point for trying to save me. I push him out of the way, as my eyes narrow on my dragon. "Fuck Falkon! You can't do that! You almost made him go up in a blaze of glory!"

She rolls her eyes. "He's smart enough to have moved out of the way, Arabella The Chosen. The better question is do you have a death wish?"

I put my hands on my hips. "No, but I seemed to have handled myself just fine. Thank you very much."

She gives me a look of pride. "That you did. Your task is not for the faint of heart, and cowards are worthless. Your bravery means that I choose you, Arabella The Chosen. Come forward and give me your hand." Confused, I follow through on her command. Sliding my hand toward her, awaiting further instruction. Falkon uses her talon to slice a small gash in her arm, making a hiss pass through my lips as she does the same to my palm. My dragon's voice is commanding, "Place your hand to my wound, for the blood oath."

A dragon asking me to give them my blood was never a conversation I thought I'd have. "Before I do that, will you explain to me what that means?" Sebastian doesn't appreciate the side eye that I give him as the words are so fitly spoken out of my mouth.

Amusement lights her features. "A blood oath is many things, but simply put it is a joining of our minds and lifespans. We will be able to communicate much like you and Sebastian can. As concerning the other, you will be gifted with a very long life. However, if you die, I die. So, don't do that."

This is a very grown-up life decision. Do I want to live longer than my family and friends? Seeing my reluctance, Falkon adds. "It is a great honor that's been bestowed upon you, Arabella The Chosen. We will need each other in this war."

Having a dragon, especially one as fierce as Falkon could benefit my new team. Being in charge means making the hard choices. "Thank you, for this great honor, Falkon. My hesitation comes from the unknown. Living a long-life means watching all the ones you love die. Not to mention, I'll be essentially murdering you if I get killed."

As my cut touches her laceration the outside edges begin to glow, and a tingle begins moving slowly up then down my arm like ants marching to a beat. The feeling permeates through our veins as our bodies begin to glow. A bright light picks me up off my feet, creating bursts of light out of every part of my body. I fall to my knees as if in prayer as sweat drops from my forehead. Sebastian bends to check on my welfare, but I swat his hand away. Sebastian tries again. "Bell's, please let's walk back to the palace."

"Oh, I'm walking, but not with you. You're ten minutes starts after dinner tonight, and not a minute before." I stubbornly reply.

Sebastian's face is crestfallen, but he quickly masks the emotion. "As you wish." He throws a rock on the ground. The confidence that his present sexy smirk exudes, is enough to make my insides sting with need. My heart drops as he disappears into the mist that it created, because I already miss him.

"You're drooling, Arabella The Chosen." Falkon gives her unwarranted opinion, my cousins double over in laughter, I can't help but join in.

"Falkon, we have to leave for dinner. Where will you go?" I ask.

"To the palace, of course. Where you go, I go. Your cousins can walk, but you can ride." She answers nonchalantly.

My mouth opens, it takes a couple of moments for words to form. "Don't I need training?"

Falkon puffs grey smoke toward the sky. "No training needed. Hold on, and don't fall off." My dragon is fucking crazy, but our lives are intertwined. She trusted me, now I'm going to trust her. Falkon lowers her leg, while I slowly ascend her scale ridden side.

Jeremiah shakes his head. "I think this is a bad idea. It can take months to learn proper protocol."

Deen nods. "Yeah, what he said, also Falkon I'm offended. Why can't we ride?"

Settling into the middle row of her horns, I quickly grab the one in front of me with both hands as she moves her head to the side and blows fire in Deens direction. He only laughs and jumps out of the way. "Falkon," I scream! "You can't do that!"

"But can't I? We've played that game since they were children, besides he moved out of the way." She bends down on her hind legs, then flies into the air in one giant thrust. We fly higher than the trees. While the cool evening air greets my face like a long-lost friend. Strands of my hair roll into the wind and I can't stop the giggle that escapes making Falkon chuckle in return. Regrettably, the palace comes into sight all too soon because I could ride Falkon for hours. The need to get out of my head is real. If I could be granted the ability to not think about the coming trials or the battles that'll turn into war for a day, I'd take it.

I send Falkon a message with my mind to see if the blood oath works. *When can we go again?*

Falkon whispers. *Soon.*

* * *

Sebastian

I've waited a hundred years for her, and if it takes me a hundred more to get her to forgive me, I'll pay the penance. Because she's finally mine.
-Sebastian

HIDDEN WITHIN MY SHADOWS, I watch the evening sky for Arabella's return. Knowing Falkon, she won't be able to resist giving her Chosen a ride. The cantankerous dragon is younger than most but still wise beyond her years. She was born to be Bell's champion. That's her birthright as mine is to save the world riding by her side.

A flash of Arabella's face as she came on my fingers infiltrates my mind, it almost brings me to my knees. She will be my undoing, so tender and sweet. She tastes like vanilla and strawberries on a warm sunny day. My cock aches to be inside her, as it tightens against the zipper of my pants. Tonight, I have more plans for her. After groveling, of course.

A ghost of a smile touches my lips as I hear their arrival, laughter fills the quiet air. No matter what Arabella goes through, I hope she keeps the goodness that is in her. Especially since she'll bear a terrible burden. The fate of the world will be on her shoulders. Billions of people whether they know it or not will be counting on her. Folding under the pressure will not be an option for her. With great responsibility, often comes great personal sacrifice. Will she be willing to make those sacrifices? Our way of life depends on every decision that she makes, as well as the peace of all humanity.

A knot forms in the pit of my stomach. Mayra, and the escaped convicts are after my beloved, but I'll kill anyone who touches her. A part of me died the night I defeated death in the Valley of the Decayed. Now, fucking Death Duvessa Raven herself is after, my Bell's. I'll burn this world to the ground before one hair on Arabella's lovely head is touched by that bitch. If Duvessa thinks I won't come back down into the valley, she'd be wrong. I'll rip her spinal cord out through her mouth, ending her once and for all.

My soul no longer sees things the way that it used to. They are no longer black and white, only gray. Placing Arabella under compulsion was a necessary move to ensure her safety, because our love story was forged into the stars many years ago, and Ethan will not take her from me. I need her light, just like she'll need my darkness.

Chapter 19

My Sweet Aunt Adalia

Arabella

Sometimes you meet someone and it's like you've known them forever.
-Arabella

MY COUSINS ESCORT me back to my room so that I can get ready for the celebration tonight. Uncle Jo left word that he's still in meetings and will see me at the dinner. A light tap sounds on my bedroom door. Deen and Jeremiah are standing guard, so it won't be an enemy.

The coo-coo clock hanging on the wall beside the window alerts the hour. It's a red and gold dragon, very similar to my powerful yet beautiful Falkon. The clock states it's seven, and the feast starts in about an hour. There's still plenty of time in case it's Sebastian coming to brown nose me.

Instead of shadows greeting me, Aunt Adalia stands at my door. She's one of the prettiest women I've ever met. She smiles warmly at me and an unexplained connection instantly forms between us. Her toffee colored skin is flawless, her red and black braids are pulled into a high bun as her ruby gold crown proudly sits on top of her head.

"Hi," I say nervously.

"Hello, Arabella. We have waited for this day for so long, and although the circumstances are not ideal, I'm thankful that our family is now complete." She reaches up to wipe a stray tear from the corner of her eye, making me wipe a tear of my own.

My words come rushing out. "Aunt Adalia, so much has happened these past couple of days. I'm confused, and I don't know how to do any of this."

She holds up her hand to halt my words, walking past me as she beckons me to follow her to my bathroom. Aunt Adalia is everything a leader should be, regal and graceful. I try to walk like her but give up after almost tripping over my "graceful" feet. She stands with her back to the full-length mirror in our new bathroom. "Arabella, look in the mirror. Tell me, what do you see."

Hesitantly, I gaze at my reflection. Taking my forefinger I touch my hair, my cheeks, and my nose in the process. What do I see? A scared little girl, who is a skilled warrior, but without all her training. A daughter, a niece, a best friend. I say none of this, only look shyly back at Aunt Adalia. Shaking her head, she points back toward the mirror.

"Well?" She asks.

Aunt Adalia apparently doesn't beat around the bush, that's probably a Queen thing. "I se-e-ee a girl who is wonderfully made, but one that's not sure of herself. A skilled warrior, but not trained in all the areas that matter. Her heart won't survive if she fails because seeing her friends and family die like her parents did is not an option. This ordinary girl has been asked to do an extraordinary thing, and I'm not sure she's the one for the job."

My aunt stands behind me, placing the palms of her hands gently on top of my shoulders, where she locks eyes with me. Unwavering, I meet her steady gaze. "Now, let me tell you what I see." I nod, because my emotions won't allow me to speak. I need her to speak life into me, because this self-doubt is killing me little by little. My nerves are frayed at the edges. "Arabella, I see a girl on the brink of womanhood that has the beauty of the Creator living deep within her. A warrior who hasn't had the chance to reach her full potential. A granddaughter of a great Aztec warrior chief, a daughter to two of the best warriors of this century, and a niece to a King and a legendary master swordsman. But there is even more greatness within you. You're a child of the light, you cannot fail. Being uncertain is natural, but it's in those times that you find out what you're truly made of." She lets go of my shoulders and comes and stands in front of me.

Reaching out my arms I embrace her in a big bear hug. She told me exactly what I needed to hear, and uncertainty can't be allowed to rule over me. Aunt Adalia kisses my forehead and leaves me to get dressed while the seeds of confidence she planted start taking root in my heart. Walking back into my room, I contemplate my outfit for tonight. Sebastian will be at the dinner, so I need to look my best. Clothes and jewelry were delivered to my closet earlier in the day.

An above the knee gold dress in the corner catches my eye. It's a V-neck that flares at the bottom with thick tank top straps. It reminds me of something Marilyn Monroe might have worn back in the 50's. Next, I decide on bright red jewelry that compliments the dress well.

After hair and makeup, I look expectantly at my reflection in the mirror. My bold red lips stand out, but pairs well with the jewelry. I'm nervous, this is a big deal, because it'll be my first time as The Chosen at a function, and all eyes will be on me. I've never been one to shrink back against the wall, but I'm not the life of the party either. Being the center of attention has always been something I've tried to avoid. Middle ground is where I like to stay, and with my Chosen status, that's about to change.

Taking a deep breath, I leave our apartment. My cousins left to go get ready a while ago, stating they'd meet me there. More than likely their Mama made them leave, they take this watching over me seriously.

I'm not a hundred percent sure where the dinner is being held. My cousins said, there was no way I could miss the Hall of Zohar.

Thankfully, people are walking ahead of me and following them is probably my best bet.

A painting on one of the high ceilings grabs my attention. A mural of a great battle scene is sketched there. I close and open my eyes several times, in hopes that the scene before me will change. It doesn't, which makes the hairs on my neck stand up in anticipation of the battle to come. I'll never back down from a fight, but that doesn't mean we're not still fucked.

In the scene, I'm wearing all black while my cousins are standing beside me. My expression is one of determination, as an army of what looks like thousands are behind us. Which in theory, should be awesome, however, the opposing enemy before us is so big that it takes up over half of the ceiling. Their army looks eerily like demons from the pits of Hell. My arm is raised indicating we are about to charge into battle! Falkon is hovering above us, her eyes slits of fire. Shivers run up and down my body as I stare at the scene before me. Did someone dream about this scene? I wonder how it came to be and also what its outcome is.

Taking a deep breath, I move on, even though I'm shaken to my core. Someone touching my elbow pushes me out of my reverie. It's Sebastian, in all his shadowed glory. He's wearing an all-black suit. His raven tresses are halfway pulled back in a hair tie while the remaining strands touch his shoulder. He looks like a walking red flag, and I'm here for all of it.

"Hello." He whispers, as his answering smirk lets me know he's in my mind. *Asshole.* I hate how he makes my heart pound, and how my palms get sweaty. He stops breathing as his lust filled gaze sweeps over my curvy body. "Go change. Now!" Sebastian's jaw is clenched so tight I'm surprised it doesn't snap.

"Hey." I ignore his command; my voice is hoarse from wanting. "I was just heading to the dinner."

My dark Prince's eyes narrow, as a shadowed arm shoves me against the wall. Hoisting my legs around his waist he grinds his erection into the seam of my now soaked panties. He smells my arousal in the air, making an almost savage growl leave him. "You. Are. Mine."

My lust addled brain turns to mush, forgotten is his earlier betrayal. I don't care what he's done, what his reasons were. At this moment, I want to be his. The need my body feels for him is different than anything else I've ever experienced. This is raw, and real, and new. My body is greedy, and she won't be ignored. This frustration of every event that's taken place since my arrival needs to be released.

His touch, his mouth, his cock. *Mine.* His heart shaped mouth meets mine halfway, my answering moan makes him grow even harder. Every emotion is poured into this earth-shattering kiss. Sebastian's possessiveness drives me wild with need. He wants to be my sole reason for breathing. On at least that one thing we agree.

The clack of stiletto heels startles me out of my trance. He holds me firmly against the wall, multiple shadowed arms capture my wrist and ankles, as Sebastian envelopes us both in a cloud of gray mist. "No one will be able to hear or see us. You're so wet for me, Bells, so wet."

A woman in a red dress and heels walks swiftly past us oblivious to the fact that Sebastian is reaching underneath my dress to rip my panties with one snap of his fingers. "Bash, please."

He smiles against my lips. "Please what?" my dark Prince growls.

"Please," I shamelessly beg again.

A shadow hand grabs my throat applying pressure, igniting a blaze from where his fingers tightly graze my neck straight to my pussy. "Don't make me ask you again."

Like a rabbit caught in a cobra's snare, I can't look away from him. Shamelessly, my lips move, my voice is almost unrecognizable. "Fill me up."

* * *

Sebastian

> *Fill. Me. Up. Fuck, and fill her up I shall.*
> *-Sebastian*

THERE's no time for foreplay, she's ready, I'm ready. With my magic, I remove our clothes. Inch by inch my thick cock enters her tight little cunt. My elongated k-9's come out to play, making her whimper as my teeth sink into her neck. Her blood tastes better than anything I've ever sampled or could have ever imagined. It's not just the fact that we're Bound making it that way, it's her. She's a heady aphrodisiac, setting my world off its axis. Finally, for the first time since coming back from the dead, I feel like I can breathe again.

Taking my fill, I nip a line from her neck down to her breast. Leaving my mark on her, because alerting everyone that she's mine is crucial to my sanity. My hips plow into her over and over, the soft heat of her walls are beginning to clench around me. I've never felt such pleasure. The sounds of our moans and the slapping of our meeting skin bounces off my shadowed cocoon. No one will ever hear or see her this way again.

"You're such a good fucking girl, Arabella. You're embedded into my very DNA, and I'll never let you go." I capture her mouth and kiss her so deep our mouths may wind up bruised.

She meets my tongue thrust for thrust, as my fingertips bury themselves deeper into her soft tawny skin. "Give it to me. Now. Let go."

She shatters around my cock, yelling my name for only me to hear. Arabella will be mine forever. She sends me over the edge, I bite into her skin as my cum explodes inside of her. Leaning my forehead on her shoulder, I can't release her yet, not until I become soft, and our heavy breathing subsides. With her, the screaming inside of my head stops, and I feel alive again. I'll never stop chasing the high she gives me.

Reluctantly, I release her, but not before kissing her plush pink mouth thoroughly once again. She's everything I've ever wanted, and more.

Chapter 20

The Hall of Zohar

Arabella

Trouble is coming, and we need to get two steps ahead of whatever it is.
-Arabella

He sets me down on shaky legs and nips at my lips again. He cleans us up, much like he did at the marshes, as we continue our walk-in silence. My experience is limited, but no one has ever made me feel like Sebastian just did. The dirty things he whispered, the feel of his fingers around my throat, how he relentlessly took me over the edge was better than anything that's ever been done to me.

A shadowed fingertip caresses my cheek, sending shivers down my body. "You're welcome." I yank my arm out of his ironclad grip, his face is expressionless, but he sends a laugh inside my mind. *Asshole.* I pinch his arm, making him yelp which brings me explicit joy. He takes my hand into his, and we continue our walk.

I can't stop my pout. *It's not fair that you can hear my thoughts, but I can't yours.*

He nods. *Now that we've mated and solidified the mating bond, you can.*

My side eye comes out. *What do you mean by solidified?*

He shrugs. *It was never my intention to take you before explaining but nonetheless, I don't regret it.*

I roll my eyes. *I told you I'd only give you ten minutes to explain yourself, but now you're only getting five.*

He turns to me, his lime green eyes glowing. *No Bells, you're wrong, I get forever.*

There is no more conversation after that, the closer we get down the hall, the louder the sounds of people talking become. My grip tightens on his hand, he's a jerk, but a jerk that surprisingly makes me feel calm. The sound of dueling pianos and people cheering engulfs us. My intestines turn inside out, and the present company excluded, I've never been this nervous.

This will be my first big outing as The Chosen. I would rather be on the battlefield than have to make small talk with people I don't know. Swords are easy, people are not. Light radiates from the entryway of our destination. Sebastian tries to say something, but I don't hear it because of the sounds around us. He smiles, takes my hand, then kisses my knuckles. A goofy grin spreads across my full lips, he is breathtakingly beautiful.

My cousins rush to my side and gently take my hand out of Sebastian's. Startled, I take a step back. Deen looks at Sebastian with a raised eyebrow while Jeremiah sways his finger back and forth in front of his face. Ethan nods in understanding and shrugs his shoulders at them. Giving me a wink, he disappears into the crowd. Each cousin offers me one of their arms so that together we walk inside my first dinner as The Chosen. The pianos shout, and the people grow quiet. Every eye bores into me, while the expression of all the onlookers is one of awe.

Running away would be ideal, but that can't happen, gone is the carefree girl from Savannah. The old Arabella can't come to the phone right now, because she's dead.

The Hall of Zohar exceeds my expectations. A million candles line the room and are on the tabletops. The walls are gold, and the ceiling is a glittery black making it look like a dozen stars on the darkest night. There are two oval tables overlooking the room. King Aramayus, Amelia, and Kamila Kelli and her husband sit at one. My uncles and Aunt Adalia are sitting down at the other. They have been awaiting our arrival. Why isn't Sebastian sitting with his family?

Surveying the room, my mouth runs dry. There must be at least 300 pairs of eyes staring back at me. I thought we would have a low-key meal with family, some Guardians, and maybe some high-end military officials. That is not the case, as the crowd looks back at me expectantly. I hope they don't want me to talk or anything. I look toward my aunt and uncle for direction.

Aunt Adalia smiles encouragingly at me, then back at the crowd. She raises her hand, and they stand. "Lux, and Pyralis factions, The Chosen One has finally come home. We will soon be on the front lines, for the Great War is almost upon us. While under her leadership, we will be ready. Arabella, address your people."

No. Nope. Never. My mind rebels, but my body obeys. I move to the center of the stage and Uncle Jo whispers behind me. "You can do this, Arabella."

I spot Sebastian in the back of the crowd, and he gives me an encouraging wink. Breathing in and out, for the first time in my life I try not to overthink things, I'll just speak from the heart. "Thank you for supporting me and my family tonight. As you know, I didn't grow up in this world, so I feel like a fish out of water, but someone once told me that leaders aren't born, they're made, and no one will work harder for you than me."

I look behind me at Aunt Adalia before turning back to the crowd and finishing. "A wise woman reminded me today that I was chosen for a reason, as this is all our destiny. Before my mother married my father, she was a Pyralis. Isabella Grace St. James was fearless and the best of the best. My father was Lux, and he never backed down from a fight. I come from a long line of rulers and masters of their trade, it's in my blood. We will win this war as a united front. We can't idly sit back and do nothing as terror comes our way. The world may never know who we are, but we don't fight for fame or glory, we fight in the name of hope, peace, and justice for all. As it is written, there is a time for peace and a time for war. The age of peace is almost over, but the era of war is coming quickly."

The crowd erupts in applause, I calmly take my seat next to Uncle Radix, my cousins are on the other side of me. All the members of my family are grinning from ear to ear, which tell me it must have been a decent speech, I'll take it. The adrenaline rush has left my body, and now my face feels somewhat numb.

There is a feast set before us, every type of meat including brisket, steaks, pork chops, seafood, not to mention there are sides galore. Mac and Cheese will be my first thing I reach for, my mouth waters as I spot chocolate cake to the left of me, that will be my last thing.

"Thank you, Arabella. Such wise words from someone who thinks she doesn't know how to lead! You're halfway there, dear girl. Societies let's feast! In one week's, time the first battle for the Lux's top two begins." Uncle Radix squeezes my hand lovingly as King Aramayus addresses the crowd.

My cousins pat me on the back, so I take the opportunity to ask them a question. "I think everyone knows who will be in the top two for the Fire Trials, but my question is, which one of you will finish first?"

"ME!" They both shout at the top of their lungs, earning a disconcerting look from their mother.

"You both can't finish at number one, boys." I fire back.

"Men. You mean men." Jeremiah rolls his eyes at me.

"That's right, men, Arabella. Don't worry, Jeremiah, you'll probably finish only about a few seconds behind me. That's nothing to be ashamed of, bro." Deen says with a mouthful of mashed potatoes.

"If that's what you need to tell yourself to make yourself feel better, you go right ahead. Just know, I will beat you so bad that even our mama won't be able to comfort you afterward." Jeremiah barely makes out the words before he starts laughing.

Deen spits out his drink and laughs. "Man, that's cold." Then holds his hands up in a W and whispers, "Whatever..."

Jeremiah shrugs then turns his attention to me. "The Fire Trials will be unlike anything you've ever witnessed; this moment is ours. We've trained and worked our entire lives for this great honor."

Deen gives me a toothy grin. "We've pulled out all the stops for this one. We Pyralis' as a whole can be a little extra."

"But ain't no shame in our game. Lions plus fire, what could go wrong?" Jeremiah winks.

"Bro, when you're right, you're right!" Deen laughs.

My eyes dart back and forth between the two of them. I'm amazed how they can go from almost fighting to laughing like hyenas. I wonder if what Uncle Jo said was true. Will the participants in the Fire Trials really ride out on lions?

Which reminds me, I need to talk to my family, then to King Aramayus. I'm not sure how they will feel about my promise, so ripping the band-aid off is best. I blurt out my declaration. "I've decided to enter the Trials, I can't expect the future Guardians on my team to do something I haven't done."

Uncle Jo looks like he's about to have a heart attack, but Uncle Radix and Aunt Adalias faces are beaming with pride. Uncle Jo mumbles under his breath. "Damn freshwater mermaids."

Aunt Adalia pats Uncle Jo's hand. "Let me speak with Aramayus first. He will not be on board with this, but we will come to an agreement of some sort."

I nod. "Thank you, this is important to me."

Turning my head back to Frick and Frack, I start to ask my cousins questions about the lions when suddenly, an explosion happens in the center of the room. Knocking the table over, they jump in front of me, interlocking their arms to form a small fortress around me with their bodies. The others at our table draw their weapons. I can't see much through the tiny gap my cousins have left open.

Sebastian, in the distance, instructs some of the people in the crowd. His voice is authoritative yet calm. His expression is not to be fucked with though. There is a blue gray smoke charging throughout the center of the room. Someone better have a good reason for being here, or it's about to get real bad for them.

As the smoke settles, a man with blue-black hair and beady eyes emerges. Hairs on my arm stand up, and I instantly feel repulsed by the man. Everyone is still in attack mode, waiting on their leaders to give their seal of approval to take out the the unwelcome guest.

My uncle Radix is the first to speak, "Thaddeus, you're bold to show up at our niece's welcome feast unannounced. Not to mention without an invitation."

Thaddeus greets the royals with a halfhearted bow. "Forgive me, dear Aramayus, Radix, and sweet Adalia, but I assumed my invitation had gotten lost in the mail. I..."

A voice I've never heard stops him before he can say another word. The voice is soft yet commanding. "You will address them by their rightful stations, or you will be escorted to Inferno where you can stay the night, free of charge."

Thaddeus' lips are smiling, but his steel blue eyes betray that emotion. He doesn't like that the man talked to him like that. "Yes, of course. I meant no harm in my lack of formalities. Dear Kings Aramayus, and Radix, and sweet Queen Adalia, my King Diodyous has sent me to talk to the girl. You will understand that I must see her in private. It's what he wishes."

I detect a slight Russian accent, it's in the way he rolls his r's. Glancing toward my aunt, her demeanor gives nothing away, but her hand is balled up into a tight fist at her side. That can't be good. "Surely, Diodyous knows his wishes are not the ones that we will grant. We deny your request, it is our wish that you tell her your message in front of us all. However, be careful, Inferno is especially menacing this time of year. All our high-ranking officials are listening, so unfortunately they will get to you before I can."

Uncle Radix nods his head in our direction. "Deen, Jeremiah, it's time to release her. Arabella, come forward. Thaddeus, this is The Chosen to all our people, even yours." In one swift movement, the "twins" glide apart ending up at each one of my sides. With the protective cocoon they offered me gone, all that's left is the coolness of the air and the deafening silence set before me.

Thaddeus' pale skin is impeccably flawless making him look almost see through. He has small, smoky gray eyes, with dark circles underneath. His chin is pointy, as is his nose. He lifts an arrogant brow; his lips transform into a thin fake smile. "Thaddeus, it is a pleasure to meet you." I paste on a fake one of my own.

"Splendid indeed, The Chosen, it is my pleasure. King Diodyous of the Kori sent me here to give you a warning..." My cousins jump off the stage moving so quickly that I almost fall on my butt.

Jeremiah makes it over to Thaddeus first and wastes no time getting in his face, "Warnings can be perceived as threats. You better watch yourself, Thaddeus."

Deen's tone is low but deadly. "I wish he wouldn't, J. Come on, Thaddeus, I've been itching for a fight."

Jeremiah looks over his shoulder. "You'll get first dibs, little bro."

Deen, satisfied with that promise, backs up just a bit. "Alright, sounds fair. Now, what do you have to warn her about?" Annoyed at my barbaric cousins, I jump off the stage and storm toward them. This is my fight, so I'll get first dibs if someone needs a punch to the face. *Stupid oafs!*

Growling, I elbow my way in between them. "Boys, I can take it from here. Thaddeus, this is YOUR only warning. You better choose your words wisely."

A gasp sounds through the crowd, as someone in the back happily shouts. "Yes! Better watch out, Thaddy. She gets it from her Mama!"

Embarrassment creeps in, my temper gets the best of me again. I can't hide my redness, but I'll still hold my head high. Thaddeus puts his clothing back in place as he looks over at Jeremiah and rolls his eyes. He's not happy with all the new wrinkles. I gently bite the inside of my cheek to keep from smiling. My cousins don't feel the need to hide their smile, which makes me have to bite down a little more.

Thaddeus' clothes look like something out of one of my aunt Georgia's historical romance novels. I may or may not have borrowed them and put them back before she realized they were gone. He looks like he's straight out of the Regency period. Yeah, I've got questions. His ensemble even includes a cravat—Oh, a fancy Jackass.

He bows before me and finishes by placing a top hat on his head. I hadn't noticed he was holding the hat. I mean, does all of the Kori dress like this? Or is it just him? "May I call you Arabella?" He tries again.

I stifle a reply from my cousins. "Yes."

He winks at me, making me feel sick, then proceeds. "Good. Arabella, my warning is not to threaten you, it's for your own protection. The King asks that when you travel to Barrowice Falls for the Ice Trials that you take the route of the Shadowlands. He has closed all mirror portals between the societies. The Resistance has given him no choice. He fears for your safety if you travel any other way, because they have figured out how to manipulate the end destinations within our mirror system. However, it's imperative that you not be caught in the Shadowlands after midnight."

"Why is being there after midnight a bad thing?" I curiously ask.

"Monsters, even too scary to be nightmares, lie within the Shadowlands, and they only come out after midnight. You don't want to face any of those nasty creatures. After the Light and Fire Tournaments, King Diodyous will be expecting all of you. Remember, stay safe, for the night has no eyes." As if he is a magician, Thaddeus throws some rocks down and disappears within the smoke.

I look over at my family, and they don't look pleased. The veins in my cousin Jeremiah's forehead are jumping violently, and Deen has his fire lasso at the ready. That must mean there isn't an alternative route to take. As the saying goes, it is what it is.

Chapter 21

The Treachery Runs Deep

Sebastian

I like her in the moonlight best, the way her skin shines in the darkness breathes life down into the depths of my shadowed heart.
-Sebastian

As THE SMOKE CLEARS FROM THADDEUS' departure, I walk slowly toward Arabella. Deen and Jeremiah have formed a protective magical barrier around her as they exit the room. Using my shadows, I teleport to outside the great hall and await to see what direction the brothers take her.

The smell of her clings to my hands and mouth, causing me to inhale deeply at the memory. Her tight little cunt felt like Heaven wrapped around my swollen cock. Finally, she's mine. Since I found out about my part in the prophecy a few months ago, she hasn't been far from my gaze. Ethan would have killed her, but I couldn't let that happen. Arabella was made for me, and because of that, he hates her. The Ethan I knew died years ago; the replacement is a conniving fuck. The sole reason I was sent down into the Valley of the Decayed was because of him. His heart will be on the end of my sword, the way revenge is best served, and it will happen *soon*. All that was left for me to do was claim her, and now that's finished. I follow Arabella, as I've done for months. Always in the background, forever out of sight. There are positives to having shadows.

After they change into their workout gear, the trio head toward the practice field. Again, my feet tread after her, because she's the candle to my darkest midnight. The air is brisk for this time of year, and through our bond I can feel Arabella shiver. My shadows itch to reach out to her, to protect her against every discomfort. Caring for someone on this level is a foreign notion to me. I'll incinerate every enemy in our path and will lay them down at her feet as an offering of tribute. Arabella's a Queen, and I'm but her lowly subject.

Encased in shadows, I watch on the sidelines while her cousins teach her advanced defense techniques. Besides myself, there are no better teachers than Deen and Jeremiah. They've fought against thousands, and still they stand. Falkon lets out a roar as she soars high above our heads, keeping watch and making sure there is no threat coming from above the clouds, for she'll be ready when it comes. And come it shall.

Watching Arabella in this way makes my darkened soul happy for the first time in years. Her hair is the color of the horizon at daybreak, it's the perfect kaleidoscope mixture of orange and red. Proving once again that she is a light unto my darkness. Being around her even in this capacity makes me forget what the chokehold of death feels like. That is a price far above rubies.

From this angle, I can just make out the slight pout of her lips as she concentrates. The erotic pucker reminds me of how good her silken mouth felt as she wrapped it around my cock. Tonight, after our talk, she will in truth become fully mine. Nothing will be left to reveal. I will tell her everything, as promised. Ethan will be desperate when he finds out what I've done, but she won't be taken from me. She is as much mine as the air that we both breathe. We will never part!

* * *

Arabella

Training with Deen and Jeremiah may be the death of me. They suck ass!

-Arabella

MY BODY HURTS, causing me to let out a hiss as soon as my aching thighs touch the scalding bath water. Sebastian never left my side tonight, even now he hovers outside my bedroom. With the bond came an invisible string that tethers us together. I'm constantly aware of him, his mood, his everything. It's weird, but not unpleasant.

Washing my hair, I dunk underneath the water to rinse off the suds. 1, 2, 3, 4...I count the seconds I'm under the safety of the water, like a game. No rhyme or reason, I've just done this since childhood. Springing up, my heart almost lunges out of my chest as Sebastian makes my scream die in my throat with his magic. My family is in the next room, so there's no reason to worry them unnecessarily. I cover my small breasts, for the sake of propriety. With a quickness I don't possess, one of his shadows removes my arms, making my teeth clench. "Privacy!" I angry whisper.

"Are you trying to get me killed...again?" He hisses.

A diabolical smile forms on my wet face. "I would take immense pleasure in seeing any one of my parental units kick your ass."

One thing I'm learning about Sebastian is that he loves my sassy nature. He visibly smirks, while pulling me out of the tub. "As for privacy, that went out the door the minute we sealed our bond."

Putting my hand on my hip, I raise my eyebrow in defiance. "What do you mean sealed our bond? Falkon said that being bound could be undone."

He nods. "That's true as long as the bond isn't sealed."

I'm about to go ape shit crazy on this shadowed asshole. He's infuriating, and I may kill him. "Sebastian, pray tell, what does sealing the bond mean?" My voice is eerily calm.

He pulls my soaking wet body against his, then positions me to where I'm sitting on the bathroom counter. Sebastian growls when he smells the scent of my arousal. "Well Bells, it means that the moment I came inside of you, there was no going back."

My inner independent woman knows that I should be disgusted by what he's done. However, my heart is a stupid bitch that wants to understand why he went to such extremes to ensure I became his because she may like it. "What the fuck Sebastian?"

He runs his fingers through his hair. "I'm sorry, okay. You don't understand what's at stake here." Sebastian bites his lip in frustration. "Damn it Arabella, you've got to listen to me! Ethan means to kill you and your entire family. Yes, that means the whole damn line of you. He wants your power and the only way he can do that is by killing every last one of you."

I push him away from me, so that he backs up enough for me to be able to walk into my bedroom. I'm not understanding his reasoning. Why does he care? "So, you mean to tell me that you did this out of the goodness of your heart? Something's NOT adding up Sebastian!"

He stomps towards me furious, his jaw set in a hard line. "No, I'm not that noble, Arabella. I've never done anything out of the goodness of my heart, not even before I became this monster you see before you. Our path together was written long before either of us was born. I'm a selfish creature by nature, and I couldn't let Ethan have you. I saved him from killing you, not because it's the right thing to do for our people, but because my darkness can't survive without the light that is you. I'll never regret what I did, even if that means you'll hate me for the rest of our life. You'd better be damn rest assured I'll never let you go. You. Are. Mine."

Sebastian's anguished expression kills me, he's so at war with how he feels. My heart slams in my chest and falls all the way down to my toes. My lips move to speak, but I'm not even sure of what to say. I don't understand all of what he's just said. How does he know we were written? Why does Ethan want to kill me? I can't deny how my body reacts to him, because it's not just sexual. It's as if my very happiness depends on if he's nearby. The unformed words stop as one of his ten shadows caress my cheek. "Arabella, Bells, even before I became the shadowed abomination before you, I was not a good person. However, the first time my eyes sought you out I knew that you were the light to my darkness. We were the Yin and Yang to each other's soul. Your inner goodness calls to me, makes me want to be a better being. I know it's a shitty deal for you. I bring nothing to the table, but please don't hate me. Ethan couldn't be allowed to harm you. I couldn't let him turn you into something dark and evil. Your goodness and light are like sunflowers in the midst of my dark stormy night."

My forefinger traces the scar over his eye that stretches across the bridge of his nose stopping just above his other eye. My dark Prince shivers under my touch. I want to scream and make him tell me who did this to him so that I can end their lives. Sebastian's story must be one full of pain. "You're not a monster or an abomination, Bash." He kisses the palm of my hand while leading me toward the bed. Undressing, he pulls me into his arms, as the demons of his past make a plethora of gut-wrenching emotions run across his beautifully scarred face. "What happened?"

He's quiet for so long, I'm not sure he's going to answer. "No one but Ethan knows how I wound up in the Valley of the Decayed, because he's the one that sent me there. We've always hated each other but I never suspected he would succeed in handing me over to Duvessa."

Fevered rage burns through me, that's the second time I've heard that name today. "Who is she, Sebastian?"

"Duvessa Raven is The Queen of Death, The Grim Reaper of the Fae world. She makes bargains for souls, and reins over her kingdom with an iron fist. Only a handful of us have ever made it out of the Valley of the Decayed alive. We aren't without suffering for the crimes we committed to scratch our way back up to the surface. There's a reason I have ten shadows connected to me, Arabella." Sebastian lays my head on his chiseled chest then begins rubbing me in soft rhythmic strokes.

Ice chills in my veins at the thought of this otherworldly creature, as well as the things she's put him through. My silence encourages him to continue. "A few years ago, there'd been a change in Ethan. Where he was once kind to others, he'd turned monstrous, vile even. It was enough to make me take a second look. We'd both been knights then, frenemies, both equally trying to prove to my father that we should be The Head Knight." A shiver runs down his body as he remembers. I massage his chest and stomach gently to let him know I'm here in whatever capacity he needs. His pain runs deep, he's seen things I've never had to, yet still he stands. Sebastian is strong, even though I don't fully know the story yet, hatred burrows its way down into my heart towards Ethan. Fuck him, for whatever he's done to my Dark Prince!

Sebastian kisses my forehead, then slightly chuckles after reading my thoughts on the matter. "We'd been on a security detail for a high-level councilman, an Alpha from the Blue Ridge pack, it's there I was attacked from behind." He takes my fingertips and guides them along a wide gash down the entirety of his right side. "The hearing is the last to leave you when you're dying. Had it not been for that, I may not have gotten my revenge on all but one. Now that you've arrived, his time is coming. I was given a paralytic agent much like your parents and my mother. They couldn't have gotten to me otherwise. As I laid there, I listened as they damn near tried to gut me. Ethan didn't do the dirty work. He was there as the other two took turns taking their knife to my side and face. The last thing Ethan said to me was, 'Mors vincit omnia,' *death conquers all.*"

Understanding runs through me, almost shattering my last bit of control! "Ethan made a deal with Duvessa, for your soul?" The answer is clear, making bile rise and gurgle up from my stomach.

His hands still, as his breathing hitches. "Yes." He answers even though he doesn't need to. How awful! I don't push down the sadness from coming. How long my tears have fallen, I'll never know, but stopping them is not an option. We hold on to each other for dear life, the things he must have suffered at her hand, at their hand. I make a solemn vow to not only myself, but also to Sebastian. Ethan will die at one of our hands!

Chapter 22

Being Bound

Arabella

He's my person for eternity.
-Arabella

WE LAY SNUGGLED in my bed for what seems like hours. For the first time in a couple of days, I relish in not having to play my part as The Chosen. With Sebastian, I'm still me, the girl from Savannah. He's lost in his thoughts, but he doesn't have to tell me that he's not ready to talk about what happened in the Valley, it's apparent from the grim expression on his face. When that time comes, for him to confide in me, we'll hold each other like tonight. I'll never judge him for his past.

It's not fair what he's endured. If only I could help him see that they're the monsters, not him. "Sebastian, what does being Bound truly mean?"

He turns to me for the first time since we began our talk, genuinely smiling as he laces our fingers together while we turn on our sides. "Only true mates can be Bound. Or, as my forefathers called it, *infinitus*. Simply put, it means we are one in mind, body, and spirit. We will be together, always, in this life and into the next."

Confusion furrows my brows. "I know that sometimes humans can be mates with one of the others, but it's rare. How did you realize I was meant to be yours?"

"Several months ago, I learned that there was another prophecy by combing through Ethan's mind. We three were to be in a love triangle, which is the only reason he's still alive. No one, except Ethan and I, know that he was my persecutor. I've held the secret all these years, waiting to exact my revenge. Now I know why it never felt right. That's why he had me killed in the first place, so he wouldn't have to fight for your hand against me. Even more rare than for a human to have a supernatural mate, is for that human to have more than one. I didn't fully believe it until I touched you for the first time, when you literally brought light back into my shadowed touch." Sebastian says the last part as he kisses the spot in reference where he left his mark on my body that night.

Understanding dawns, before getting to know Ethan's true nature, there was an attraction and an initial spark between us as well. Sebastian growls as he reads my thoughts. Serves him right, always an invasive possessive asshole. I place my forefinger on his lips, making him bite back his curt remark. "Your spark was bigger." I laugh.

He gives me a coy smirk. "Everything about me is bigger."

I make a big show about trying to get out of bed. "I've never seen his. Let me —!"

Sebastian pins me to the bed. "Watch it, Bells! You mess with me; I'll fuck you in front of everybody so there's no doubts that we are truly Bound."

Taking him by surprise, I flip us over. "Is that someone's secret kink?"

Sebastian gives me a smug grin, "I have several, but voyeurism isn't one of them."

Straddling him like this, makes my knee rake across his injured side, stilling me. A solitary tear slips past my defenses, as my Dark

Prince catches it with his lips. "I'm so sorry, Bash. For all the shit you've been dealt. I can't change it, but I promise you that I'll do my damnedest, to make you happy for the rest of our days." Sebastian traces my bottom lip with his thumb and chuckles when I try to bite his finger. We haven't known each other for long, but being with him in this way is easy. So, in turn, I'm honest with him. "Even though you should have gone about it in a different way, I'm glad you won."

His hungry mouth crashes down on mine, while we fight for dominance. He brings out my competitive side. In the end, Sebastian allows me to win, if only for a moment. Feeling bold, I reach below to grab his thick cock with my hand. His lime green eyes glisten with dark desire as he moans my name on his full lips. Kissing down his body, I greedily lick the precum off the top of his shaft. His hips buck in rapacious satisfaction. "Be a good girl and show me that you can take it all, Bells." He wraps us in shadow, so that my family won't hear us having sex. I need him like the air I breathe. My eyes water as he fucks my mouth. One of his hands holds my hair back out of my face so that he can see me take every inch of him.

"Look at me, Bells." He closes his eyes for a moment. "Yes, like that. I want your throat raw, so you'll remember to whom you belong."

Sebastian

I have many devious proclivities. Tying her up is just the beginning of what I'll teach her.
-Sebastian

ARABELLA's bright blue eyes shine with tears of a different kind as I vigorously fuck her mouth. She was made for sin, made for me. The thought of Ethan even in the same room with her drives me crazy, let alone the reminder that she felt their initial spark. It made me almost turn savage with rage. With one more tug, I come with a shout, branding the back of her throat as mine. "Get on your knees and place your cheek on the bed." Slapping her ass, she whines prettily. "Open wider, let me see how wet you are for me." She does as she's told. "Good fucking girl." She's so wet that the evidence of her arousal trails down her thighs, making my mouth water. I slide under her and lay on my back, bringing her pussy close to my lips. "I want you to ride my face, beautiful." I slap her other ass cheek when she doesn't comply fast enough. "I'm hungry, Arabella! Feed me!"

She's rewarded for following instructions when my tongue connects with her clit, as her answering moan makes me smile victoriously. The smell of her arousal is intoxicating, almost enough to send me back over the edge. The sounds of our labored breathing and soft moans bounce off of my created shadowed haven, which will be with me always. The perfect moment, with the perfect mate. I hook two fingers inside her, while I suck on her clit. Grabbing the headboard, she moves her hips with chaotic precision. "Please, Bash."

Grabbing her wide hips in my hand, I set a rapid pace. Both of us are lost in a lustful haze. She comes on my tongue, but I hold her hips in place before she can move. My tongue lingers on her clit after I devour all of her sweet cream. Arabella will be sensitive, though I can make her ready and panting again in no time. She's a very receptive lover.

There are many things we can teach each other. Flipping her over on her back, some of my shadows tie her arms to the headboard and her legs to the bedpost. I kiss my way down her body, paying special attention to each breast and nipple. "Bash," she moans with pleasure.

"What beautiful?" Placing my nose near her pussy, I inhale. *Fuck.* The scent of her arousal just may be the death of me! Arabella is magnificent like this. With her red hair laid out on the pillow. Her cheeks are flushed, and her bright blue eyes are darkened with desire.

"Please," She whispers.

I slap her pussy with my hand. Arabella yelps, her wetness once again running down her thighs. "Please, what? Tell me what you want." Rubbing between her folds, she begins to buck against my hand, so I slap her clit. "Tell me!"

"Fuck me, please!" She begs.

"Whose pussy is this?" I ask vehemently.

"It's yours, always!" She moans. The echo of which makes me grind into her harder. I enter her without warning, making her breath hitch. Her thighs quiver, as I slam over and over into her tight pussy. Arabella loves it rough and raw, and I plan to give it to her, just how she likes it. Letting go of my restraints on her hands, I allow Arabella to dig her nails into my back and ass. Which drives me crazy. She needs me with the same intensity that I do her. "Now, come for me, like a good girl!"

Arabella screams my name and comes almost violently; I fall on top of her as my seed shoots inside. Her walls clamp down on me, and nothing else matters. She is mine, forever!

If this had been anyone else, I would have shut the door as soon as I reached my gratification, but not with her. She is my life, my love, and now, I need to hold her as she sleeps. My only ambition in life forevermore, is to ensure her every need is taken care of. Arabella's safety always comes first. My fingers rub her naked skin as we drift off into a blissful sleep.

* * *

The Shadowlands: Dream Sequence

Arabella

THE MIRROR that led us to the Shadowlands was a black hole. As we fell into the darkness, all I could sense was agony and despair. This place lives up to its name. The area is gloomy, but enough light filters through the trees that we can see a few feet ahead of us. Creepy marshes line the forest, as an owl screeches nearby, making me jump at the unexpected sound. My heart skips a beat with the realization that I am the one in charge of this mission. Nausea rolls in my belly, but I squash it quickly. Throwing up in front of my new lover is NOT an option. Sebastian watches me curiously while his sister Amelia awaits my direction.

A faint mist starts falling from the darkened sky, because a storm is brewing. I shiver, because something is coming. It's probably a terrible omen to have a storm in your dream. Traveling through this godforsaken place to get to the Ice Palace has made me thankful for all the times I haven't had to travel here.

"Everybody, stay close. It's now two hours until midnight, and we don't know how long it will take us to find answers." Jeremiah looks toward me, then at his brother as Deen comes to stand beside me. They nod at each other, an unspoken request made between them. They have made it clear they consider themselves my own personal protectors. Once again, my cousins have placed me in the middle of them, with determination sketched on both of their handsome faces. It's weird seeing them acting so serious with how much they like to joke around.

Our postures are tense, and we are all on high alert. This road is not traveled often, and I wish we could have just gone through one of the other portals, but Thaddeus clarified that every mirror that led to the Ice capital had been compromised. I don't trust him. I don't trust this place either.

We move toward the openings at the edge of the forest and there are three visible pathways leading into the heart of the unknown. The path directly in front of us calls out to me for some reason. My gut feels drawn to wherever this leads so we're doing it! Cutting back the foliage will be a challenge while taking this route, and the clock won't stop ticking any closer to midnight. I second guess myself as look at my friend's expectant faces. Is this the correct decision?

Sebastian looks at me and shrugs his shoulders, "Bells, which way would you like to go? Your crew, your decision." He unnervingly looks around at everyone, daring them to object to what I have to say. My dark Prince is intimidating even in dream form, which I love. My first impulse is to shake my head in resistance. I'm not ready to be the one to give the final answer, but I can't cower under pressure either. Ready or not, this is "my crew," and I don't think they are going to like my decision.

I give the team my best smirk. "I've always heard the road less traveled is the best one to take."

"Yeah, but that one looks like it ate whoever traveled down it last," Amelia laughs. She's not wrong, because the area does look darker than any other part of the Shadowlands, but I will no longer second-guess myself. My female intuition is telling me to go down this passage.

With closer inspection of the clematis vines, we notice they are covering an archway of some sort. I remove my billy club, aptly named, Billie, to cut back the weeds, gently at first, with no success. Frustrated, I rear back and go in for the kill—a light so bright sparks from the impact of the hit, blinding me as electricity flows through my body. I fly through the air into the murky waters that Eleanor warned me against.

Drums beat inside my head, and my ears ring in perfect cadence to the rhythm of the thump. Sinking to the bottom with a thud, I scream as a pale hand reaches for my wrist. A Maritime woman with silver hair and alabaster skin speaks to my mind. Only, it's Eleanor's voice that I hear. My vision blurs as I fall into a trance-like state. "Arabella...Arabella! Wake up! It is me, Eleanor. You must come to me. There is information that must be revealed. The Ice King's treachery runs deep, but do not be wary. Come alone, for I do not know whom we may trust. Come, Arabella. I say, come!"

The spooky woman pulls a ring out of her pocket, placing it in the palm of my hand. This time, it is her harsh voice I hear. "This is a ring carved out of a moon tree from the lands of Feyord, not a lot is known about its magic. It's dangerous and powerful, for it will only work in darkness and shadows. Hurry, The Chosen, the dark Prince is looking for you, and his shadows are growing restless. He won't like that you need to travel this way. Quick, you must think of Eleanor, and you will be transported to exactly wherever she awaits."

The ring has a thick black band and the pearl sitting on top is generous in size. For the first time, I realize I can breathe within the icy depths of the dark waters. Focusing, I close my eyes and think of my mother's best friend, Eleanor. Her fair skin consumes my thoughts, her blonde wavy hair, the way her dress sparkled as she walked out of Lake Luminous, and the bittersweet look she had on her face when she thought of my mom.

My eyes bolt open, my heart is beating erratically, and just when I think it will explode, it stills. My body begins going in and out of focus. A scream dies in my throat, and panic sets in as Sebastian appears out of nowhere. Every time he tries to grab hold of my hand, his fingers can only graze my skin for a fraction of a second. My hand fades in and out, making his hand fall back into the water. His menacing gaze lands on my ring, as he tries to take it off my finger again, only to have the same scenario play out. Somehow, his shadows are a fraction faster than he is. Two of them manage to pull me out of the water.

The whole group surrounds me, my cousins are freaking out because my body can't focus. Merrie-Beth is somehow here... She looks like she is about to have an aneurysm. Sebastian starts whispering into my ear, but it comes in clipped words that I can't make out. It sounds like he is telling me to let go.

Let GO??! I don't think so! That would mean I'd have to relinquish control and face the unknown. No, this was a fucking mistake. I just can't.

I wake with a jolt, the part of the dream where I'm fluttering in and out is now real. My heart contracts in on itself as my body continues to go full blown Houdini with all the disappearing and reappearing acts. My dark Prince is beside me, he appears calm, but his worry slices into me like a knife. With his magic he slips my clothes into place. "Ara—a...L-t go. You must do th----s!" Sebastian's words still fizzle in and out, but it calms me all the same. He says I have to do this, and Eleanor wouldn't hurt me.

Closing my eyes once again, I concentrate on Eleanor and the conversation we shared. That night seems like forever ago, so much has happened since. I'm finally able to let go and the last thing I feel are his lips on my forehead before I'm teleported away.

Chapter 23

The Maritime in Me

Arabella

Moon travel is different than through the mirrors.
-Arabella

ALTHOUGH, I am calmer than seconds before, my chest still feels heavy, and my breathing is labored. All I see is darkness mixed with fragments of light and shadow. I'm flying toward something, but what? Finally, a great beam of light that doesn't disappear in the distance, makes the ring on my hand start to glow. My anxiety lessens the closer I get to the light. My inner peace returns, and seeing Eleanor is my only concern. Her sweet murmurs of comfort begin entering my thoughts.

I land on my feet somewhere in the middle of the forest and Eleanor seems frantic, rushing to my side. "Sorry, but there was no other way you could travel to me except by way of the Moon, sweet child."

Flinging myself into her arms, she holds me. "What's wrong, Eleanor?"

"First, I must apologize, Arabella, because traveling by the light of the moon can be deadly. Many never return from its shadows, but you did well, just as I knew you would. However, they can sense these things, so you must return another way." She squeezes my hand and beacons me to follow her.

"Who's they?" I already know the answer, but I need to hear it from her.

She leads me into the heart of the forest, so I take out my necklace to give us some light as we travel. "No, put that away. Quickly. We mustn't be seen Mayra has eyes everywhere. That's why I didn't want you traveling through the palace. Those that mean you harm are many, Arabella. An evil is growing in this world, and Duvessa is at the root of it all."

The mention of Mayra and Duvessa makes me cringe, causing me to move as close to her as I can get without being a weirdo. From this moment forward, I must be careful in all things. The Umbra having spies planted in this very place. I whisper, "Do you think they have lots of spies?"

"Yes, more so than anyone else believes, and I don't think they captured all of Mayra's supporters before she went to jail. They hid in plain sight, draped in silence, waiting for the time and place you were born. They knew that their wait would be limited, so they've been preparing for war. I watch when no one else is watching and have witnessed the evil things that the "honorable" men do. There are whispers at home. I'm afraid some will side with Mayra when the time comes. No one will be spared from choosing a side." She shivers while holding my hand tighter.

How will I know who to trust? When I'm one step ahead, I fall two steps back. Mama's warning about the one who wears the ice dragon tattoo filters through my thoughts. Who else is on that list? My head hurts, and it's about to explode!

Eleanor brings me to the edge of Lake Luminous. Startled to now be so plainly out in the open, and without the safety of the trees, I feel naked. She feels my hesitancy and that I'm getting ready to bolt back to safety, so she grabs my hand tighter. "Trust me. Please, follow." I trust her but I'm questioning my sanity as my feet follow hers into the cool blue waters. When Eleanor is shoulder deep, she turns to me with a smile. "Do not be anxious. I want to see something. Ok?"

I nod and continue walking, almost disturbed because my very soul already knows what the outcome will be. I'll be able to breathe. My knees buckle as shivers encase my body. In a few short days my entire world has blown up in my face. So many changes are happening in my life, but I'm learning that sometimes change can be good. As we continue, warmth surrounds me. Without needing to hold my breath, we make our final descent into the depths.

"Open your eyes, Arabella. Tell me what you see?" With some reluctance, I comply. My eyes see everything, looking down at my feet reveals they are planted firmly on a cobblestone road. I'm not floating. In fact, it feels as if I'm not underneath the water at all. Lifting my head, I look towards the surface that's merely inches above my head. The moonbeams are dancing happily on top of the water as confusion furrows my brow. "My dear sweet, Arabella. It's as I expected. Oh, this is marvelous!"

Eleanor doesn't move her mouth to speak, but there's no doubt that she is visibly excited, her face is radiant with joy. My face is the opposite, add annoyance and being fucking done with the confusion. It's anyone's guess which emotion is more prominent at this point. I swear if one more thing proves different, I'm going to have a full-blown meltdown.

Eleanor laughs, causing my irritation to grow. How can she laugh at a time like this? She laughs again, but I just can't handle it. With a huff I turn to make my way back up to the surface. "Stop!" I bring my gaze back to Eleanors. She's trying hard not to smile.

"Why?" All that comes out is a bubble, no sound. Covering my mouth with my hand, I whisper the question in my mind this time.

She looks perplexed, not sure of how to answer my complex question. Without a confession, I still know she's been privy to every thought I've ever had around her. "Yes, I can read your thoughts, but this is the first time I've allowed myself to do so. It takes practice to control our gift, and in time you will learn to do the same. My sweet, Arabella, you are half Maritime. I suspected as much but didn't know. Your great-grandmother was one, it skips generations until it falls upon whom it may."

"Eleanor, this has to be some sort of mistake! I have been under water plenty of times before. This has to be some kind of fluke! I won't believe it, I just won't."

Eleanor comes to stand in front of me, her hair gliding behind her as she moves. Her hands squeeze mine gently. "I'm sorry that it comes at a time when you're not ready to hear something new. You have every reason to be upset, but you must listen. When someone is not born of the water, and they live outside its parameters they will not exhibit signs until their 18th year. It was the same for your great grandmother, Charlene. I called out to her from the water in a dream, and she heeded to my voice. She went on to be a part of the First Five, which is the reason we won the second world war, and you're the reason we'll win the 3rd."

That does give me some comfort. "Does my family know?"

She shakes her head. "Everyone knew it was a possibility. This is a significant moment for both your kind, Arabella. I'm fearful because I know this time we will be forced into this war. The Maritime will fight if one of ours is on the front lines, you will be the very first out to battle."

The puzzle pieces are beginning to click together. "They will follow me even though I didn't grow up in this world?"

"To us, blood lines are everything. We will sacrifice anything to help one of ours that's in trouble, Arabella. You will need the help of our people before this is over, I saw it once in a dream that your mother had." She whispers. Chills creep down the hairs on my neck, and I'm done with words. I'm a warrior, but I am still only one person. So many people are counting on me, everything will have to go perfectly. "Everything will be alright, Arabella. You will see, follow me." Her face lights up in a smile, and I can't help but return the gesture.

186

The weirdest thing about this whole situation is that besides my hair floating up and down every so often, it feels no different than walking on land. Even breathing through my nose is the same but when I attempt to breathe out of my mouth, a long succession of bubbles come out. Something is really weird here.

We make our way into the business part of town which is small. The buildings, and wooden pathways remind me of a movie set from a western. Well past business hours, the place is empty. I can almost picture Doc Holiday and Wyatt Earp at the jailhouse delivering the outlaws they've just arrested into a dirty old cell. Uncle Jo loves all Westerns, I tolerate only that one.

As we finally make our way to the outskirts of town, I stop in my tracks when I realize the houses are all made of glass. Some windows are covered while others you can see straight through. Some are big, and some are small, but all are perfectly beautiful. The Maritime people have no qualms about blatantly staring at me. Families are lined up in their driveways to get a good look. Some smile, while others just raise a brow, but no one says a word. I can only imagine what they're saying in their minds. Landers are not trusted down here.

"You're not a Lander anymore, Arabella. They are saying they can't believe The Chosen One is Maritime. Some are already planning to join the efforts to keep you safe, because you must be special, which I agree." She smiles encouragingly.

Our final destination is a mansion so big I couldn't get a full picture on my cell phone, unless I was standing 200 feet away. Good thing, mine is not in my pocket.

Eleanor stifles a laugh. "Welcome to our home. The Governor, my father, is away on business." The butler opens the front door before we make it up the front porch steps. He is surprised by my appearance but manages to mask his reaction quickly. "Ms. Eleanor, I have a fire built in the common room. Do you wish to retire there?"

How do you build a fire in water? The butler smirks, obviously hearing my thoughts. He's handsome, very Bruce Willis-ish. He has a shiny bald head on top, with closely trimmed hair around the back of his head.

The common room, as the butler called it, is extravagantly furnished. Red drapes cover the windows, and the walls have painted portraits of mostly men. They are from different centuries, as well as every walk of life. A minuscule number of women are on the walls. I smile broadly at Eleanor when I see her picture, walking closer to get a better view.

No more than a teenager, the artist captured the freckles across the bridge of her nose, beautifully. A glowing smile spreads across her face, while she plays the harp. The word angelic comes to mind, because you can see her inner goodness shining from deep within her. Next to her portrait is one of a raven-haired beauty, who is the dark of night to Eleanor's light of day. It's Eleanor's older sister Geneva, the traitor married to the Scotsman that is trying to kidnap me. When my eyes meet Eleanors, her expression breaks my heart, because of the sorrow radiating there. No matter the crimes her sister has committed, she still loves her.

"I'm sorry, Eleanor." My would-be captors may be assholes, but before they became the villains in my story, they were average beings that were loved by their families and friends that they betrayed.

"Geneva, was not always bad, you know? We loved each other and because of our age difference, we hardly ever had disagreements. She had a bright future set before her, one destined for politics, just like our Papa. The summer she came back home after her Finishing School graduation, everything about her was different. She was no longer the optimistic sister I knew and loved, in her place was a cruel vicious young woman. She was so full of anger and self-righteousness. Our father caught most of her wrath, as she spewed hate and screamed about how she was tired of living in the old ways. Geneva was done with living in what she called the shadows of society. She had fallen in with a bad crowd of misfits at her school in London. Blaine Ramsey was a young, highly decorated officer of her Majesty's Maritime Navy. It was love at first sight for those two and it didn't take long for him to poison her mind against us all. If only we could have stopped that chance meeting." Her smile is sad, yet hopeful.

She hopes that her sister can one day come back to them. The realization of that makes my heart break even more for her. The chances of that are extremely slim. She must know that. It's not fair because Eleanor deserves better.

Blaine sounds like an opportunist, and I just know that once he's done with her, she'll be discarded like trash. Geneva is the daughter of the most influential man in the Maritime community, and that's no secret. I don't believe their meeting was by chance.

Eleanor gasps, and I want to facepalm myself. She can read my thoughts, I'm such an idiot. "I'm sorry."

She takes my hand and directs me towards the sofa against the far wall. "It's ok, Arabella. I have thought those same things a million times! He targeted her for a reason. His heart is too evil to love. I choose to believe that she's not too far gone. Redemption, once lost, has a way of coming back to us all. It is up to us on whether we accept the gift or not."

"I believe that too, Eleanor. But look at all they have done. How can you think she's not too far gone?" I hate to say those words, but they are true. Geneva is a ruthless criminal, and I don't understand Eleanors fierce loyalty. She turns from me, I've made her feel sad, which in turn makes me feel like shit. "The words are hard to hear, but they are warranted. Geneva no longer has my loyalty, but she will forever have my love. When she's brought to justice, hopefully peacefully, I will be by her side. There are no excuses for her behavior, and she must pay for her crimes, but I will not make her do it alone."

Eleanor becomes lost in thought, and I hate to interrupt that. I may not fully understand her every emotion but do understand her reasoning.

"Arabella, you mustn't be gone for much longer, there is much to discuss. Great rumblings are coming from all directions, we've received some intel from as far as East Asia. Mayra is looking for a secret weapon that was hidden by your society's forefathers many years ago. This weapon is said to be indestructible and has obliterated entire nations. Mayra's top General is said to be the one searching for it. The pieces have been scattered throughout the world. It is crucial we stop her, whatever this is, it cannot be good." Eleanor looks almost nauseated as she tells me the newfound information.

Nervous energy flows through my veins, I would like to know sooner rather than later what this weapon of mass destruction can do. "Who is her top General? How many top-ranking officials is she said to have?"

Eleanor holds her hand up and begins counting them down. "The top General moves in and out like a ghost, no one knows his true identity, we only know him by his nickname Phasma. He has two Generals below him: Elaine Rickles, and Jameson "The Chainsaw" Dixon. They were unashamed supporters of Mayra and have been on the Nation's watch list for years. Despite Kamila Kelli's best efforts, they have not been able to connect them to any terrorist activities. That will change since the great prison escape. Their army will be ruthless, as her numbers grow daily. We need to find out what this weapon is, that way we know what we will be fighting against."

I agree, it's not a matter of if they attack, but when. "Do you know where any of the parts are located?"

She gives me a devilish grin. "Of course, dear child, that is why I called for you. Rumor has it that Phasma has acquired one piece already, and they're keeping it in a heavily guarded facility in the heart of the San Francisco Bay. It used to be a prison for mobsters or something like that. I've heard numbers as high as two thousand guards being there protecting it. Be careful, Arabella. Mayra will stop at nothing to find every single piece."

"That's Alcatraz. There's no telling how lethal that weapon will be, Eleanor. I can't even imagine the destruction that's coming for us all if we don't figure it all out." My voice shakes on the last word, an inky heaviness sinks into the depths of my every pore.

Eleanor begins pacing in front of the sofa. "Mayra will show no mercy when the time comes for you to face off, and that kills me. It's hard to see you running towards danger and not be able to stop it, but please never lose hope, Arabella, because you will win this fight. You must, because our very futures depend on that success." Eleanor reaches inside her pocket and pulls out a picture, then looks around the room, before turning back to me nervously. She whispers so low I almost don't hear her question. "Have you ever heard the name Solomon Flint?"

My interest is piqued. Why is she whispering? I hope he's not some new enemy of mine, because I've reached my quota of those. "No." I whisper back.

"Ella, what I'm about to tell you, cannot leave this room, at least not until you find out who you can trust. Solomon Flint is what we call a Wanderer of Time. No one knows how old he is or where any of them originated from. I've known him since I was a child and in all that time, he hasn't aged one ounce. He's been missing for a year. Suspiciously, around the same time the new Ice King took the throne. I suspect he's being imprisoned in the Ice Palace. Arabella, you must find him." Eleanor takes something else out of her pocket and holds it to her chest, a solitary tear falls down her left cheek. I watch in awe, because how can that happen in water?

So many questions sound off simultaneously, that I'm not able to stop them from tumbling out of my mouth one by one. "What is a Wanderer of Time? Why must I find him? Can he be trusted? Why are you crying? What's on that piece of paper?"

Eleanor kneels before me and tries without much success to hide her amusement. "I know this has to be tough for you, being thrust into this world and knowing absolutely nothing about any of these things. I feel for you, but this is how it had to be, one day you'll understand the importance of it all. Now, to answer your 659 questions, Solomon Flint is from an ancient order that was formed long ago. Each member can travel through time, with their main goal being to fix the wrongs of the past. Your mother trusted him to a point. She said as long as it served his purpose, he would do what was right. You must find him, because your mother said you couldn't complete your journey without him. This letter is from her to me, I only found the note this afternoon in the back of a picture frame. That's why it was so urgent I reached you before you traveled any further in your journey."

Eleanor hands me the note, and I run my fingers over the words my mother wrote. She loved Eleanor, they were true best friends, parallel to my relationship with Merrie-Beth. My heart aches for our loss, but there is no time for tears. It's nice to be around someone that knows my parents better than most.

Dearest Eleanor,

You've taken on a tough role as confidant and protector of our Arabella. We are forever grateful for the wisdom and guidance you will give her. Sweet friend, our time is nigh, for we will not be on this earth much longer. Our knowing this was the hardest secret we have ever had to keep. I wanted to tell you many times, for that I'm sorry. We had to allow things to happen in just the right way for our child's sake. For her to live, we had to die.

Our Arabella will grow into a great leader, she will be just, and nothing will stand in her way of winning the war. Not only will Mayra fall once and for all, but so will Duvessa, The Queen of the Dead. Before Arabella's journey to compete in the Ice Trials, you must speak with her. I had a dream several years ago that Solomon would be taken, he laughed when I told him. He's very prideful and vain, and he never believed he could be captured. Our dreams are sometimes a burden, but we must listen to them. Solomon is one of the keys to winning this war. As you know, he and I had a love-hate relationship, but he will help her find the artifacts that our ancestors hid in plain sight. Mayra has been searching for them for years. However, Arabella must find them first. Through Solomon, I've seen the devastation of billions being murdered because of this device. They must be stopped!

Tell my beautiful girl, in my dream Solomon was being held captive in the highest tower on the eastern side of the castle. Some kind of massive beast was guarding his prison cell. She must be careful but tell her that we believe in her. We love and miss you both terribly.

Eleanor, my dearest friend, and most trusted ally, thank you.
Until we meet again,
Isabella Grace

PS. See if she is like you, Eleanor. I feel deep down in my gut that she will be! It's in our blood and could help to unite our brethren if she is Maritime. I pray she is.

I reread the letter several times, until the tears fall so hard my vision blurs. For once, I don't try to stop the waterworks. My parents had to die so that I could live. It's not fair, and I want to lash out, to scream, to throw things against the fucking wall! Nothing will ever heal this tiny void that their loss has put inside my soul. I don't know when Eleanor took me in her arms and started holding me, all I know is that I felt more at ease when she did. She smells of lavender, and it helps to soothe me. "Eleanor, it's obvious my parents didn't tell you of their impending deaths, but did you sense anything at all?"

She nods. "I knew they were hiding something big from me, but I didn't know what. I certainly didn't think it was their demise. I want to chat with Solomon, Arabella. I want to know if he knows anything. You must find him."

"I have to, Eleanor. You read what she said, he will help me. This is hard for you, too. Thank you for helping me." My eyes are misty, but I can't cry any more tears right now, because the numbness has crept in and seeped deep into my bones.

"Ella, we are family. My best friend is still alive, because she is a part of you. I will help you until my last breath, and I will fight in the war that's coming. Consider me your first Maritime recruit." She hugs me. "You must be getting back. I can only imagine how antsy your cousins are getting."

I laugh despite the feeling of a knife repeatedly stabbing me in the heart. "My cousins aren't in my room, Eleanor. However, they are a little protective."

Eleanor huffs. "Yeah, when you left, everybody busted in your room, and I mean everyone! Just remember, as annoying as their protectiveness will probably be for you, don't be too hard on them.

They're just playing the role they were designed to play. Protecting you is their destiny. They were built with that very instinct in their DNA. We will all have a role to play in this, we were all built for something more."

I smile at her, because she's right, they mean well. I grimace as Sebastian's handsome face pops into my mind. He's probably killed somebody in my absence. Wait, when she said everybody, does that mean my uncles because I'm not ready for them to know I'm Bound. *Fuck!*

"As much as I hate leaving you, it's time. How will I travel back?" She leads me into the library in the next room and removes a book from one of the shelves revealing a secret door. A smaller room is revealed within that has a full-length mirror standing against the wall. She walks to the side of the mirror and comes back with a small bag which contains three small peach-colored pebbles.

We hug each other fiercely. "Never fear the shadows, Arabella. For its proof that when the darkness comes, it can never truly over-power the light. When you think it's over, and you've had enough, please remember it's always darkest before the dawn. The light deep down inside of you will find a way." Not trusting my voice, I smile at her. Standing in front of the mirror, I wait for her to throw the pebbles inside. "Arabella, to free Solomon you'll need to take the throne back for the Fitzgerald's first. That will be your first true battle on the road to the war. Trust only those that are worthy of that admiration. King Diodyus will harm you in any way that he can. He controls his people by something dark and sinister. That's why they are too terrified to overthrow him, but the Resistance against him grows in numbers every day. You must rid them of the darkness that's controlling them. Rally them towards our cause because we will need them in the fights to come. They will not trust you easily, we've idly sat by as rumors circled our kingdoms of the horrors they have faced. It is up to you to right our wrongs."

"I will help them first, Eleanor. Then finding Solomon will be next on my list, because we need answers." I feel sorry for the members of the Kori, and my irritation grows towards all the higher authorities that did nothing to stop their suffering. My family did nothing, and that's not right.

Elenor hands me the small bag and gives me instructions. "This bag is filled with rocks that will get you to me, no matter where we are. They're magically linked with our DNA and were a present from your mother to the both of us. This is your bag. Take it with you wherever you go. Travel safe, trust very few, and right our wrongs."

She speaks so assuredly but I just don't know, because it's just not that simple. She throws the pebbles in her hand, and a swirling gray circle forms faster and faster as it churns, until an explosion happens in the mirror. I gaze at her sweet face one more time, then jump in without hesitation. A smile forms on my saddened heart, I'm finally getting the hang of this mirror travel thing. "Until next time, my sweet Eleanor!"

Chapter 24

The Plan

Sebastian

Moon magic can be lethal, and had she stayed gone for much longer, I would have traveled into the Moon Realm and killed the one who had tried to take her from me.
-Sebastian

JEREMIAH SLAMS his sword into the bedroom floor for the hundredth time, frustration is so thick in the air that even Falkon couldn't burn through it with her fire. "Who the fuck gave her a moon ring?"

"A Maritime wraith gave it to her in a dream, she meant Arabella no harm. Eleanor sent for her." I combed through the wraiths mind myself as it was happening. Had she meant Arabella any harm I would've reached in and gutted her myself. "Listen, I don't like it either, but our bond shows me she's still with Eleanor and that she's okay."

I don't add that just mere minutes before, my heart shattered into tiny fucking pieces because I could sense that Arabella was upset, which filled me with a murderous rage. No one will ever harm her again, and thankfully, as quickly as her overwhelming sadness had come, it passed just the same. "Eleanor better have a good fucking excuse for giving her that damn ring or I'm going to lose it the next time I see her."

Arabella's cousins slammed open her bedroom door the second she had left, alerting everyone that I was butt ass naked in her bed awaiting her return. Fuckers. Everyone wanted to move to the living room, but I wouldn't budge. She left this room, she'll return here. I'm certain of it. Josiah St. Grace's stare hasn't left me since his arrival. My father came in shortly after the King and Queen of fire, and Merrie-Beth and my sister were the last to walk on in. The gangs all fucking here. Yay.

King Aramayus, my father, was furious at first, until he noticed the bonding tattoo. Now, he's sitting in the purple chair beside the window with a smug smile on his aging face. With one look, all the worry for my future left him. Although he was grateful for my return, my newfound shadowed status along with my excess in women and alcohol has caused more than a few of those gray hairs on his head. Being bound works two ways, not only did Bells choose me but I chose her. He gets it, and he's happy.

My gaze slides to Merrie-Beth and Deen. She doesn't know it yet, but a prophecy was also written about her way before her birth. It's not by chance but by fate that she and Arabella are best friends. Merrie-Beth will help to unite two kingdoms herself. Arion and Dante are even more ruthless than I am, and that's saying a hell of a lot. I wonder what's going to happen when they see her, their mate, at the Light Trials. Deen better start keeping his flirting with her to a minimum. They are crushing on each other, but it's not meant to be.

The floor length mirror on the wall closest to me begins to glow making me jump up and await her return. She crashes into my arms and buries her face into my neck. Josiah stands next to me and rubs her back with his hand. He hasn't tried to kill me yet, so that's comforting. Arabella shyly looks over my shoulder. She looks at our Bound tattoo then back at everyone else. "Well, I guess the cats out of the bag. King Aramayus, can you call a meeting with Kamila Kelli."

He nods. "Will 8:00 AM sharp be, okay?" She shakes her head

while putting the death grip on my hand, so I whisper to her mind to assure her. *It's okay, he won't tell you no. Remember, even now, the armed forces are yours to command.*

Arabella smirks which is sexy as hell. "No sir, it has to be tonight, and Ethan is not allowed in the meeting." That's right baby he's not allowed near you. My father stands and makes his way toward the door. "She'll be notified. Meet in an hour in my study?"

She shakes her head again. "What I have to say is super classified, and I'm being paranoid. Where can we meet that can never be compromised?"

My father looks toward me. "I'll take care of it." I answer softly. My father nods and leaves the room, but not before turning to look at us with a determined brow, and an all-teeth smile. As I read his thoughts, my heart falls from my chest, because of all the things he could be thinking about, his mind is focused on having grandkids after the war.

* * *

Arabella

They say to keep your friends close and your enemies closer, but I say, fuck that. My circle is small, and it will always be small, and it will never consist of any of my enemies.
-Arabella

WE FILE one by one into the greenhouse on the edge of the property that's chocked full of floating fairy lights. Once everyone left, Sebastian told me that this place had been his salvation, but now that great honor was all mine. He said when the walls of darkness threatened to close in on him, he had always gravitated toward the light.

Checking in with Falkon, I make sure she's close enough to read my thoughts, so that she's privy to all information. *Falkon, do you copy?*

Her voice is hoarse when it comes through. *Yes, and my spies say Ethan is secure inside the palace.*

I reply, *Thank you.*

Falkon has the answer to everything. *If you'd just let me eat him, he'd really be secure.*

I laugh despite my best effort not to. *Not yet.*

She huffs. *Pity that.*

I'm not sure how everyone will take the news that we're taking the throne back for the Fitzgerald's but that's exactly what's going to happen. Kamilia is alert as ever, gone is her red lipstick, but her penetrating stare is still intact. She watches me like a panther waiting for a command to do my bidding. She's really a bad ass bitch, and I love it. My gaze lazily falls to my uncles. Uncle Jo took Sebastian being in my room well enough, he only threatened to tear him to shreds once before he left us alone to go get ready. Uncle Radix is nestled close to Aunt Adalia, both are pictures of strength and grace.

Nodding my head at King Aramayus, I'm ready. "Tonight, I visited with Eleanor, and she laid some information in my lap that has rocked me to my core. There is a weapon of mass destruction that has multiple parts scattered throughout only God knows where. Nobody knows how many parts it consists of but Mayra's General, Phasma, has secured the first. The society's forefathers are the ones that separated and hid them because it has the potential to wipe out billions. It's being kept at Alcatraz and is heavily guarded by at least two thousand men. Have any of you ever heard of this weapon before?"

I survey the room and everyone but Merrie-Beth nods. Uncle Jo answers. "We've heard whispers all our lives, and rumors are based on at least an aspect of truth. I can't speak for everyone else, but that's worse than I was ever told."

Kamilia slaps her thigh, the sound coming out as a squeak off of her leather pants. "I've been after Phasma for years. Let my team go, Arabella. You have my word we will retrieve it."

"I want your team to be a part of the extraction, but it's not time yet. The timeline has changed. The Light Trials must come first. Before the remaining Trials can begin, we need to take the throne back from the Fitzgerald's. After all those things are complete, and we have crowned the remaining four victors, my team will be the one at the helm of the search for the missing pieces." It has to be in this order.

Aunt Adalia grabs my hand. "Are you sure that's the way this needs to play out?"

I squeeze her hand back gently. "I am."

She looks at her husband then at her old friend, King Aramayus. "Then that's how it will be sweet child."

Kamilia doesn't look happy, because she's out for Phasma's blood. However, she nods in agreement all the same. My next question is for King Aramayus. "Is the date for the Light Trials set in stone?"

He looks perplexed. "If you want it moved, tell me and it will be done."

I exhale. "It needs to be. Mortem will attack us soon, so we need to throw a wrench in their plans. It only makes sense that they would choose the date of the Trial. How soon could we have it?"

"You give the word, and it could be as soon as tomorrow. All guests and contestants have already arrived." He assures me.

"Tomorrow sounds good, they'll never see that coming." I tip my chin up in a newfound strength and confidence in this new plan.

Chapter 25

The Beginning of the Trials
Arabella

None of this is for the faint of heart, thousands have died today. My heart aches for every single one of them.
-Arabella

AUNT ADALIA LEFT Luxington Valley after our meeting last night. She has gone home to rally the troops before we go to war with Diodyous. Uncle Radix stayed here to escort me to Dragoncrest City after the Light tournament. Uncle Jo is on patrol duty, so I'm meeting up with Uncle Radix at the private entrance of the arena. From what I've been told, because there are three different factions, there will be three separate trials today. King Aramayus, reluctantly, has agreed to let me participate in the second one.

The first trial is one dealing with water, and since it's been discovered I'm Maritime, my being able to compete in that one is a forfeit. He said the last one had only been designed for the last three contestants and there wasn't a fourth spot available. Someone had a dream a long time ago, and it is already recorded who the remaining three will be. It's sealed in the archives. Whatever the hell that means.

The butterflies in my stomach flutter with a vengeance, each task is secret, and all they told me was that I could bring my Billie club, because the others would retrieve their weapons in the first task. Uncle Radix has the biggest smile on his face when he spots me. His smile reminds me so much of Aunt Georgias. His reddish hair gleams in the sunlight, and he even has the same freckles running across his button nose.

My cousins are taking Merrie-Beth to her designated seat on the floor, and they are going to stay down there so they can see all of the action up close. "Arabella, remember, this will be a televised event, so don't be nervous. All you have to do is act as if the cameras aren't here. The more you're in the spotlight, you get used to them, and almost forget they are there. Our people have a right to see what's going on, seeing this tournament is everything to them. They also need reassurance that you're safe. That's the only reason King Aramayus allowed the media access to the palace grounds."

I nod my head nervously. "Do people suspect I'm not safe?"

He shrugs as he opens the door to the balcony where we'll watch the Trials. "You know how rumors are, one person says something contrary to the news, and it spreads like wildfire. A tabloid reported that you had been captured. We are about to prove them wrong."

I almost don't hear his explanation, because I'm having a hard time making my mouth stay closed. This arena is magnificent! The open-top arena is three levels total, and seats about ten thousand. We are on the second floor, which offers the best views in the house. The walls are made out of white marble with gold trimming. The stone floors are cut straight from the mountains. However, the competition part of the floor looks different, no fuss or fluff. Just a bare wooden floor, with a dark blue mat that covers over half. They even have two places where you can buy concessions in the back.

I'm amazed. Uncle Radix explains that they've had the blueprints for this place for several years. They started construction about eight months ago, intending to have it completed by my 21st birthday. As the plans changed, they worked day and night to finish this place. It was all hands-on deck to get it done. I swell with pride as I look at all the detail they put into this place. It's smaller than they intended, but nothing to be ashamed of. I'm starting to see just how hard our people work. When there is a problem, they don't blame anyone else. They find a solution, band together and fix whatever needs fixing. Unity is more important than anything in a society.

A Vampira with silken black hair waltzes into our box. Her mysterious smile is alarmingly beautiful. Danger leaks from every one of her pores, and the feminine precision in which she moves is in total contradiction to the predator that she is. No one has to hide who they are in Luxington Valley, so her lips painted red, with her canines extended. She's here for the blood contract. "Arabella, welcome home. As King Aramayus has explained to you, I'm here to render the blood oath."

I nod weakly up at her and hold my finger out to be pricked. He explained that in the task I'm participating in today that each of us would have to sign a contract in blood. After writing our signatures, only death or victory will get us out of the contract.

She takes a long needle and pricks the top of my forefinger, then draws up as much as she thinks we will need. She inserts my blood inside of a fancy looking pen.

"What's your name," I ask.

She looks down at me in surprise, as she hands me the pen. "Brambri, from the shores of Azure."

I smile at her, she's beautiful, as all Vampires are. "Nice to meet you, Brambri."

She nods in turn, and I stare at the contract for only a minute before I literally sign my life away. *Freshwater mermaids are the worst.*

She leaves us with a bow, and I go back to people watching. With twenty minutes left to go, the TV cameras are out in full force. I'm thankful that, at least for now, they have not discovered my where-abouts. I lean over to get a better look at the people standing to the far right of the stage. My eyes casually dart between two men and one woman. They must be announcers, because they look like celebrities. The woman is tall, lean, and platinum blonde. She wears a metallic blue mini dress with electric blue stiletto heels. She's gorgeous. The man to her left has short spiky hair. He's wearing a solid black suit with a bright red bowtie. The other man is about two inches taller than the first guy, and all I can think is, Hello, Daddy! His thick dark hair is graying at the temples, making him look distinguished. His pants and shirt are black, but is sporting a bowtie that is shiny gold, and his sports coat is the same, polished gold with a design trimmed in black interwoven into the coat. I take the binoculars beside my seat to get a closer look at the design. It's my sun. He's wearing my sun.

Uncle Radix laughs. "Your sun is a pretty big deal around here, Arabella. You better get used to it, sweetie. I have a similar coat myself."

A giggle erupts in my throat. This is not real life. I can't believe what I'm hearing but tell me more! "Really? Why is my sun such a big deal?"

"Arabella, you are a beacon of hope and peace. The purpose for your life was set before you were born, and you're going to save billions of lives. Mayra won't quit until she rules the entire world, but you're going to stop her. The people are excited because this generation will see all this come to pass. You don't understand the impact the Prophecy of the Chosen has had on every single one of us. Even I was told the story of you as a child. You're a legend, and we were chosen just as much as you were. You will lead us. Then we will win." He grabs my hand and flips my wrist upward, so my sun is visible. "This sun, your sun, gives new purpose to us all. To think that our family line is the one to have been chosen, that's humbling. Who are we but servants hiding in the shadows."

Everything he says comes crashing down on me all at once. I'm no one special, and that makes his words even harder to process. "My mind is having difficulty believing this is my new reality."

"You've had everything thrown at you in a short period of time, and that isn't fair, but that doesn't change the fact that war will soon come for us all. There is no time for you to get acclimated." He takes my hand and gently squeezes.

"I wish there was more time, but I know that isn't going to happen." Desperately needing to change the subject, "Uncle Radix, who are those people? They look important."

"The woman is Estrella Fitzgerald, she's the beloved daughter of Jarret Fitzgerald, which makes her a princess and Kori royalty. She's no fan of the Diodyous, and she has done everything she can to get her father sober. Because of her open hostility toward the new regime, she lives in exile in the valley. The Resistance still loves her, and they are patiently waiting for her return."

"I've heard of the Resistance. How many of them are there?" I have so many other questions.

"Nobody knows the exact number, but I would say it's a signifi-cant amount, because the Fitzgerald's are still very popular. I don't know exactly how many there are. They cause quite a stir in Kori territory, and steal from the palace daily." He chuckles. He doesn't like Diodyous either, I can tell. Maybe I can meet with Estrella before we leave here tonight. I would like to get a read on her and let her know that although my family sat back and did nothing, I won't.

"The gentleman in red is Alberto Ferrari. He's Pyralis and the lead investigator for the UGN. He's very popular, and the ladies love him. Mr. Sunshine over there is Damien Killyorn. He's Lux and the Undisputed Heavyweight Underground Champion of the World. He's been in fifteen title fights and has won every single one of them." My brain goes into information overload. So many people, places, and things.

Uncle Radix gives me an encouraging smile. His good mood and smile are infectious, and because we've been talking for so long, I hadn't noticed the arena filling up. Not many seats are left, and the crowd is growing restless and loud. This is going to be awesome. The lights go dim, and the crowd goes wild. The announcers walk to the middle of the arena and a spotlight captures their every movement.

We're all sitting on the edge of our seats. I see Eleanor in the box diagonal to ours. She's smiling, and excitement is etched all over her pretty face.

The announcers bring out the remaining twenty competitors, thousands have competed in different tasks today, and these are the last ones standing. As loudly as I can, I scream out Amelia and Sebastian's names. My uncle covers his ears, which makes me shout even louder. He laughs and starts cheering too. Estrella Fitzgerald signals for the crowd to calm down so they can begin. "Luxington Valley! The day has finally come!" The crowd goes wild again, and she throws her head back and laughs. I see why she still has loyal supporters. She's not only beautiful but also charismatic. "Okay. Okay! Let's settle down."

She has to wait a couple of minutes for the arena to quiet down before continuing. "We have only twenty remaining competitors. Each has passed every grueling test set before them today. Tonight, their limits will be tested even further. Each of the three tasks is timed. If they do not complete the task before the buzzer goes off, they will be disqualified."

The camera cuts to Alberto. He has dimples when he smiles. The ladies start yelling, and several whistles ring out throughout the place. "You're sure looking good tonight!" The women scream, and I can't help but giggle. He's handsome. Estrella rolls her eyes, and Damien flexes his biceps. That makes me take part in the screaming. I swear I hear Sebastian growl in my ear, which makes me laugh. My uncle puts his hand over his eyes in embarrassment, and I shrug my shoulders at him. He's wearing my sun on his jacket so I gotta represent.

Damien smiles at the camera. "We've waited our whole lives for this moment. Our Chosen has come home, and our generation has been given this difficult burden. We will not run away from our calling. We will fight!"

The crowd erupts in applause. Even Estrella can't help but cheer. She looks up to where I am seated on the balcony, and a spotlight is now on us. "Before we get started, we would like to direct your attention to the second-story balcony. I know there was much speculation on if the Chosen would be here in attendance tonight. Arabella, stand up. Your crowd wishes to see you."

Since running is out of the question, I stand. I smile toward the camera and the crowd. My uncle gently nudges my hand, and I remember what he said about showing them my sun. I raise my fist in the air so they can see the birthmark that they so curiously want to see. The crowd is so silent that you can hear a pin drop. The look of awe on their faces makes me blush. Uncle Radix stands up and starts proudly clapping, and the crowd quickly follows. My gaze catches Estrella before I sit down. She is looking back at me cautiously. She's trying to determine what kind of leader I'll be. The answer is simple, the one that takes the throne back for her family.

ARABELLA

Chapter 26

The Trial of Light

Arabella

Today I found out that I'm good at killing people, which in theory is good considering I'm supposed to win a war, however, I'm not sure how I feel about the fact.
-Arabella

ALBERTO TAKES AN ENVELOPE FROM ESTRELLA. "The contestants have not been told of the remaining tasks they will face today. I'm holding the directions for the next one in my hand." He deliberately takes forever to open the dang envelope, which makes the crowd scream and me laugh. Finally, the eternal wait for the envelope to be opened is over. "The first task is an underwater assignment. Each contestant will have ten minutes to locate a weapon that we have hidden within the depths of the saltwater tank. This weapon will aid them in their next round."

Damien looks gravely at the camera. My heart races with antici-pation. "In the water they will encounter one of the sea's most venomous creatures. The purple-dotted octopus. Small but extremely deadly, there are hundreds down there hiding within the depths of the tank. This is a very serious situation that will test their abilities under pressure."

Estrella turns to the contestants. "Please, be careful. If you are bitten, you have one minute to make it to the surface. If you are even a second later, you will die. Our experts are the creators of the only anti-venom for this species in the world, and it only works if administered within that time frame of being bitten." The fact that they could actually die is intense.

I look at Sebastian and my heart melts when I see him staring up at me. He gives me a knowing smirk. *Don't worry about me, Bells. I eat razor blades for breakfast, lunch, and dinner.*

I laugh despite myself. *Great, now everyone thinks I'm crazy, because they think I'm talking to myself.*

He shrugs. *You are crazy. For me.*

My smile grows bigger. *Just don't die, okay?*

He rolls his eyes. *I'm already dead.*

I turn to Uncle Radix. "I've talked to Sebastian all day and I know thousands have already died in the preliminaries. Is it necessary for the trials to be this dangerous?"

"Arabella, our jobs are dangerous. Since birth they have known dying young is a real possibility. Not all of us will make it, but we pledge our lives to keep everyone safe." He grabs my hand and gives it another gentle squeeze, which I know is his way of calming me. "They've been given the rules, and they know what the outcome will be if they don't make it back to the surface in time."

The hosts and contestants move over to the far side of the stage. The bottom of the floor starts to open up, the saltwater tank is underneath. They announce that the tank is twenty feet deep and fifty feet wide. They also show the crowd the body suits the five will wear. Each of them will be given a helmet that will help with their breathing underwater.

The first contestant, Derek Jones, carefully puts his suit on and dives into the blue depths without hesitation. Multiple screens have come down from the ceiling so that we can watch every move he makes. I'm nervous for him and can't help but think of his family. I bet they are a nervous wreck right about now.

Whoever created the ocean habitat did a great job. It's got everything, even fish. Thankfully, I don't see any sharks, and have yet to see any of the purple spotted octopuses. Never knew those poisonous assholes were a real thing. As Derek makes his way further down, hundreds of luminescent purple dots make their television debut, covering the bottom of the tank floor. I don't know how any of them will be able to find their weapons with that mess of venomous creatures on the tank floor.

Taking a stick from a nearby plant he starts his search for the weapon he will use in the next round. Derek has five minutes left on the clock, so he better get his ass in gear. He looks around every plant and through the garden of seaweeds and finds nothing. He has no other option but to comb through the tangle of little killers down at the bottom. He does so almost violently, agitating the creatures. He quickly becomes their target and while he tries like hell to wave them off, there are just too many.

He swims furiously to the surface which tells me he must have been bitten. A team of Healers are waiting for him to emerge, at the docking station. He's clutching his stomach and is writhing in pain. They have to inject his bite with the antidote twice before he becomes stable. Then Derek is sent to the recovery room so they can monitor his condition, but it's announced shortly after that he has passed away. My heart aches for him and his loved ones. His picture flashes on the screen with his birth and death date at the bottom.

A woman with bright pink hair wails in the crowd, I stand up and look at her, my heart caught in my throat. That must be his Mama. The resemblance is uncanny, she's devastated but she doesn't look at me with hatred. She lays her arm across her chest, as tears roll down both our faces. I whisper, "I'm sorry," and mimic her motions.

The crowd including my uncle do the same. Derek's mama bows her head slightly and walks toward the recovery to gather her son. Instead of celebrating, she will have a funeral. Uncle Radix squeezes my shoulder, and we sit back down. It feels wrong to continue the competition, but that's what we do.

We sit on the edge of our seats for the entirety of this task. Thankfully, the remaining contestants find their weapons, and no one else dies. Sebastian finds his weapon in record time. The entire time he was down in the tank, a million questions are firing off in my brain. When he says that he's already dead, what does that mean? Do I need to worry that he could die or die again? Caring about someone like I do him has its perks until it doesn't. Uncle Radix stopped me more than once from running down the stairs to help him.

The weapons hidden within the depths of the tank were brass knuckles, nun chucks, and billy clubs. Amelia and Sebastian were gifted with billy clubs for the next challenge. Amelia's time was only a second behind her brother, she should be proud.

There is a slight intermission before the second round starts, only ten rounds remain. The tank has been covered up, and Estrella Fitzgerald makes her way back to the full stage. "Chosen, if you will please come down, and bring your weapon. We have a special treat today. Arabella has so graciously offered to fight in the forthcoming battle. The next round will test not only everyone's abilities to work together, but how well they handle high pressure situations. Together they will fight against one thousand of Inferno's toughest death row prisoners. If you lose, you die, and if they win, they are set free. We don't care if this takes all night. We will remain here, patiently waiting."

The crowd only has eyes for me as I slowly walk toward the stage, and after hearing that we're going to fight all these rabid criminals, all I can think is fuck those freshwater mermaids, and what the hell was I thinking agreeing to be a part of this? Hopefully my face doesn't betray me and reveal what I'm feeling.

The gasp throughout the arena is all that can be heard when Sebastian grabs my hand as I move to stand by his side. Since we had our talk, there is no reason for our Bound tattoos to be covered up with magic. A camera closes in on the matching tats, and the people grow loud with excitement.

Damien comes out in a referee outfit, and that tight shirt should be against the law. Sebastian rolls his eyes. *Stop looking at him like that or I'll push him in the water tank after stirring up the poisonous octopuses with my shadows.*

I bite the inside of my cheek to keep from laughing. I love the fact that he's jealous. He clearly doesn't need to be but teasing him may be my new favorite thing. *Please, you'll always be my only, but I'm not dead.*

Damien smiles over in our direction, which makes me have to slap one of Sebastian's shadows away from trying to hit him. "Here are the rules. One hundred fighters will be released every ten minutes, and if you fail to defeat all one hundred in that time frame, your battle will only get harder, because the next hundred will soon be on their way. It is advised that you defeat them all within that amount of time."

Alberto walks up casually and takes the mic. We're all dressed in black as if this will be a funeral for some of us, and the nausea rolls deep in my belly as I realize that this is a kill or be killed event. The contract we all signed in our blood cannot be undone. For the first time, I'll have to take lives today, because it can't be me that gets placed in a body bag. The weariness that comes with being a savior to our people rests heavily upon my shoulders.

Looking toward my fellow contestants, they don't appear upset or fearful, only determined. Maybe this is normal for them, but it's not for me. I can't stop thinking about how we must face a total of one thousand opponents. Without any warning, Damien lifts his hand and throws a rock down on the floor, transporting us out of the arena and into a makeshift battlefield. The field is overgrown with weeds and there is a breeze blowing through the pine trees. The pink and purple sky of dusk looks like it was hand painted by an artist. It's quiet, too quiet, because it's the calm before the storm.

As if on cue, Damien takes out a whistle and blows, signaling the start of the second challenge. Sebastian grabs my face for a kiss. *Stay close. We'll fight together.* My lips find him, and I pour everything into our earth-shattering kiss, because what if it's our last? *Where you go, I go.*

The ground shakes in front of us as it splits in half, parting the soil beneath. Black smoke leers from the opening like a premonition to a forthcoming nightmare. My body shivers in anticipation, not only with excitement but with the realization that we could die. The hairs on the back of my neck stand on end when the high-pitched wails start. The sound travels through the air slowly, promising death to all who listen. It starts as a whisper then grows louder, until I have to fight the urge to cover my ears, because I know everyone is watching, and I can't show any weakness.

Sebastian holds me close as a mist explodes around us, lightning crashes in the distance, then all hell breaks loose. Otherworldly creatures surround us on all sides, my companions wait for my signal to attack but they won't receive it, because I was taught to wait.

A seven-foot-tall beast with a high ponytail and six arms grins when recognition of who I am lights his unpleasant features. He stomps toward me, but I hold my ground. My dark Prince stands in front of me, but I push my way past him and can feel his anger from doing so. *You may be my partner, but I am still the leader.*

He rolls his eyes. *What's that got to do with me trying to keep you safe?*

The Beast seems to be the leader of this group of one hundred. He takes six swords out of their sheaths then charges me. Sliding in between his legs, I take billy club, that I call Billie out to play. Jumping up two of his muscled arms, I bash his head in with the nails on the top of my club. Turning around I charge toward the next, not allowing myself the time to think about what just happened or what I just did.

It's not until the fourth round that one of us is killed. Her body is carried away, but there is no time to mourn. We are tired, bruised, and sweaty. I've killed so many I've lost count. Sebastian slaughters even more since his shadows can take out twenty targets at once. The only wound I have is on my right arm, the cut is superficial, but my dark Prince disemboweled the man for his insolence. His words, not mine.

With the tenth round came more giants, and supernatural's. Amelia and Sebastian have been bickering on and off about who is the best. They've been keeping record on their kills and Sebastian is ahead by fifteen but it's not from her lack of trying. I fall to my knees when the fighting is over. The bruises on my body are begging to be soaked in Epsom salt. I'll need to be healed by Merrie-Beth soon, we'll all need our Healers when we're transported back.

Chapter 27

The Beginning of the Woes

Arabella

*I couldn't watch one more person die today, but little did I know,
Death was right around the corner.*
-Arabella

I'M STILL on my knees when we are sent back to the arena, nausea swells inside of me from what we've had to endure, and the exhaustion is beginning to set in. With our appearance, the crowd goes wild screaming our names, and excitement can be seen even from the rafters. Only four of us remain, the others are dead. More funerals will need to be planned, along with more families that will be without loved ones tonight. Sebastian helps me to my feet, and Uncle Jo is there to escort me back to the balcony. Guilt pierces through me, because I get to rest now, the others do not. How is that fair?

When we get out of sight, Uncle Jo takes me in his arms. His strength engulfs me and causes me to lose it. All the pent-up raw emotions leak from my eyes. My tears are for all those who have died, for those of us that remain, and for the fact that I don't regret killing any of those monsters in the last round. That last thought is the one that breaks me.

Uncle Jo kisses my forehead and holds me until all the tension departs my body, and I'm grateful he doesn't feel the need to try and make me feel better with words. I just need to be held. With a deep breath I step away. "Thank you." I whisper hoarsely.

"I will not only stand by you through the good, but also through the darkest times." He kisses my forehead.

Merrie-Beth opens the door to the hallway and rushes to my side. Her cheeks are flushed like she ran a marathon to get to me. "I was so scared, Arabella, but you were awesome. I've never seen you more in your element than on that battlefield. I'm so proud of you!"

I smile at her words. Leave it to my best friend to turn a grave situation into something positive. "God knew I needed you Merrie-Beth."

She smiles. "I am awesome."

I laugh. "Definitely, and very humble."

She shrugs, and her back stiffens as the door opens behind her. Two men hover in the double door entrance way, both are tall and intimidating. Not to mention, hot. Their intense stares are locked on Merrie-Beth's back. My first instinct as always is to protect her. Grabbing Billie from the wall, I move to a position where it would be easier for me to shield my best friend if need be. "Can I help you?" My tone is not friendly, but not overly bitchy either. Growing up southern means I wouldn't normally be so borderline rude, but it's clear that they are making her uncomfortable, and that is not okay with me.

Both of the Fae males are very attractive, and royal. The proof of which is in the lime color of their eyes. The first has darker hair than even my dark Prince has. Wearing nothing but black from head to toe, his whole demeanor exudes danger. He ignores my question. "Merrie-Beth." His deep voice is more of a command than a greeting.

Merrie-Beth's beautiful doe-like eyes widen even more, not replying. She grabs my hand instead and pulls me toward one of the bathrooms. Confusion slaps me in the face.

The second Fae's hair color is very similar to mine, only his has streaks of blonde throughout. He beats us to the door and places the tips of his fingers underneath her chin. "Merrie-Beth, we mean you no harm. May we have a word with you? Please."

She stares at him for a long moment, then looks toward me because she's unsure of how to respond. A blush is spread prettily across her face. How they know her name is a mystery to me, maybe even to her. They are both dressed in traditional Fae formal garb. Which is only still worn by the Fae that choose to live in other realms besides the human world. I like the one touching her better than the grumpy one over there, so I throw him a bone. "What do you want to do, Merrie-Beth?"

Grumpy rolls his eyes, but I look straight ahead into my best friend's face ignoring his attitude. The red head still has a light grip on her chin, he takes that as his cue to bring her eyes back to his. "I've only ever said please once in my life, don't make me utter it again." He gives her a roguish grin that has her melting in the palm of his hand. I'm intrigued.

She smiles up at him shyly. "As soon as the last task is done, I will meet with you. I need to heal Arabella first."

He nods and gives her a panty dropping smile. "Thank you, Sunshine. Intermission is almost over, and they are about to start the last task. May we walk you back to your seat?"

She looks at Grumpy and he surprisingly looks hopeful. Merrie-Beth nods, then gives me a hug. "Do you need me to heal you first?"

"I'm good for now. I'll see you after. If you need me or Billie, just say the word." My gaze wanders between the two of them but stays a second or two longer on the dark-haired Fae prince.

Walking back into the box, Uncle Radix greets me with a hug. "You did well, Arabella, our people have so much to be thankful for."

I smile genuinely. "Thank you."

The intermission music fades into the background, alerting people that they need to get back to their seats. Looking over the edge, I spot Merrie-Beth wedged in between the two mysterious princes. She was sitting in between my cousins during the first round. I can't wait until she and I get a chance to talk more.

Estrella Fitzgerald takes the stage. "The next round will test not only the contestant's agility but also their durability."

Regrettably, Damien is back in his evening attire. Sorry, Sebastian, but I really miss that ref outfit. "Our next task will be a challenging one. War is unpredictable. Things can change at the drop of a hat, and our last three competitors need to prove they are capable of handling those type situations." Squeals ring out through the arena and without needing to look I know the spotlight has been placed on Alberto. "This is not an ordinary obstacle course. We've made it hard on these last individuals, and only the best two will emerge victorious."

Estrella gives instructions to the remaining three. Her description of what this round will be is harsh. "Each of you will be given a package. Its contents are something that is quite, shall we say, flammable. There is no special antidote. If your package explodes, so will you." Damn.

Damien's face is full of pride as he looks at the remaining three with admiration. "Lux members, your names will forever be in our history books as the fiercest three, and I am proud of each of you. Princess Amelia, your strength and courage have made me want to be a better fighter. No one thought you'd be standing here, even me, and for that I'm sorry. I'll never doubt you again. Prince Sebastian, your ability to pull apart your opponent has made me evaluate my own fighting skills. I'll never get in the ring with you! Anthony, my man, you're making me look scrawny! You're a beast, and I don't wanna face you in the ring either!"

The lights go dim, and the arena floor changes once again. A multidimensional platform replaces the flat surface, and I can't believe how much detail has gone into every crevice. Magic is the only answer. I've never seen anything like it. There's a small forest along with a dirt road that has multiple twists and turns and is completed with mountain highs and valley lows. A true masterpiece of ingenuity. My adrenaline goes into hyperdrive. In just a short while the next two members of the Guardians of War will be named. I'm nervous and excited.

Each of them is given a package, and a hoverboard that lifts off the ground. They have to go around the arena three times before they can discard their explosive packages. Ten minutes have been placed on the clock. Thunder crackles in the distance, and a flash of lightning almost strikes down Sebastian about a second later. Thankfully, my dark Prince proved agile and moved out of the way before it hit him. Amelia screams, but quickly regains her composure.

My heart is racing as the smell of burning wood enters all our noses, making us all turn in the direction of where the lightning struck. Smoke rises from the top of one of the pine trees. A light rain begins to fall on the area of the platform where they stand. Loud thumps sound through the arena as white balls of ice drop down on the floor.

The rumbling sound of a train filters through the air and lands in our ears. Grabbing Uncle Radix's hand, I look from left to right but see no evidence of a funnel cloud. Lightning strikes again in the middle of where Amelia and Anthony are standing.

A little girl with blue hair in the next box whimpers loudly, as she points towards the sky. Her little fearful eyes are my undoing. Taking a deep breath, I follow where she's pointing, and unease settles in my bones. A tornado begins to form in the sky.

In seconds, it touches the ground, and the remaining three jump on their hoverboards and scatter in different directions. The time clock finally starts. The tornado is small, but incredibly fast. Despite the rain, the lightning strikes have caused a small fire in the forest, and as the tornado whips through the trees, the fire and the tornado merge into one.

It grows in size, angrily swirling around the course. Even from here we can feel the heat that's radiating from it. Not able to hold it in any longer I voice my worry, "Do we need to start evacuations?"

Uncle Radix shakes his head firmly. "No. Despite appearances, they have everything under control. We are safe, even though they are not."

War is hell, but this is barbaric. They were trained to handle the first two events, but I highly doubt they were trained to survive this kind of catastrophe. Thankfully, the final three have managed to go around the track twice, without being harmed or killed.

The final lap starts, and I hold my breath. Anthony grabs the handle of his hover board and takes a sharp left. It was too sharp because he tumbles off, rolling down a steep hill. We all watch in horror, because he's not moving, and the fire breathing tornado is coming.

Jumping up, I can't stop myself from yelling down. If he doesn't get up soon, he's going to die. "Get up, Anthony, get up!"

The crowd jumps to their feet and starts chanting the same. A big man who must be his dad starts running toward Anthony. He's muscled and well over six feet. Security tries to stop him, but he barrels past them. If his father can get to him in time, he will be disqualified, but at least he will live!

Please, God, let him get to him in time. My heart is pounding as he grabs Anthony and starts running away from the direction of the incoming tornado. I grip the edge of the balcony tightly, but he won't make it. It's too close, he's too late.

Closing my eyes, I can't watch. A small gentle whisper comes to me. It's my Eleanor. You have the power to stop this, use your necklace. Hurry, before more death happens this day. Startled, I look across the arena into the awaiting blue sapphire eyes of my mother's best friend. *Do it now!* Her voice is commanding and so unlike her. I snap out of my self-doubt and grab my necklace. Visualizing the water underneath the forgotten stage, I reach out my hand as an electric current flows from my fingertips. Focusing on only the elements inside of me, I tune out the noise around me. The mind is a powerful thing, and I visualize holding the water in my hands, but it's not enough to put out the fire. Taking it a step further, a form of me is transported into the saltwater tank.

The familiar scent of salt surrounds me, and a strand of seaweed touches my cheek. All my senses are on fire. Floating to the surface, I hold my hands up above my head. The water heeds my command, as it rises above me, and over the racing track. The water attacks the fiery cyclone and eliminates any remnants of its existence. Vanishing without a trace, the water dissipates.

Waking from my trance, I slowly become aware of my surroundings. My slack-jawed uncle still stands at my side. The crowd watches me in silence, as the competition looms on. This is a powerful moment, one for the history books.

Uncle Radix bows on one knee before me, igniting the same desire in everyone in attendance. The competition looms on while every eye is focused in my direction. I am humbled by their attention and support. I just couldn't bear witnessing another death today. But little did I know, Death had already entered the building.

Chapter 28

Ambush

Arabella

Someone let them in, we have a traitor in our midst.
-Arabella

WITH THE SOUND of the final buzzer and a shout from the stage, all our attention snaps back to the Prince and Princess of the Lux. Amelia zooms in front of Sebastian, almost causing him to wreck. Thankfully, much to my heart's jubilation, he stays upright.

Excitement radiates through the crowd, as cheers ring out through the arena. Princess Amelia beat her brother by only two seconds. However, a win is a win! By the look on my Dark Prince's face, he wasn't expecting her to beat him which makes me laugh.

The crowd is going wild, chants of Amelia's name are on the lips of everyone including mine. No Princess has ever passed the test to become a Guardian. Princess Amelia has set a new standard for future princesses.

A mirror appears from behind the stage, and a flash of lightning sounds right before a loud popping noise. *Fuck.* The track disappears and the flare stage reemerges, all without so much as one finger lifted. The sinister gray smoke, like the one from the lunchroom, seeps from the stage, and the icy coldness returns making me shiver. Dark magic in all its evil glory.

Uncle Radix looks toward me with a horrified expression in place. No words pass between us, none are needed. He grabs my arm, but I take it away from him. His mission is to keep me safe and mine is to fight. I won't leave.

Turmoil is everywhere. Bile looms in the pit of my stomach. Uncle Radix tries to grab my arm one more time, yet again I move out of the way. He screams my name, but I am already gone.

Running down the staircase all my thoughts are of Uncle Jo. Something is about to happen to him, deep down in my gut a weariness sets inside. I don't understand this feeling; however, my intuition is telling me to find him. After he left me with Merrie-Beth he could have gone anywhere. Family above all else.

As the black smoke starts to clear, I look for a sign of my would-be captors. Yet none of the villains in my story make an appearance just yet. I know they are looming somewhere, waiting to bring chaos to us all. My bones ache as the shock and cold finally settles in. They've come for me again, but this time I've got Billie and she's got a score to settle with the Cohen twins.

The screams have subsided, as I take in the scene unfolding before me. It is eerily quiet as the truth of what's about to happen settles over the crowd. All Guardians in attendance are standing with their swords held upright. The Healers are on the outskirts with their weapons drawn on as well. They will only fight if it is an absolute necessity. Merrie-Beth is nowhere to be seen; I spot her parents looking for her. After I make sure everything is okay with Uncle Jo, I'll find her myself.

All we can do for now is wait for our enemy to make itself known. Slowly, I push myself toward the front lines, because that's where he'll be, he's the bravest man that I'll ever know. Sebastian's warning about Ethan taking out my entire line in order to secure my power resounds in my mind. He can't be allowed access to any of my loved ones.

Another loud popping noise sounds, then hordes of masked figures come out of the huge ass mirror. The intruders start charging toward the Guardians, and they are more than ready. A million emotions run through me as I watch, searching for any sign of Uncle Jo or Merrie-Beth. The battle begins as shouts and the clanking of the metal fills the arena. Soldiers, my soldiers fall to the ground and their Healers rush to their side. Looking away, nor running away is not an option. This is my new reality, a part of my birthright. What a sobering thought, yet it's one I'm honored to have.

Taking Billie, we fight our way to the opposite side of the arena, maybe I can get a better visual of them from this angle. I slam my favorite weapon into my enemy's inch by inch. Blood pours down my face but it isn't my own. The sulfurous smell of death is in the air, making me almost dry heave. I'm not sure I'll ever get used to it.

With Uncle Jo's height and stature, it doesn't take me very long to find him. Enthralled, I watch the way he fights in between my opponents. I see why they call him a master swordsman. He is magnificent, his moves are calculated and strategic.

From the corner of my eye, the Scotsman, Blaine Ramsay, heads toward him. My uncle is oblivious to this forthcoming onslaught. I stand, horrified, as realization of what is about to happen shocks me. Uncle Jo is fighting another man, and he has no idea that the coward is coming to slaughter him from behind. Bullshit. This is why I was meant to find him, to stop this slaying.

Warning him is my only thought, I move my weapon with precision because I see a better path to block Ramsey. A masked man comes for me, his eyes light up in recognition. Yeah, I'm that bitch, now bye! When I try to push him out of the way, he grabs my arm instead. I take Billie and rearrange his face; he falls to the ground with a thud. Should have just let me go, asshole. I move on, void of any emotion about what I've just done.

My feet carry me several more feet before I'm accosted again, I let out a screech, but he can't hear me. "Uncle Jo! Uncle Jo! God, please, NO! He's behind you. Blaine's coming!"

I bludgeon the woman who stopped me, her beautiful blonde hair becoming a bloody mess of crimson and brain matter. I'm only fifty feet or so away from Uncle Jo now. He is fighting and winning against a different opponent than before. Blaine has killed the courageous Guardian, then quickly returned to his mission. The Scotsman has a smile on his face, he enjoys all this death and destruction. Disgusted beyond belief, I'm going to enjoy taking him down.

As close as I am, the Scotsman is closer. Someone comes up and grabs me from behind. This person is tall and powerful, I try to break free with no luck. Clearing my thoughts, Aunt Georgia's teachings come flooding back to me.

She taught me when being held against your will, you should make a drastic move to confuse them. So, they won't suspect what you're about to do. Then while they're still confused, quickly elbow them in the crotch! The jackass yelps, allowing me to break free. The high-pitched squeal could have come from me not using my elbow and using Billie instead.

Another person has engaged the Scotsman in a fight. I hope the person lives, but I'm glad he hasn't reached Uncle Josiah yet.

My uncle's new opponent is as big around as he is tall. I make it about ten feet before another attacker stops me. Just my luck, it's my favorite Cohen twin! He looks every bit as nefarious as he did last time. A smile grows when I notice the bruises on his face. His frown turns into a snarl when he realizes the reason for my smile. He is more intelligent than he looks.

Before I can react, he takes mixed black and silver powder out of his pocket then throws it in my face. A radiating light flashes once, taking my vision as it leaves. Gone with it is the noise of my surroundings, like I've been transported further away. Panic rises in me, but I take a deep breath allowing my calmness to return. Relying on my training, I close my eyes, and concentrate on my other senses. The smell of leather from the black vest he is wearing hits me first. Playing it cool, I wait until the sound of one of his fists comes towards me, then moves out of the way. Ducking, I land a jab to his unprotected ribs. Not wanting to waste any time, I sweep his legs out from under him using Billie. He falls to the ground and screams out in pain the deep incisions my weapon caused.

My vision is slowly returning, finally able to make out certain shapes and colors. I only get to take a few steps before being ambushed again. The man whispers something in a different language. It's the other Cohen turn, his voice is hoarser than his brothers. He backhands me, making me drop Billie in the process. That was unexpected, because I allowed him to distract me with his words. My anger boils to the surface as the copper taste of my blood fills my mouth.

However, he makes a mistake when he lets his breath touch my left ear. I throw a punch to his stomach, which he blocks. Good boy, my fist fakes another stomach punch. My vision is almost clear now, it's only slightly hazy. He has his hands close to his abdomen, and I take full advantage. When I lift my fists this time, his stance becomes tense. He is anticipating for me to go for the stomach again. So, when he makes a move to block me, I change the direction of my fists. With a quickness, I've never had the ability to wield before, I grab Billie off the ground. Then with one swing I slice his throat open. Surprise etches his angel-like face before he falls dead to the ground. I feel no remorse when his brother screams and crawls to his side.

As the illusion of the powder wears off, I realize Uncle Jo is so close to me now. His body is turned away from me. However, my screams of warning still don't reach his ears.

Right as I'm about to make myself heard, Uncle Radix reaches me, his look of disdain is apparent. He won't listen to my explanation of why I ran away. All that's left to do is look on in horror as the Scotsman closes in on Uncle Jo, with his back still turned. Blaine lifts his sword and swings. Blood trickles from my uncle's side as he falls. I am too late.

Uncle Radix takes me to the edge of the arena, and I no longer have the will to fight him. He injects something into my neck, making my limbs go numb, and my face sting. The scene from before is on instant replay in my head. Uncle Jo is a master swordsman, he could have survived. If only it had been a fair fight, one that he saw coming. But it wasn't fair, nothing about any of this is fair.

My head feels fuzzy again. Trying to get my attention, someone shakes my arm. It's aunt Georgia. Why is she here? Jumping up quickly from where I was lying down, every part of me is confused. Uncle Radix is nowhere to be seen. That's weird, but my mind still can't quite wrap around what's fully going on.

Chapter 29

Death

Arabella

Death has a way of coming for us all.
-Arabella

WHEN I LOOK UP AGAIN, Aunt Georgia's not there, and all that's left in me is bitter desolation. I'm an empty shell of the girl from mere minutes before—my soul aches. Life has taken a drastic turn for the worse, and darkness consumes me.

I no longer see the battle that's all around me. Instead, in my mind I'm walking down a long dark tunnel. A cold darkness filled with no happiness or hope abounds in this new place. I've never felt such bitter anguish. My eyes start searching for the light, because I know that even the dimmest of lights can cover a multitude of darkness. All that's needed is a tiny shimmer of one of its golden beams, but there is no light here. What will I do? We all need the light to survive. Not all battles are fought between flesh and blood, some are against darkness in the vilest of places. Only evil lurks in the shadows here. Cognitively, in the back of my mind I know that a battle rages in front of me, but the ringing in my ears won't allow me to hear anything else. I'm a million miles away, and the closer I move into the blackest of shades, the louder the ringing becomes.

As I walk into another part of the tunnel, hands shoot up out of the ground. They're trying to trap me here, to make me like them. Their coarse alabaster fingers wrap around my ankles. Kicking them helps, but they won't stop reaching for me. It's like having a thousand tiny snakes slither up and down your skin.

A raspy voice whispers from somewhere within, "Let go, Arabella. Give way to the darkness, we can be an unstoppable team. The world will be ours to rule, and all will bow before us. The darkness won't take as much from you as the light does. Come to me, my child, while the offer still stands. I will teach you the truth about your destiny, not lie like all the others. I will show you how to tame the darkness and bend her to your will. She is a mighty tool."

This is the voice of Duvessa Raven, The Queen of Death. How is she manipulating the light? My lungs fail to produce the oxygen that's needed for me to survive. My shallow breaths turn frantic. Is this what drowning people feel like when they know the end is near? Who will save our people if I fall?

"Arabella, come back to the light. You must do it now before you're lost forever. You know what to do." Eleanor whispers loudly through our Maritime bond.

Her voice is filled with worry, but she soothes me all the same. She found me; I won't be lost forever. Grabbing my necklace, I visualize the bright glow that came out of the letter my mom had written me all those years ago. A giant flame of light flows out from my fingertips, awakening me from my dark nightmare. My mind returns to the light, and the fuzzy feeling is gone.

Aunt Georgia is walking toward me, that's not possible, she's away on a mission for the King. However, there is no time to think rationally, we have to go see if Uncle Jo is okay. Plus, my people are on the front lines, they need me back out there. As she reaches me, she grabs my hand and leads me in the opposite direction. "Ella, come, we must get you out of here."

"We can't leave! Uncle Jo needs us! Our people need us!" Her hold is firm, and the skin on her hand is bruised and feels slightly different. Something is wrong.

"I've sent Jeremiah to save him, look." Jeremiah has the Scotsman in a chokehold, while Uncle Jo is now fighting on the other side of the made-shift battlefield. "Please, Arabella, come."

She should already know; I won't leave any of them. She's the one that taught me family comes first. "No!" Aunt Georgia shouldn't be here. Turning my head back toward the chaos, I scream. The scene playing out now vastly differs from what I saw mere seconds before. Blaine Ramsay is a body length away from Uncle Jo, and another scream leaves my wrecked mind. "Please, God! Oh, God, no! No."

The powder that the twins slipped me was tainted with dark magic, and nothing after was real, an ugly chuckle eerily sounds beside me. Blaine takes his sword, plunging it forward narrowly missing Uncle Jo. Sebastian's shadow comes out of nowhere saving him in the nick of time. Knowing my Dark Prince will take care of the rest, my attention flies to the Anti-Georgia standing beside me. I grab Billie, and the fraud in front of me has the nerve to smile, sending prickles of ice down my body. "Only cowards hide behind disguises."

The answering laugh is evil. My eyes light up with the realization that this is a changeling. "Aunt Georgia" slowly fades away, and Ethan stands in her place. The emerald eyes that I once thought were beautiful shine brightly in the glowing light of the dusk sky. His smile is cruel, and when he moves his neck to the side, an ombre blue and white dragon tattoo slinks up and down there. The one with the Ice Dragon tattoo is Ethan. All at once, the pieces start falling into place. It's how Thaddeus gained access into the palace, and how the Umbra knew where the mirror would be placed at the end of the Trial. "Why?"

With the nod of his head, two Umbra grab me, and we're teleported to the upper East Wing tower of the Palace. The sound of Sebastian's snarl fades through the air as I'm whisked away. His shadows are too late to save me from being taken.

As my eyes adjust to the candlelit room, my heart slices into a thousand pieces. The real Aunt Georgia is tied up to a wheel of death torture chamber. Mayra Blackwater stands at her side with a knife. A cold knot forms in the back of my throat, this can't be happening, she's not supposed to be here.

Aunt Georgia's smile is sad, she's given up. "No!" I scream.

"This is how it has to be, baby. Please, let me go." Fuck That.

Sebastian. Falkon. Upper East. Torture Chamber. I turn off all other communication, like Sebastian taught me, because I need to concentrate.

Motherfuckers forgot about Billie. Swinging her from side to side, I head for Ethan. He takes out his sword with a smile. "You should have chosen me, Arabella."

"Yeah, that's a hard pass for me." Many have already died today, but not my sweet Aunt Georgia. I need her, like the desert needs the rain.

Ethan comes for me, just like I knew he would. I flip him on his ass. Then Billie tears out a piece of his arm, because she's a greedy bitch today. "Well, Ethan, it looks like you should have chosen the other side."

He howls in pain, as his eyes turn into angry little slits. He doesn't scare me. I can't lose another parent, not to Mayra, not to anyone. This is a fight to the death, one of us will not walk away from this. The traitor comes for me again, I slide out of the way and Billie goes for his throat but only nicks his ear. "Stupid bitch." He howls.

My smile is vicious, because he has no idea, don't hurt what's mine. I go for him again, this time however, he's ready. Ethan slices a deep gash into my shoulder, causing me to cry out in pain. Blood flows freely down my arm, anger boils to the surface. My new wound won't stop me from attacking him again. This time he doesn't expect it, Billie is a good girl and connects with his leg.

Mayra yells for us to stop, but I don't take orders from murdering assholes. The two Umbra that escorted me here flank beside me, however this time I won't allow them to touch me. "Ethan, you can't kill her."

I laugh. "Mayra, baby, you're going to give me a complex. Here I thought I was the one kicking his ass."

Ethan chuckles. "That's cute. I've been holding back, because I can get a little crazy."

I swing Bilie over my shoulder. "Bring your worst."

He moves the guys out of the way, then looks back at Mayra with a sigh. "Please? I won't kill her, okay?"

"Phasma, rein your crazy in, only bring a little pain." She slithers over to where he stands kissing him thoroughly, before turning back to Aunt Georgia.

"I just threw up in my mouth." Surprise slams into me, not because of the kiss they shared, but Ethan is her fucking General!

Mayra shrugs, as she brings the knife back to Aunt Georgia's throat. "If he nicks any part of you, she dies."

No. "I'm not playing your game, Mayra. How about you allow Aunt Georgia to fight instead? It is her life after all." She could probably beat him with one hand tied behind her back.

She smiles. "No can do, I'd much rather witness what The Chosen can do."

I stare at her not backing down, gone is my bravado from before. "Phasma, make her." She hisses.

His answering grin is sinister and a little unnerving. Phasma leaps toward me, as razor sharp nails extend from his fingers. Shock almost gets me cut, but I escape just in time. I extend Billie out, just as shadows encase me and move toward my aunt. Hope fills me because my dark Prince has arrived.

Mayra growls, just before plunging the knife in Aunt Georgia's chest as Sebastian is within a hair's breadth of saving her. Mayra throws rocks down allowing them to escape. Leaving us with no chance of retaliation.

I run to Aunt Georgia's side and hold her dying body in my arms. There is nothing I can do to save her. Her uneven breaths come out in spurts, but still, she smiles at me. Lifting her fingers to my cheek she caresses me there. Tears fall and land on her face. Don't—cry—baby."

I wipe the stray tears that fall out of her own eyes, kissing her forehead in the process. "I love you forever and always."

"Remember, this—is not the — end. I love -you." With that she's gone.

Sebastian wraps his arms around me as I scream. Loud sobs wreck my body. "NO!!! Don't leave me! Please don't leave me!"

My uncle's breakthrough then, Uncle Jo grabs his wife with a screech. "Georgia! No!"

I'll never unhear his anguished cries for as long as I live. Guilt grabs hold of me because I was the one that got to say goodbye. He never will. Uncle Radix falls to his knees beside his sister, as he places a comforting hand on his brother-in-law's shoulder. With one swift cut of a knife, he became an only child. The pain stabs my heart in thin angry slashes, this hurts worse than even my parents dying. I never got a chance to really know them, but Aunt Georgia was my constant. She understood me when others did not.

I sense Falkon before she calls me. I was too late to save Aunt Georgia, but not to help my people. Running to the window I peer out. A fire rages below, as the fight continues on. Sebastian hovers behind me, taking his shadow he gently rubs my back. "Your Aunt Adalia has brought reinforcements, dragons included."

Good, I need a distraction. He opens the window, and we jump down into the wind. My dragon awaits. She catches me with one fell swoop, taking me swiftly to the ground. Sebastian's shadows form into giant wings that carry him down to meet us.

She nuzzles up against my back, affording me a sense of comfort. Through our bond, she senses the pain of my loss and the betrayal that slapped all of us in our faces. Her anger burns even brighter than mine. Falkon wants to make them pay in both blood and fire.

What can I do? She whispers to me telepathically.

Turning on my heel towards her, I grab my Billie out of its protective sheath while rubbing the side of Falkon's cheek with my other hand. My answer is a simple one, no other request will suffice. *Burn them all.*

Yessss. She roars before taking off into the sky to join the other dragons.

"Where is Merrie-Beth?" I calmly ask my lover.

He kisses my forehead, reluctant to tell me the answer. "She's been taken by the Moonland Fae princes."

"Why?" I can't muster any other response.

"She's their mate, Bells. They thought whisking her away from danger was best." He replies.

I nod. "Well, I need her back."

He nods back in agreement. "They've already said they will help our fight, but they needed to have a ceremony of sorts first."

"Will they hurt her?" I ask.

He shakes his head. "I don't believe so."

Sebastian places his forehead against mine. "What do you need?"

"To make them pay, Bash." His smile is devilish, before he teleports us back to the battlefield.

"Where you go, I go." He whispers mimicking my words during the second round.

We charge into the fight. I let Billie do all my thinking. Every being that comes in contact with her regrets it. She's out for vengeance. All my eyes see when I look at their faces are those of my enemies. Ethan, Mayra, even Duvessa. They can't feel my wrath, yet. But they will. I'll kill them all. My weapon will be soaked in their blood.

When the chaos is over, blood and guts cling to my clothes. A terrible stench floats through the air. Falkon screeches as she soars above the clouds, huffing an all-consuming fire on all of our remaining adversaries. She made good on her promise, burnt flesh can be seen and smelt for a mile.

My cousins find me shortly after. Jeremiah holds me while Deen rubs my back. "We're so sorry." One of them whispers. I cling to both of them, because tomorrow is not promised. I've only just found them.

Someone hands me to Sebastian. He carries me to his room, then turns on the shower. Where he quickly washes us both. Taking leftovers out of his fridge he hands me some warmed-over soup.

"Eat, my love, you need your strength for tomorrow." Sebastian kisses my forehead before settling down beside me.

Mindlessly, I nod. Managing to bring my soup up to my mouth a few times. Tears drop down my cheeks without abandon, because with Sebastian I can be vulnerable. Tomorrow we must bury our dead. It's Lux custom that when killed in battle, burial must take place within twenty-four hours of falling. They will start tonight, Aunt Georgia's will be tomorrow, as she is higher in the hierarchy.

After eating half of my soup, we make our way to his bedroom. Sebastian places my back to his front, spooning with me. War is hell, I'll never be the same. However, in my aunt's honor, I make a solemn vow to not let it change me for the worse. I'll become better, not bitter. However, the Umbra will still feel our wrath. Phasma, Mayra, and Duvessa are at the top of my list. Soon, I will be the one to send them all straight to hell.

"Thank you for everything today, Sebastian, it's because of you that Uncle Jo lives. I couldn't bear, if I'd had to bury them both tomorrow." Grabbing his hand, I kiss his fingertips. "I love you, Bash."

He stills behind me, then flips me over. "I've loved you since the first moment I laid eyes on you, Bells. I'm sorry, I couldn't save Georgia, but from this moment forth, I vow to always slay anyone who comes against you and those that you love. They will all perish; I won't fail again. What Mayra doesn't understand is that she is expendable to Duvessa we can use that fact in our favor. Today was about taking those you love to make you suffer, to make you change, to harden your heart."

I don't understand. "I know they are evil, but why that tactic?"

He kisses my forehead gently. "Because that's how they can

defeat you. Mayra and her armies will do Duvessa's bidding, they will come for all of us. Because through us they can get to you."

* * *

Sebastian

I haven't dreamed in forever, and now my worst nightmare will one day come to pass. My dreams have never lied.
-*Sebastian*

YAWNING, I rub her hair while she sleeps. Arabella was almost taken from me today. I can't lose her is the last thing I think about before sleep pulls me under.

Dream Sequence

I growl as Arabella is ripped from my arms. Looking down, my shadows are fighting with the hands that are coming up from the ground. A scream leaves her throat as she falls into the pit of darkness that leads to the Valley of the Decayed. "I'll come for you. I won't let her have you!" I shout after her, then without another thought, I jump in.

Epilogue

Beginnings

June 21, 1758
Savannah, Georgia

John William Lightfoot

LOOKING up at the beautiful sky, my breath hitches. Dawn is breaking, and the sun is peeking over the horizon. This is my favorite part of the day. The oranges are perfectly intertwined with the tinge of pink in the sky. I'm in awe of the Creator. Every morning, one is given a new beginning, a fresh start. For better or worse, life is a series of choices. What will you do with them?

Savannah, Georgia has been my home for nearly ten years now, and during that time, it has been a place of refuge for many, including me. It's near enough to the coast that we're slowly becoming a trader's paradise. We're a city built on the dead, but that didn't deter me from settling here. The dead can't hurt you.

I walk across the wide, nearly deserted street. Still too early for most shop owners to even be out and about. Mama used to always say, "Early to bed and early to rise makes a man healthy, wealthy, and wise." It's how I've lived my life. Passing by a couple of street merchants getting their items ready for market, I send them a wave.

After a short distance, the sound of boots hitting the boarded sidewalk behind me catches my attention. Turning around quickly but seeing no one, I reach inside my bag and place my hand around the pearl handle of my knife. A trusted friend gave it to my great grandfather years ago. No need to panic yet but something is off.

My imagination is working overtime. I'm not sure if my lack of sleep is making me paranoid or if my being trusted with writing the words of the sacred declaration has. There are Umbra spies everywhere, and they want nothing more than to see us fail. For all our sakes, that can't happen. We will not allow them to take over America like they have Europe. I face forward and start whistling a happy tune.

In mere seconds, the sound of the clickity clack of expensive boots starts up again behind me on the boardwalk. My paranoia has been confirmed as a reality. I resist the urge to turn around. The culprit will just hide once more—the coward. The sound is getting louder, the person must be within feet of me now.

Briskly turning down one of the darkened streets, I hide against the wall of one of the buildings. As he turns the corner behind me, I'm able to grab ahold of my assailant's arm. Slamming him up against the wall and placing my knife against his throat, the handle is almost glowing in the dim light.

"Why are you following me, and who sent you?" I growl at him.

He smiles, giving a small grunt. "I didn't know small-time merchants had skill sets that included taking down perpetrators."

Raising an eyebrow, I wait. What else does he know except who I am? Giving him a once over he's more pirate than a spy, with chin-length dark brown hair, and an eyepatch over his left eye to boot. An odd splotch of facial hair between his bottom lip and chin is visible. Very peculiar indeed. "This one does, when threatened. It seems I'm at a disadvantage, sir. How about you tell me who you are." I put the knife closer to his throat leaving a mark. "Now, as opposed to later."

The stranger raises his hands in defeat. "I'll tell you everything in due time. If you let me go, there is an artifact in my satchel that you need to see."

I cock an eyebrow. "Not going to happen, son. Not until you tell me what I want to know. Who are you? Where do you come from? Who sent you?"

He rolls his eyes. "Listen, bloody Lightfoot, I haven't got all day."

I tighten my grip even more, and he winces in pain. "We can do this the easy way or the hard way, you decide. I'm not afraid to kill a man in self-defense."

He sighs in defeat, in turn making me loosen my hold in response. "My name is Solomon Flint the IV. My point of origin is not that simple, and sending myself to this timeline was a difficult task. My great-grandfather made a horrible grievance against you and your kind. It hasn't happened yet, but it's coming. If you don't listen to me, all will be lost, and the world will perish."

My uneasiness about the man doesn't let up, but I let him go, still holding my knife out in front of me just in case. This man is either crazy or telling me the truth and my gut instinct is to trust what he says. Reading people is my job, and I'm never wrong.

Confusion envelops me. My dreams, when I have them, are always powerful. They have always come true in one capacity, or the other, and last night a glowing sun turned black in an instant. People screamed, and a war raged all around me. Weapons were used which I have never witnessed. All goodness and mercy were gone, and only darkness remained. That dream is connected to this individual.

My throat constricts. "Have any proof?"

Rubbing the spot on his neck where my knife had been, he picks up the pouch he dropped at the beginning of our scuffle. Reaching inside the bag, he pulls out something wrapped in purple lace silk. Purple is the color of royalty. A slight glow is coming from whatever is hidden inside. A sun, perhaps? I know it before he even shows me. "What in the world is that?"

A sense of urgency crosses his face. "This good fellow is a vital artifact. One that will be given unto you. There is no other way. You must take it, and I give it to you freely. My only request is that you hide this most precious gift in a place where no one will ever be able to find it, including me. I may not be able to part with it again. It holds great power, one that can ultimately lead to massive destruction.

More confusion hits me as I struggle to piece together every word he is babbling on and on about. Solomon isn't making sense. Maybe I should turn around and leave, but in the end, my curiosity overtakes me. He unwraps the package, and I must shield my eyes from the bright light coming from the object. A most beautiful light springs forth, it shines brighter than all diamonds in any of the realms. The precious rays, although still bright, are not so radiating that it hurts my eyes anymore. Solomon is holding a glorious sun made of pure gold. The absolute replica of the one in my dream. This is no coincidence. Perfect are its lines and its curves. I reach out to touch the tip of one of the sun rays with my index finger, feeling its warmth. "What in the world is that?" I repeat.

He gives me a bewildered look. "This was made long ago, with the hands of a Mayan warrior, Xabier the Great. He was not an evil man, but he built this device not knowing what it could do, what it would do. This is what caused most of the Mayan and Aztec populations to dwindle. Very few know what purpose it was built for. I only know that when activated, it will destroy everything in its path."

My curiosity is no more as I turn my back to him, because I want nothing to do with this cursed object. My beliefs are simple. I believe in love, truth, and light. Long ago my decision was made to enter the narrow gate of the road less traveled and do what was just, what was right. No, I shake my head and try to walk away. "I'm sorry, Solomon, but you're asking too much. What if it were to fall into the wrong hands?"

Shrugging his shoulders, a look of melancholy falls on his youthful face. "It won't, leave that part to me. I have chosen you because the sun's power won't seduce you. No one else is capable. Please, take this blasphemy away from me."

I bow my head in defeat, not fully understanding the calling. I must do this. I'm filled with a new purpose. I was given the dream to prepare my heart for this task. "I don't want to do this, but I know I must accept."

A look of relief washes over his face, and a genuine smile replaces the frown on his lips. He wraps the sun once again into the silk. "You're a good man, Lightfoot. Hide this artifact in a place no one knows about. May the Creator help us all if it is ever found."

Nodding my weary head, I'm most eager to be on my way. "I will guard it with my life."

He pulls a golden rock out of his pouch. His mission accomplished; his confidence has returned to his demeanor. "Lightfoot, in tomorrow's meeting, you will strike up a secret alliance with Balefire and Polarice. Each of you will become great leaders in the fight against the darkness. Although they will become your most trusted allies, you cannot tell them about this. They can be trusted, but some of your future descendants cannot be. Never forget that. This is a secret you will have to take with you to your grave."

Mr. Flint takes a few steps down the alleyway, creeping further into the darkness. He abruptly stops and motions for me to come closer, so I oblige. A look of mischievousness is upon his face. "In a few years, when another Solomon Flint comes to your mountain home and asks if he can come in, politely tell my great grandfather that I highly advised against his request. If possible, slam the door shut right in his smug face."

With a laugh, he turns and takes a few more steps down the alleyway. Hearing someone's movement a slight distance behind us, we turn around with urgency. Looking diligently from side to side, but I see nothing. No one is there. Was the sound a figment of my imagination? The look on his face tells me he heard it, too. It is eerily quiet, as if time has stopped itself.

Solomon takes a small leather bag out of his trouser pocket.

Opening the bag, he pours tiny translucent-looking pebbles into his outstretched palm. "I hope I'm right about this old chap. If not, you better take out that knife and start fighting."

Walking to his side with my body on high alert, if a fight is what they want, then a fight is what they shall get. Solomon makes a fist and throws the tiny pebbles in the direction of where we heard the sound. Nothing happens at first, but as the pebbles disperse into the air and fall to the ground, two translucent figures stand below a window on the right side. The outline of one is curvy and more than likely female. The other is most assuredly a male. Is this real? Closing my eyes, then quickly opening them up again, the figures go from translucent to actual flesh and blood.

I barely get a glimpse of the young lady before her companion makes a move to stand in front of her. She has long, wavy brown hair and big brown eyes, and looks as startled as I feel. The man with her looks exactly like Solomon Flint the IV. Are they twins? That's the only explanation I can fathom. Looking back and forth between the Solomons, neither is paying attention to me. They are only staring at each other with smirks etched upon their faces.

"Solomon, who is this?" I whisper to the one beside me.

It takes him a minute to answer. He turns his full attention to me, clearly amused in the new situation we now find ourselves in. "This, good sir, is future me. I'm a Time Wanderer. It seems that future me has come to re-witness this conversation between us for some reason or other."

Future Solomon nods his head in agreement. "It is once again a pleasure to see you, good Lightfoot. We must be going. Neither of you is supposed to meet my companion just yet. There is a time and a place for everything under the sun, and not enough has happened in your time."

Both Solomons give each other a military salute. "For The Chosen!" They shout in unison. Future Solomon throws something on the ground, and a hole begins to form. Instinctively, I back away, but it doesn't come close to our location. The girl, whom we're not supposed to meet yet, jumps in first. He quickly follows, and they disappear into the hole.

I am flabbergasted, shocked, and in need of a warm bed. Shaking my head, I'm too tired to comprehend any of this. It's been a full twenty-four hours without sleep.

The remaining Solomon Flint gives me a sheepish smile. "It will all make sense one day."

"I hope so," is the only response I can muster.

Solomon throws that golden rock against the wall. A vortex opens, and he leaps into the chaos. I stand there for a few minutes, shell-shocked. Touching the wall, it's solid. Without the silk in my hands, I would blame this encounter on my lack of sleep.

Making my way home, I try to think of hiding places, but nothing seems right. Finally getting into bed, I chuckle to myself and drift off into a restful sleep. What a hell of a day.

The End...For Now

What happened to Merrie-Beth? Find out in 2024. She will be getting her own novella. Why Choose. Curse breaking. Prophecy. Spicy Spice. You're welcome.

Trial of Fire will come out at the end of 2024, be prepared for the wild ride. This will be darker, and spicier than Trial of Light. Arabella will continue to grow in each book. Sebastian's origin story will be explained, it'll be dark so beware.

Most of my 2024 will be spent in my new Pixie Hollow University series, which will be a fairytale reimagined series. All standalone but interconnected. Thanks for sticking with me! I love you all!

Acknowledgments

Thank you, Jesus!

Thank you to my readers, and followers. I don't know what I would do without you. Your kind words and encouragement make the hard days worth it. I love you, without your love and support I would not be here! You're everything to me.

A big thanks goes to my PR Team, exposure to an Indie Author is everything. Y'all have gone above and beyond for me. I love you all.

To my besties at Sweet Magnolia Author Services, I could not have done this without you.

Elizabeth- My forever Alpha reader, you've held my hand during this whole process, and as you know I've cried so many tears. This book almost didn't happen and would not have without you. You believed in it, and me! I love you. Nicole- My forever Beta Reader, thank you for everything from the bottom of my heart. You're amazing. I love you.

Jess Houseman thank you for helping me edit this book. Your encouragement has meant so much to me! I love you, and I appreciate everything you've done for me.

Thank you, Nisha, from Passion Author Services for the prettiest cover I've ever had. Thank you for it, and for the edits! You are appreciated, and my 2023 would NOT have been so great without you.

A massive thank you goes to my husband who supports me no matter and is okay eating sandwiches on big writing days. Which is often!

About the Author

Ellis Worth

Ellis lives in rural South Georgia. She is a Pharm Tech by day, and an aspiring author by night. Growing up she fell in love with her mama's romance collection and stole them from her bookcase frequently. She always made sure to put them back in exactly the same spot and was never caught.

Ellis has a cinnamon roll husband, a stepdaughter, two beloved dogs (Chance and Doc), and a cat (Fattie Mama). She is thankful for every post, every view, and every read. Thank you.